Michal

Michal

ANN BROWN

iUniverse, Inc.
Bloomington

MICHAL

iUniverse books may be ordered through booksellers or by contacting:

iUniverse
1663 Liberty Drive
Bloomington, IN 47403
www.iuniverse.com
1-800-Authors (1-800-288-4677)

ISBN: 978-1-4620-3724-7 (sc)
ISBN: 978-1-4620-3725-4 (ebk)

Printed in the United States of America

iUniverse rev. date: 07/20/2011

Chapter 1

"Of course you are a pretty girl, Michal! Whatever made you think you weren't?"

Michal's covert glance at her sister was not lost on her mother.

"We—ll, you are only thirteen—"

"I'll be fourteen next month!"

"So—you're fourteen! You cannot expect to compete with Merab's classic beauty. In another four years, you will be just as beautiful as she is. But if your father—if he doesn't . . ." Ahinoam's voice broke.

"Please don' cry, neither, Mother. I talked with the captain of the guard; Phaltial is certain the musician Father sent for can perform miracles with his harp."

"Don't be a fool, Michal," said Merab haughtily, as she brushed her long, black hair. "Don't you know if all the wise men, soothsayers, and wizards in Israel can't help Father, a silly old harp player is not going to cure him?"

"Merab! Must you do that?"

Michal was startled by the sharp tone of her mother's voice, which was usually so soft and sweet.

"And what would you suggest I do?" asked Merab icily.

"You could go down and how your father—uh—find out if the musician has arrived."

"Oh, Mother! You know that old faker won't do any more good than the others." But the hurt in Ahinoam's voice apparently checked Merab. "Let Michal do it," she said plaintively. "You know how those soldiers smell, and I don't like the way they stare at me."

Saul's younger daughter leaped to her feet, eager for the chance. "But think how you'd feel if they didn't stare at you," Michal quipped. A mischievous smile relived the tension of her face, and two elusive dimples

1

appeared near the corners of her full, red lips as she hastened to do her mother's bidding.

Merab hurried her hairbrush at her sister's retreating back. "Mother! Why don't you make that stupid child keep her sassy mouth shut?"

"Merab! How many times do I have to tell you Michal is not stupid! Nor is she any longer a child. Even if she is only thirteen, she is taller than you and I, and becoming quite beautiful. But if you and your brothers keep telling her she is stupid, she may begin to believe it."

"What do you mean my brothers! Aren't they her brothers too?"

"Well, I always thought so. But she says Jonathon is her brother, and the other three are yours."

Now that's what I mean: Why do you let her get by with that sharp tongue?"

Ahinoam sighed. "She should curb her tongue, I'll admit. But there is generally so much wisdom in what she says, I find it difficult to make her keep quiet—especially when the rest of you torment her so."

"Well, you mark my words: If she does not learn to control that sharp little tongue of hers, it will dig her grave one of these days!"

Michal's face burned. She drew her thick, black curls over her cheeks to hide the crimson, and gathering up her volumous skirts of many colors worn by the virgin daughters of the king, she ran up the cold, gray marble steps to the judgment hall above. She never intended to annoy her sister, but somehow everything she said or did always to be wrong.

In fact, everything about her was wrong. She did have beautiful black eyes like her mother and sister, nor their lovely ivory skin. Her eyes were only a little darker than her father's. She had also inherited his high cheekbones, and—fearfully—his height. She was already taller than her youngest brother, much to his displeasure—and hers.

Only Jonathon and Michal were tall, strong, and straight like King Saul. Abinadab and Melchisua were of average height. Merab was small and dainty like her mother, and, Ishbosheth was short like his mother but broad like his father.

In spite of the rich furnishings and lavish appointments, the atmosphere in the palace was as dismal as the weather outside. Dull gray clouds hovered the flat roofs completely hiding the dome that set the palace apart from its neighbors, and dense fog filled the courtyard.

As Michal reached the stair landing, she heard a wave of muttering voices drifting down the stairs, accompanied by the stench of stale sweat.

The ominous cloud that had hovered over the palace for weeks seemed to have erupted into a violent storm. Now all Israel was filled with fear.

The temper tantrums and alternate fits of depression that had possessed Saul for months were growing increasingly worse. All day long the king had been slumped upon his throne as if turned to stone. He would touch neither food nor drink. His eyes were wide open in a vacant stare. His beetling black brows and iron gray hair were in disarray. He appeared completely deaf to all entreaties from family, servant, and counselors.

The mute figure on the throne bore little resemblance to the mighty warrior who stood head and shoulders above his fellows, and had delivered Israel so gloriously for many years.

Michal avoided the front entrance where the milling, muttering soldiers stood guard. She also passed the side door where a smaller crowd gathered. At the back of the hall was a huge window, and beneath it a tiny door which opened into a small foyer. In the niche behind the wall of heavy blue and scarlet draperies that formed the backdrop for her father's throne, Michal had found a secret hiding place. It was a private sanctuary where she could dream her little-girl dreams.

Saul's youngest child arrived late in the family, and had never quite seemed to make a place for herself. So she dreamed of the time when she would be a beautiful princess, and a handsome prince would carry her away and make her queen of a kingdom even greater than her father's Israel. Surely, then she would be recognized along with her brothers and sister as a real member of the royal family.

Even the royal dress did nothing to increase her status. She had been so sure when she was permitted to dress like a princess her brothers and sister would treat her as an equal. Her eyes stung with tears of disappointment.

In addition to being a sanctuary for her dreams, Michal's hiding place enabled her to keep her young fingers on the erratic pulse of her father's kingdom. She knew the whole palace was in an uproar.

When the king fell into the trance, the wise men insisted he was held in the clutches of an evil spirit. Their best efforts at casting out the demon had failed. Now they were waiting in brooding silence for the musician Saul sent for before he fell silent. The harpist was their last hope.

Suddenly a bubble of exited voices penetrated the curtain. Michal peered cautiously between the fold of the draperies. The two messengers dispatched to fetch the musician were standing before the throne. Between them stood a shepherd lad. A harp hung across one shoulder, and a leather bag was suspended from the other.

The youth and simple attire made little impression on the girl; she was too entranced with the beauty of his face. His skin burned bronze by the desert sun turned the youthful pink of his cheeks a ruddy color. His soulful brown eyes were nearly obscured by the ringlets that escaped the red band tied around his head to keep his almost should-length black hair out of his face.

Michal admired the boy's broad shoulders and strong profile, but she was certain the charming dimple in his chin was the key to his character.

After she recovered her breath, Michal slipped from her hiding place, gathered up her skirts, and raced back down the stairs to the family living quarters.

"The musician is here!" she cried.

Ahinoam dropped her needle, but Merab did not miss a stroke with her hairbrush. "So—?" she shrugged.

But—perhaps now—Father—. Merab, don't you care at all that our father is so ill?"

"Don't be foolish, Michal; our tears will not help Father any more than our prayers have. And that old man won't do any more good than the other witch chasers have done."

Michal looked at her sister in total disbelief, then she smiled, and lowered her eyes before Merab could see the gleam in them.

"But he's not old, Merab; he's young—and—he's so handsome!"

"Oh?" Merab paused. Perhaps I should take a look."

As the girls went out the door, Michal glanced back at her mother; she was on her knees, her face lifted toward heaven, and her lips moving in silent prayer.

Not even such an important occasion prompted Michal to share her sanctuary with her sister. The two girls peered into the throne room from among the sweaty soldiers at the side door.

Saul sat on his throne. His eyes were wide open in a vacant stare. His massive frame slumped like a bag of stones, and his chin almost rested on his chest. His long powerful arms were folded dogmatically across his broad torso, the only incongruous note in his posture. His sandaled feet were turned disconsolately sideways.

The shepherd boy carefully tightened the strings on his harp, and stroked them soundlessly.

The king's counselors waited in taught expectancy.

"Michal! Must you always be a fool! Handsome? Ha! Why that beardless stripling is nothing but a common sheepherder."

The young princess shrank from her sister's contempt, but in that instant the lad's fingers caressed the strings of his harp, and heavenly music began to swell and echo through the vast judgment hall.

Chapter 2

The melody reached a crescendo, then became softer and softer and softer until Michal strained her ears to catch it. Almost imperceptively, Saul began to respond.

"We-ll," Merab temporized, "he could be an Edomite or an Amalekite for all I care. If he can charm Father out of the clutches of the evil spirit, who cares what he looks like! If word gets around the king of Israel is a lunatic, we may all be back herding sheep."

"If we still have any sheep to herd!" Michal quipped absently, while she questioned if the joy bubbling in her heart was all for her father's recovery.

Merab gave her sisters a condescending look of grudging admiration.

While the princesses watched, a miracle seemed to take place. As the soothing, caressing music bathed them in the throbbing, pulsing melody, the tension went out of the king; his vacant eyes closed, and his massive frame relaxed as if he were in a deep sleep.

Gently the soldiers lifted their unconscious monarch. While a servant sponged his master's face with cool water, another tried to coax a few drops of wine between his lips. In less than an hour Saul was sitting up, eating and drinking, and talking with his courtiers.

Michal could hardly take her eyes off the musician long enough to appreciate the miracle of her father's recovery. The joy and gratitude she felt was overshadowed by wonder: What kind of power did this handsome stranger posses? One thing she knew: Such beauty of face and soul surely was divine.

The word spread quickly. Sounds of rejoicing filled the palace.

Two burly members of the palace guard hoisted the young musician to their shoulders, and bore him in triumph around the judgment hall. Their fellows cheered wildly.

"For heaven's sake, Michal! What's wrong with you now?" Merab pinched her sister to get her attention. "Where is all that concern you had for Father? Come on; let's tell Mother,"

The girls ran up the steps two at a time to give their mother the good news. But her woman's intuition had preceded then, and she was already busily preparing a feast for the evening meal.

"Haste, Michal, find your brothers. Tell Jonathan to have the servants kill the fatted calf. Ask Melchishua and Abinadab to bring wine and corn from the cellar. Merab, see to the table; use the best cloth."

"Don't you even want to know what happened?" Merab objected.

"But I do know; your father is back with us again."

Michal observed Ahinoam's flushed and smiling face with delight, and turned to do her bidding. But Merab balked.

"Mother! Why must we be so common? Other kings have hosts of slaves to wait on them."

"Other kings also have harems; that, I could never endure. So I shall leave well enough alone."

"Other kings also have power," observed Michal calmly, "and everyone knows Samuel still rules this country the same as he did before father became king."

"Don't you dare let your father hear your father say that, young lady. The kind may not have power to tax the people and fill the royal treasury, but he does control the army, and he could have the prophet killed."

"Don't you think Samuel knows that, Mother? Why do you think he has not been near the palace since he hacked up old King Agag, and had the row with Father that sent him off? If you remember, he's been in a state ever since."

"Of course your father has been upset. Samuel told him God had rejected him as king over Israel because of his disobedience in letting King Agag live."

"That wasn't quite all, Mother; Father also kept the best of the flocks and herds God said destroy. But what really upset Samuel was Father's offering the sacrifice before he went into the battle."

"Oh! No! Michal, are you sure? Who told you?"

"I—I—heard it downstairs."

"Mother, if that child is so smart, let her round up the servants and look after the table for you. All this commotion has given me a headache." And Merab retired forthwith to her room.

"Never mind, Mother; I'll take care of the table as soon as I get back." Michal dashed down the stairs. She was relieved to evade further questions, and delighted to get another look at the proceedings below.

But in the jubilant crowd she saw nothing of her brothers. The palace guard still stood faithfully in their appointed places by the doors. The big captain greeted her kindly.

"Can I help you, little princess?"

"Thank you, Phaltiel. I was looking for my brothers; Mother wants them."

The captain turned to the man on his right. "Find the king's sons and bring them here at once." He smiled at Michal. "Consider it done, my lady."

Michal bowed gracefully, but her head came up a trifle higher, and she walked sedately back up the stairs. After all, if she was going to be a queen some day, she needed to practice being a lady.

When Saul came to his table, it groaned under all the food he loved. The aroma of parched corn and freshly baked bread filled the palace. The king brought the young musician with him, and seated him on his right hand in Jonathan's accustomed place.

"This is David," he said proudly. "He is to be as one of the king's sons. He shall eat at my table, and stay always within my call. David, my sons: Jonathan, Melchishua, Abinadab, and Ishbosheth. My wife, Ahinoam. My daughters: Merab and Michal."

David bowed graciously to each in turn, but his eyes lingered upon Michal. She could feel herself blushing again. She lowered her head so her hair would hide her face. She could not hope to compete with her beautiful older sister, but then Merab was not interested in the newcomer—or so she said.

"Tell us," asked Ahinoam, after the plates were served, "about your family. Was your father not unhappy to see so young a son leave home?"

"No, my lady; my father was honored to do service to our great king who has delivered Israel so gloriously."

"Has your father other sons?" asked Jonathan.

"Seven—and three daughters."

"Older or younger, my son?" asked Saul.

"I am the youngest of my father's house, my lord," David apologized.

"What did you do at home?" asked Jonathan.

"I kept the sheep. My brothers preferred to tend the cattle and the camels."

"Wasn't it terribly lonely?" asked Ahinoam.

"Not really, my lady. I had my harp, and I practiced with my spear, my sling, and my bow. And—I write psalms."

"You can write?" blurted Michal.

Merab pinched her sister into silence, but Michal's heart seethed, and she controlled her tongue with difficulty. Some day—when she was a queen—she would say what she pleased, where she pleased. And she would learn to write whatever the cost. How could a queen send accurate messages if she could not write?

"How nice that you write songs," Ahinoam was saying. "When we've finished eating, will you sing for us?"

"My pleasure, my lady." David bowed humbly but unabashed.

"Are you good with your bow, my son?" asked Saul.

"Quite good, my lord," replied David modestly.

Ishbosheth nudged Abinadab, and smirked.

"What is a sling?" asked Jonathan.

David drew from his pocket a long piece of rawhide with a leather loop at each end, and a patch of leather laced through the middle. He held it up for inspection.

"How does it work?"

David took a small smooth stone from his pocket. "You put a stone in this." He placed the stone in the leather patch, and deftly caught the two ends of the rawhide thong. "Then sling it around your head until it gains sufficient speed, turn loose of one end of the thong, and it hits your target—if you're luck."

"Are you as good with the sling as you are with the bow?" asked Saul.

"Yes, my lord."

Ishbosheth and Abinadab nudged each other, and they both smirked.

"Then you shall be my armor bearer," announced the king triumphantly. "That will keep you by my side."

"But what about Adriel?" asked Merab quickly.

"Isn't he the chief ogler?" whispered Michal.

Merab pinched her sister harder.

Michal said nothing, but she shoved her sister's hand away.

"He's been anxious to get back to his flocks and herds anyway," said Saul. "His father is getting old and needs his help." The king's eyes began to twinkle as he watched his elder daughter. "Some time ago my armor bearer offered me a king's ransom as a dowry for my daughter. I told him you were only interested in marrying a prince."

"My daughter!" seethed Michal. "Is my Father not aware he has two daughters?"

"But, Father! It's Michal who wants to marry a prince!"

The brothers laughed. David looked speculatively at Michal, but she was so engrossed with her resentments she did not notice.

"Well, I meant—I'm not interested in marriage," blushed Merab.

"Of course you're interested in marriage! And I must see to the arrangements as soon as I get my own affairs under control. Now that David is here to keep the evil spirits away I'll get my house in order." Saul paused briefly. "If everyone has, let's have that song he promised us."

David picked up his instrument and seated himself on the edge of a deep casement window. He touched his harp strings lightly, looked up into the starry heavens and began to sing:

> "Our Lord our Lord, how excellent is thy name in all
> the earth! Who has set thy glory above the heavens.
> When I consider thy heavens, the work of thy fingers,
> the moon and the stars, Which thou has ordained;
> What is man, that thou art mindful of him?
> And the son of man, that thou visitest him?
> For thou hast made him a little lower than the angels,
> and hast crowned him with glory and honor.
> Thou made him to have dominion over the works of thy
> Hands: thou hast put all things under his feet:
> All sheep and oxen, yea, and the fish of the sea, and
> Whatsoever passes through the paths of the seas.
> O Lord our Lord, how excellent is thy name in all the earth!"

When the song ended, the royal family breathed deep as one person. Even Ishbosheth and Abinidab wiped the smirks from their faces. The shepherd lad's voice was as sweet and compelling as his music. Michal felt as if she were drowning in his limpid brown eyes, and could think of no desirable way to go.

"And the Lord bless you, my son," breathed Saul in benediction. "Jonathan, take David and give him the best bed in your quarters. He's had a hard day."

As Jonathan escorted their guest away, the three younger sons held a whispered caucus. Each nudged the other, then Melchisua spoke. "Father—ah—do you really mean we are to have that sheep—shepherd boy as a permanent guest in our home? And surely you don't intend to make him your armor-bearer. Why you'd be putting your life in his!"

"Can you think of better hands, my sons? Did he not save your father's life today—or is that not important to you?"

"Of course it is, Father. But playing music is one thing: being a warrior is something else. He's too young—too—"

"I'm still making the decisions here; David shall be as of the king's sons. See that none of you forget it!'

"Yes, Father," replied the three sons in unison.

After Ahinoam coaxed the tired monarch to bed, Ishbosheth exploded! Did you hear that? 'As one of the king's sons,'" he mimicked. "Ha! Sounds to me as if he were to be preferred above the king's sons."

"At least we can pretend he's not here," suggested Merab.

"I didn't see any sheepherder. Did you see a sheepherder?" asked Ishbosheth.

"I didn't even smell one," sniffed Abinadab, and they all exploded with laughter.

Michal hesitated as she cleared away the dishes. "Could the king's sons be jealous of a shepherd boy?"

"Jealous? Of that" Why he's little more than a tramp," snorted Ishbosheth.

"Armor bearer!" exclaimed Melchishua. "Can't you see that little shrimp carrying Father's armor? He couldn't carry his spear. Are you sure are seeing straight, dear little sister? Jealous? Of what!"

"All right, stupid! I've had about enough of your sharp tongue for one day," said Merab as she advanced menacingly toward her sister.

Chapter 3

Ahinoam returned barely in time to rescue her youngest child from the wrath of her brothers and sister. At their mother's firm command, they all went to bed.

It was as if the sun were rising on a whole new world. Peace and joy reigned once more in the royal household. The king spent his mornings in the counsel chambers with his advisors, his afternoons hunting with his sons, and his evenings in the bosom of his family. David was usually near by. Frequently his deft fingers plucked sweet melodies from his harp. Michal was certain life in the palace was too good to last.

On David's first morning in Gibeah, Saul commanded Jonathan to acquaint the lad with his duties as the royal armor bearer, while he conferred with his counselors and Abner. He needed to catch up on the affairs of his kingdom and his army.

Michal bided her time. While her brother went to fetch his father's armor, she caught David alone in the corridor. Her heart was in her throat, but she was determined to speak before she lost her courage.

"I'm glad you are going to live with us," she said with childish candor. "And will you grant me, I pray, a great favor?"

"Your wish is my command, my lady."

"Will you teach me how to write?"

"My pleasure! But can you read?"

Sadly, Michal shook her head. "Merab says it is unbecoming for a girl to want to read and write—and, besides, there's been no one to teach me. But I must learn to write; I must."

"First I'll have to teach you to read. Have you any books?"

Again Michal shook her head.

"Never mind; I have some psalms with me, and I can write more. But where shall we study?"

As if she had been waiting for him all her life, Michal led David to her little sanctuary. He viewed the lighting and the cushions on the floor with satisfaction.

"Quite a place you have here. A small table and some writing materials are all we need. But can you study with all that noise out there?" he gestured toward the hum of voices coming from the throne room. "How do you stand it?"

"When I get to be a queen, I'll need to understand affairs of state." Michal saw amazement on the boy's face, and something else that could have been disappointment.

In the weeks that followed, David proved to be an effective teacher, and Michal an apt pupil. Her greatest difficulty was in restraining herself from sharing the joy of her newfound knowledge with her family. But for the first time, she was glad the royal family took so little interest in the youngest member; their neglect gave her ample time for her studies.

The same was not true, however, for David. Although he was ignored by the presence almost constantly; and Jonathan spent hours instructing the lad in the ways of life at court, and the art of warfare. Only the proximity of their classroom to the judgment hall enabled David to find any time at all for his happy pupil.

Often in the midst of a lesson, the young people heard Saul's voice rising in anger. David promptly took his harp, slipped through the curtains, and played for the troubled king; always he was refreshed.

As the months hurried by the visits of the evil spirit became farther and farther apart. And at last he seemed to have departed altogether, and Saul appeared to be himself again.

All was apparently well in Israel. The king found ample time for fellowship with his sons and with David.

Surely, now that the evil spirit has departed, God will not take the kingdom from me. I have searched carefully among the wise men of Israel, and found none who would make a better king then you, my son, Jonathan."

"And nothing would please me more, my father. But God does not always see men as we see them. We can't be sure whom he has chosen until he reveals his plan to us. What does Samuel say?"

"I fear the prophet is avoiding me even as God evades me. Samuel has not been near the palace in almost a year now.

"Yes, and nothing has happened in the year. Perhaps it was only Samuel who threatened you," said Melchishua.

Saul meditated for a few moments. "No, my son, Samuel would not speak anything for God he was not told to say."

"I'm sure you are right, Father," Jonathan agreed. "In fact, I felt Samuel was grieved when God rejected you as king."

"But if God wants to take the kingdom from you, why has he not already done so?" asked Abinadab.

"That I do not know. The ways of God are an eternal mystery to me. I've never understood why he was so angry with me for offering the burnt sacrifice. I was afraid to go into battle without making an offering, and Samuel was not there. And I still can't see anything wrong with keeping all those herds of fine sheep and cattle of the Amalekites. They would have fed thousands of our people. Is God not happy when we feed the poor?"

"I could tell them if they asked me," whispered David to Michal as laboriously copied a psalm. God's time is not our time; ours is limited—his is not. We cannot hurry God. He can see to the end of our lives. The Lord knows what is in store for us, and what is best for us, he will bring it about in his own good time. All we can do is trust him; he had rather have obedience than sacrifice."

While Michal listened to her teacher in curious silence, the next words from the throne room gave them immediate cause for concern.

"If the evil spirit no longer troubles you, Father, why do you not send David home?' asked Ishbosheth. "I'm sure his father needs him to herd the sheep," he added piously.

"Yes, Father, why not?" insisted Abinadab. "We are not at war; you don't need an armor bearer."

"But I like the boy. I prefer to keep him here."

"Of course! We all like him," adding Abinadab hastily. "But we are thinking of his father and—and of David. Perhaps the boy is homesick; he has been here almost six months now."

"What do you think, Jonathan? Should I send the boy home?"

"The decision should be yours, of course, Father. But why not ask David if he wants to go?"

Michal lifted suffering eyes to David's face. "You won't go away?" she whispered.

David smiled. "Why not, little princess? You can read and write now. Your father no longer needs me. Perhaps I should go home."

"Do you want to go?"

"What I want is not important. As long as I'm where God wants me, doing what he wants me, doing what he wants me to do, or there herding sheep, it matters not at all."

"But how do you know where God wants you to be, or what he wants you to do?"

"I ask him. Every day I ask him to guide and protect me."

"But how does he answer you? Does he talk to you, or do your answers come through visions and dreams?"

David was thoughtful. His soft brown eyes half closed in dreamy contemplation. In the unaccustomed confinement of the palace, the shepherd lad had lost his bronzed, ruddy appearance; and his natural olive coloring had returned.

"It's hard to say how God answers me. It's like explaining how I know I'm alive. I just know. Sometimes he speaks to me through others, the prophet, the priests, and the Scriptures. But usually what I want to know, I ask him. Sometimes he says 'yes,' sometimes 'no,' and sometimes he says 'wait a while,' but always he my prayers."

"Oh come now! Tell me one answer you've had to a prayer."

David smiled. "Only one? Let me give you at least two: Once a lion attacked my sheep; I called on God, and he gave me the strength to kill that lion. And another time I killed a bear."

"With your bare hands?"

"With my knife."

"David, you couldn't."

"I didn't; God did."

Michal gazed at the earnest boy with a mixture of awe and unbelief. "But how—?"

David sighed. "If God talked to you the way he does to me, you wouldn't have to ask. It's like the wind: Have you ever seen the wind? But when you feel it blowing, you know it's there."

"You mean anything you want, you ask God—like—you ask my father?"

"No—not like I ask your father. First I must find him, then I have to be sure he isn't busy—and that he's in a good mood. God is always available, and always kind."

"You mean any time? Anywhere? You don't have to be in the Tabernacle, or before an alter?"

"Why should I? God does not live in the Tabernacle or on altars He is everywhere. It seems I can get closest to him when I'm wrong; I love to go to the Tabernacle, and we always have an altar beside our home where we worship regularly. But those are special times of spiritual renewal and public worship. I worship God every day in my heart."

"And you can ask God anything you want to, and get an answer?"

"Yes. I'm asking him something now every day, and every day I get the same answer: I must wait for God's own good time to reveal his plans to me. It's not because I'm impatient that I keep asking; I want to be sure I know what God would have me do each day. He wanted me to come to the palace—so I came. If he is ready for me to go, I shall leave."

"But how does he tell you all that?"

"He tells me in my heart."

"Will God talk to anyone?" asked Michal eagerly.

"No. Only those whose hearts are in tune with him."

"And how do we get our hearts in tune with God?"

David drew a deep breath. First, of course, we have to believe he lives. Then there are many ways; though prayer, worship, and sacrifice. Really, Michal, I believe any way we seek God, we can find his will for our lives.

"But, if we offer to do anything God wants us to do, there is no telling what he might demand of us!"

David laughed. "Foolish little princess! Don't you know God knows all about you? He knows what will make you happy. Do you?"

Michal bowed her head; she could feel a warm flush stealing over her face. "I think so."

"But, you see, you only think; God knows. If you are wise, you will ask him to give you what he knows is best for you. Only God knows the future, so only he knows what will bring you happiness.'

"Sh-h-h," whispered Michal. "Listen! I hear Abner's voice. When he comes back, there's always trouble."

"No, my lord," came the voice of the captain of Israel's army. "It's not serious. But I think we should push the Philistines back where they belong—before it gets serious. I've already called in the tribe of Judah to help us."

"I must go quickly; your father will be calling for me."

"See you tomorrow—same time?"

"Same time," David whispered as he slipped through the draperies.

Michal did not see David again that afternoon. As soon as thanks had been offered for the evening meal, she nudged Merab.

"Where's David?"

Merab shrugged condescendingly as she nibbled daintily at her parched corn.

Michal's appetite waned; she glanced uneasily from her father to Jonathan, who was sitting in his accustomed place. David was not coming! But why, she asked herself as panic rose in her heart. Surely he had not gone without bidding her farewell. Then she forced herself to face the unusual unpleasant truth. She was only a child. David had been kind because she was the king's daughter. He'd probably never give her another thought.

From the depths of her misery, Michal realized her father and Jonathan were discussing David.

"I miss him already," said Jonathan.

"And a nice miss it is," muttered Ishbosheth.

"I miss him, too," said Saul. "But what could I do when his father sent for him? His older brothers have gone with Abner to chase the Philistines out of the country. His father needs him."

So David really was gone—without a word. Bitterness welled up in the woman's heart that dwelled in Michal's childish bosom. Tears stung her eyelids.

"Suddenly, Merab nudged her sharply.

"Why aren't you eating?"

Michal looked up into her sister's calculated eyes. She could almost see her sharpening her tongue. Michal swallowed the lump in her throat, and forced herself to speak lightly

"I was wondering if Adriel will be coming back."

"Adriel is no concern of mine," said Merab a little too quickly, as she reached for a piece of cheese. "But if we have war with the Philistines, that concerns us all."

Chapter 4

The Philistine threat proved even more serious than Abner anticipated. Every runner brought increasingly frightening news. Saul took his three older sons and went to Abner's aid. Eventually every solider in the city, except the palace guard, went to join the battle.

Weeks passed with no news from the army. The anxious women grew pale with worry.

More than a month after Saul's departure, a runner arrived. But he brought no good news. Saul sent orders to Phaltiel, the captain of the palace guard, to gather every able-bodied man in Gibeah, and bring them to the valley of Elah.

There were no casualties, the messenger said. His report was received with a shout of praise. But there had been no battle!

There was a chorus of "Why?"

The reason, according to the runner, was unbelievable. The Philistine army was led by a giant more than nine feet tall. He was clad in brazen armor from head to foot. He carried a spear like a weaver's beam, tipped with a huge iron point too heavy for an average man to lift. The giant strode up and down the valley between the two encamped armies, and shouted insults at the Israelites day after day.

"Why all these men in battle? You servants of Saul, choose you a man and let him come down to me. If he can kill me, then we will be your servants. But if I kill him, then you shall be our servants." Over and over, the giant shouted, "I defy the armies of Israel this; give me a man that we may fight together."

"The king is head and shoulders above the rest of us but he's no match for that brute. Saul offered a most attractive reward to anyone who kills the giant," the runner added with a sidelong glance at Merab. "But no takers. It would be suicide for any of our men. Our only hope is to overcome him by sheer weight of numbers."

"But how many men will be killed in overcoming him?" asked Michal. "And won't come to his rescue?"

The messenger shrugged.

"Be quiet, stupid," hissed Merab.

Michal's cheeks burned.

"Don't you worry, Little Princess," said Phaltiel. Israel has always whipped the Philistines, and we'll do it again."

On that optimistic note, the men of Gibeah left for the battlefront.

In the days that followed, the mood of the city alternated between hope and despair, then settled into a sort of anxious silence. Everywhere women huddled in groups in front of their silent houses, and even in the middle of the narrow, cobblestone streets, saying, "No news is good news." They tried to comfort each other with words they themselves did not believe.

With every rumor that drifted into the city, the giant grew taller, the Philistine army bigger, and Israel's situation more desperate. Gossip floated up and down the quiet streets like soaring vultures. Though they tried not to believe it, whole neighborhoods, swayed by the panic, rushed to the palace pleading for news, any news—even bad news.

The three women in the palace looked into each other's eyes with fear they could not conceal, as each indulged in her own private thoughts. Ahinoam knew her husband and three sons would be in the forefront of the battle. Merab was not overly concerned for her father and brothers, but she had no illusions about the danger of Adriel's place as the royal armor bearer. Michal was grieved for her father and Jonathan, but she comforted herself that David was safe with his father's flocks in Bethlehem. She knew, that if the Philistines triumphed over Israel's army in the valley of Elah, no one in all Israel would be safe.

"Surely," ventured Merab, "if Father is afraid to fight the giant, Adriel won't try."

"It's Jonathan I'm most worried about," said his mother. "He thinks he must take his father's place, and now that Saul is not the warrior he once was—" Her voice trailed off into a eloquent silence.

"But since God rejected Father as king, and Jon will not inherit the throne—perhaps—" Merab, too, was silent.

"But what if God rejects all of us?" asked Michal.

Ahinoam shuddered.

"Be quiet, stupid," snapped Merab again.

The resentment that seethed continually in Michal's heart began to boil.

Crowds formed at the watchtowers and outside the city gates hoping for news from a runner or an incoming traveler. The oddly quiet crowds grew larger and larger. There was little talking, and it was in subdued tones or hushed whispers. Occasionally the cracked voice of an old man begged for news. Instead of inciting the crowd to babbling it only intensified the gloomy silence as they heard the oft-repeated: "No runner in sight."

The mob of women on foot and in chariots grew ever larger. The heat of the close-packed bodies and the dust rising from restless feet were suffocating. The women were quiet, but their pale, rigid faces pleaded with a mute eloquence sadder than wailing.

There was scarcely a house in Gibeah without a son, husband, lover, brother, or father at the battlefront. They all waited with terror in their hearts lest death already robbed their homes. They feared and expected death; they did not expect defeat. Such a thought was beyond their comprehension.

Their men might be dying in the sun-blistered valley of Elah. Even now Israel's ranks might be falling like wheat in a hailstorm, but, the land they were defending could never fall.

Hebrews might be dying by the thousands, but, like the quail in the wilderness, thousands of fresh troops would rise up to take their places. Where these men would come, no one knew. They only knew, as surely as they knew their God was still in his heaven, that Israel was miraculous, and Saul's army was invincible.

Their knowledge of the fate of cities taken by the heathen was pushed to the back of their minds. Too many in the silent crowd had relatives who had been slain or carried away by the Philistines. Mothers did not fear the certain death they knew awaited them as much as they feared the feared the fate in store for their virgin daughters. No, defeat was unthinkable.

God gave them this land. God would enable them to keep it. They were prone to forget, however, the conditions under which God promised them the land.

Two long bitter weeks passed with no news from the army. Late in the afternoon of the fourteenth day a cry arose from the southerner watchtower: "A runner!" Ahinoam and her two daughters mounted the royal carriage, and followed the crowd streaming out of the city to meet the runner. Two soldiers from the palace guard raced ahead of the surging crowd, picked up the exhausted runner, and bore him on their shoulders back toward the city. A flock of young boys, following close behind the soldiers, turned back and raced with shrill cries toward the crowd.

"The battle is over! The giant is dead!" The glad tidings were repeated over and over in the jubilant treble tones.

"But at what cost? What of the casualties?" cried many anxious women amid shouts of rejoicing.

There was a parting on the outskirts of the crowd as the people gave way to the soldier bearing the panting runner. They bore him straight to the royal carriage, and set him on his feet.

"Phaltiel will be home—perhaps tomorrow," he gasped. "He'll tell you all about it."

"And the casualties?" asked Ahinoam.

"There were none—" The messenger was interrupted by thunderous shouts of praise. "—when the runner left," he panted. "Army chasing Philistines."

"Who killed the giant/" the crowd cried in unison.

"Don't know—runner who relayed the message to me didn't remember his name."

Chapter 5

It was late in the night when Phaltiel arrived the following day, but he went immediately to the palace and to the royal household where a light still burned. Michal was awakened by the tramp of heavy feet on the stairs. Dressing as she ran, she called her sleeping sister, and has hastened to her mother's side. The big captain stood in the doorway. He was weary and covered with dust and grime, but his pock-marked, bearded face still glowed with triumph.

"Michal, bring a glass of wine. Ishbosheth, bring water for the captain's feet." Ahinoam's hospitality took precedence over her desire for new.

By the time the captain refreshed himself, Merab joined the group. She still yawned, but not a lock of her shining black hair was out of place.

"Now," urged Ishbosheth, "tell us what happened. Who killed the giant? Was it Jonathan?"

"No," Phaltiel replied with evident relish. "It was David."

"David!" cried the four voices in unison. "What was he doing there?"

"Well," said Phaltiel with the air of one obviously enjoying himself, "It's a long story."

"Tell us," begged Michal.

"You remember David went home because his three older brothers went with Abner to fight the Philistines. When six weeks passed with no word from his sons, Jesse sent David to see about them. He brought bread and corn for his brothers, and cheeses for their captain.

"That giant, Goliath was his name, pranced up and down the valley between the two armies in battle for forty days, daring any one man to come out and fight him. You should have seen him, the big bully. Why he was twice the size of the average man—"

"Then how on earth did that—did David kill him?" interrupted Ishbosheth.

"I'm coming to that, he said, and you won't believe it. When David saw the giant, he said, 'How dare that uncircumcised Philistine defy the armies of the living God? Why hasn't someone killed him and taken away the reproach from Israel?'

"And the men of Israel laughed. 'Perhaps you would like to kill him, sonny,' they said. 'The king has offered great riches, his beautiful daughter in marriage,'" Phaltiel bowed to Merab, "'and his father's house to be free of all government obligations—'"

"Mother! He wouldn't dare! Marry me to that—to David! Never!"

"Sh-h-," whispered Ahinoam. "Let him finish."

Michal's suffering eyes went unnoticed by her family, but the captain smiled compassionately at her.

"Eliab, David's oldest brother was angry at what he considered his young brother's impudence. He accused him arrogance and pride, neglecting the sheep, and sneaking off to watch the battle. David insisted his father, and at last, he knew why. He declared he would kill the giant.

"David's boast was immediately reported to Saul, and he sent for him. The boy assured the king the army could rest because he would fight the Philistine. Saul wouldn't hear of it. He reminded David he was only a boy, and the giant a seasoned veteran of many battles. Now this you really won't believe. David said he had fought a few battles of his own—claimed he'd killed a lion and a bear that attacked his sheep. You should have heard the men laugh.

"But David insisted the Lord delivered him from the paws of the lion and the bear, and he would also deliver him from the hand of the Philistine because the giant defied the armies of God. The man jeered, but Saul gave David his permission and his blessing to go fight Goliath.

"The king even took off his armor and put it on David. You should have seen David in Saul's coat of mail; he was lost in it, and the helmet came down over his eyes. When he buckled on that huge sword, it almost toppled him over.

"The boy jerked it all off. He said he couldn't fight in that armor; he was fighting in the name of the Lord. He took his staff in his fighting in the name of the Lord. He took his staff in his hand, and that sling he always carries. He picked up five smooth stones out of his shoulder, and went out to meet the giant.

"The soldiers hadn't laughed at all compared to the giant's guffaw, when he saw that pretty, bearded boy coming out to fight him. After he quit laughing, he began to curse him by the heathen gods; 'Am I a dog that you come at me with sticks and stones? Come on! I'll feed your carcass to the buzzards and the hyenas.'

"And David said, 'You come to me with a sword, a spear, and a shield; but I come to you in the name of the Lord of hosts, the God of the armies of Israel, whom you have defied. Today will the Lord deliver you into my hand. I'm going to kill you and cut head off; and I'm going to give the carcasses of the host of the Philistines to the buzzards and the hyenas, that all the world may know there is a God in Israel. And all these people shall know the Lord saves not with sword and spear; for the battle is the Lord's, and he will deliver you into our hands.'

"Well, that speech silenced the giant. He got up and started out to meet David. And when he did, David ran to meet him. While he was running, he took a stone out of the bag and hit the giant right between the eyes where his helmet did not quite come together. That big bully dropped like a polled ox.

"David didn't have a sword, but that didn't stop him. He ran up to the monster, yanked his own sword out of its sheath, and whacked off his head.

"When the Philistines saw their champion was dead, you should have seen them run! They didn't even stop to pick up their spears. The army chased them clear out of the country. David led the way—and no one was laughing. Dead Philistines littered the valley. And when I left, our men were gathering up the food and weapons the heathen left behind. It will be a long time before they attack us again. And we owe it all to David."

"I thought," observed Michal soberly, "David said God did it."

Phaltiel smiled at the big-eyed child. "You are right, little princess; I stand corrected. We do owe it all to God, but no man in our army doubted God used David to delivered us. I doubt if they ever scold him again."

"But—Mother—Father can't—"

"Never mind, Merab; we'll talk about it later. The captain is tired; we must let him get to bed."

"Thank you for coming, Phaltiel; when will the others be home?"

"Many of them should begin coming in tomorrow. It will take a while to collect all the spoil the Philistines left. David sent the giant's head to Jerusalem and left it on display there, but he kept the huge suit of brazen armor for a souvenir. He led the army down into Philistia.

"Our men will sack at least enough cities to pay for this war before they come home. Perhaps the Philistines will think twice before they invade Israel again. David vowed to make them pay for insulting his God. You know, to hear that boy talk, you'd think God was his own personal friend. Now all Israel is waiting for him to prove it."

Chapter 6

The men of Gibeah began to trickle in the following day. And they were indeed laden with spoil. In addition to gold, silver, and weapons, they brought armor, clothing, and tents. The city rang with rejoicing. Weddings along postponed were hastily arranged now that the young men could provide rich dowries.

Abner and the regular army planned to chase the Philistines clear back to Ekron and Gath, and lay waste their cities all the way. Never in Israel's long war with their ancient enemy had the heathen been so completely routed, or so many of them slaughtered.

Eventually, reports came to the palace that the king was on his way home, but he was being feted in every city he passed through. The grateful women met their victorious monarch with singing and dancing. As the women played on their instruments, they sang praises to the returning heroes: "Saul has slain his thousands, and David his ten thousands."

There was no rejoicing, however, in the palace. Merab cried and screamed she would not marry David; she vowed she would kill herself first. Ahinoam's best efforts could not comfort her hysterical daughter. Ishbosheth gallantly offered to kill David to save his sister. His mother rebuked him sharply.

"Why don't you run away with Adriel?" Michal suggested. "Father would not dare take a wife from her husband. And if he did, David wouldn't have you then."

Merab hushed her crying. "You know," she said grudgingly, "That's the first sensible thing you ever said."

When the king's party finally arrived, only Jonathan seemed happy. He had stripped himself of his royal robes and put them on David. The young hero looked every inch a crown prince—but not a very happy one. Abinadab and Melchishua were no longer disparaging David, but they were not praising him either. Adriel's face looked like a thundercloud, and Saul was in one of his black moods again.

In response to his wife's gentle inquiry, the king stormed, "They have ascribed to David ten thousands, and to me but thousands: What more can he have but the kingdom? The Lord has departed from me. But surely he would not give my kingdom to a childish sheepherder; it's not to be borne."

"Did the boy not save your army from the giant?" asked Ahinoam meekly.

"I'd rather the giant had killed me than to die at the hands of that stripling."

"You don't really believe David could harm you?"

"Why wouldn't he? He wants my kingdom!"

"What makes you think he wants my kingdom? Did he say so?"

"Of course not! But all he has to do is ask God, and he'll give it to him."

"But Samuel says God has already taken the kingdom from you, and given it to another. If David is the man, what can you do?"

"I can do plenty! I will not let that upstart sit on my throne. I'll kill him first. Jonathan has already capitulated—put his royal robes on David, but I won't have it! My son shall rule after me, and nothing is going to stop him."

"Of course, dear," soothed Ahinoam, as she saw the emotional storm clouds erupting into a torrent.

Michal sat quietly during the king's outburst. "Father," she interposed gently, "you won't let David marry Merab either, will you?"

"Not even if I have to kill him!"

"You don't need to kill him. Anyway that would make the people angry. But if Merab ran away with Adriel, you couldn't help that could you?"

The angry monarch almost smiled. "I could collect all the dowry he offered, too. Not a bad idea at all; I'm glad I thought of it. I shall insist Merab marries Adriel whether she likes it or not."

"She wouldn't think of disobeying you, Father," Michal insisted piously.

David came back to his usual place in the palace, but he was no longer the king's armorbearer. He had been made captain over a thousand men instead. The young captain behaved himself wisely and well, and the Lord blessed him wherever he went.

But the evil spirit troubled Saul increasingly. When David tried to play for the sick man as he had at other times, the king cast a javelin at him. Only the youth's agility saved his being pinned to the wall. David tried a second, and again he was forced to flee for his life. Afterwards he avoided the king's presence whenever possible.

The more Saul persecuted David, however, the more the people loved him. And the populace clamored for the royal wedding, for all Israel knew of the king's promise. Only David said nothing.

As a matter of expediency, Saul renewed his promise to David, but asked him to wipe out a particularly stubborn Philistine stronghold before the wedding. After David and his thousand men had gone, Saul told Jonathan he preferred the Philistines kill David than having to do the job himself. The king was certain the boy's death would solve all his problems, but Jonathan grieved because he loved David as his own soul.

When a runner brought news of David's victorious slaughter of the Philistines, Saul sent for Adriel. He told him if he still wanted to marry Merab, to be ready to take her and leave as soon as darkness fell.

Merab was so excited she dropped everything she touched. After tripping on her own skirt, and falling flat on her face in the floor, she sat down and let her journey, she took off her dress of divers colors, which designated her as a virgin princess, and gave it to Michal.

"Be sure you wear it until you find a man you want to marry."

Michal was as surprised as she was grateful. It was the first time her sister ever spoke to her as an equal. "But I've already found the I want to marry."

"You've what?"

"I've already found the man I want to marry," Michal repeated boldly.

"But who? Oh! Aha! So that's why you have been so helpful about getting me married to Adriel. You want the giant-killer for yourself. I should have suspected that scheming little brain of yours. Just you wait 'till I tell father."

"Now Merab—wait. Listen to me. All Father promised the man who slew the giant was his daughter in marriage. He didn't say which one, I am the king's daughter, you know. But I can't marry until you are married—"

"And you think you want sheepherder? What about the prince you always said you were going to marry?"

"But David is a prince! Michal said stubbornly as she lifted her chin to a proud angle. And I've wanted to marry him since the first time I laid eyes on him."

"Oh, Michal! How stupid can you get?"

When Merab relayed the interesting news to her father, however, he was delighted.

"So that's the reason he didn't insist I keep my bargain. If Michal wants him, he probably wants her, too. What better way to keep an eye on him? And she is but a child; she will do whatever I say."

Merab arched her black eyebrows, but said nothing.

"Just be patient, my daughter; you may not have to run

Chapter 7

Saul sent for David immediately, and greeted his arrival with all his old loving familiarity. "I have not forgotten, my son, I promised you my daughter to wife. It's time we talked about the marriage."

David bowed low before the throne. "It may seem a light thing to you to be the king's son-in-law, but I am a poor nobody. How can I marry a princess?"

Saul smiled indulgently, but watched David like a cat watching a mouse. "Oh come now, my boy, we will be delighted to have you in the royal family. I'll even give you a choice; you can have either of my daughters. Take your pick. And as for dowry, slaughtering the giant was the richest dowry you could have provided."

David bowed his head again, but not before Saul saw the pleased gleam in his eyes. "You are most gracious, my lord, but I did not slay the giant for a wife; I slew him for the Lord."

Saul called his servants and commanded them to commune with David secretly and persuade him to consent to be the king's son-in-law. They were instructed to convince David the king was anxious to have him marry his daughter, and that the royal family and all the servants loved him.

David, however, demurred. He was not worthy to be the king's first son-in-law. And he had no dowry.

When David's excuses were relayed to Saul, he instructed his servants to tell the captain Merab was to be married to Adriel immediately, and all the dowry he wanted for Michal was a hundred dead Philistines. The servants reported back to their master that under those conditions, David would be delighted to be the king's son-in-law.

"The Philistines are mighty warriors; surely they will slay him, and my hand need not be upon him," said Saul gleefully.

But David returned victorious again from his slaughter of the Philistines, and he brought not one—but two hundred foreskins and presented them in full tale to the king. And Saul gave him Michal his daughter to wife.

David was as gentle a lover as he was a teacher. His young bride was ecstatic. "And to think," she said as she lay drowsily in David's arms, "I thought I wanted to marry a prince."

"No regrets?"

"No regrets. I have loved you since the first day you came to the palace. I even asked God to take the kingdom from my father if there was no other way I could have you. It's much better this way; God brought you to me—even if I did have to help him a little."

"You? Help God? You're but a child; what could you do?"

"I managed to arrange it so you wouldn't have to marry Merab."

"My dear girl, nothing could have persuaded me to marry Merab. But why did she want you to marry? I never counted her among my admirers."

"She thought she was spiting me—keeping me from marrying a prince."

"Why were you so anxious to marry a prince—wealth or position?"

"Neither."

"Why, then?"

"Have you been so long at the palace—wealth or position?"

"I don't recall ever discussing the subject. And I really never thought of your marrying anyone but me."

Michal felt herself bathed in a warm, sweet glow. "Mother, Father, and Jonathan were fairly nice to me, but you saw the others. If I stepped on Merab's toes, she said 'get off me.' If she stepped on me, she said 'get out from under me.' I thought if I were a queen, perhaps my brothers and sister would respect me."

"Then why marry me? You knew I wouldn't improve your status with them."

"Because, my love, I had rather have you than all the status in the world."

"And I had rather have you, my darling, than all kingdoms in the world."

"You'll always love me—never leave me?"

"I'll always love my little princess; and if I ever have to leave you, I'll always come back. Will that do?"

"That should do—as long as you are alive. But—"

"Oh, I plan to stay alive. Michal, there's something I've wanted to tell you for a long time; but your father must have never know."

"My loyalties belong to my husband."

"Always?"

"Forever and ever."

"That should be long enough. Do you remember my telling you Samuel came to Bethlehem to offer a sacrifice?"

"I remember."

"Well—I didn't tell you quite everything. It was shortly before your father sent for me to come and play for him. The whole city was excited; nothing like it ever happened in Bethlehem before. When Samuel was ready to offer the sacrifice, he sent for my father and told him to bring his sons along.

"I was out with the sheep. Father took my seven brothers, and went to worship. Samuel told Father the Lord had a special assignment for one of his sons, but he didn't know which one.

"Eliab is so big and—and handsome, Samuel was certain he was the one. But God said no. One by one, the prophet passed all my brothers before the Lord, but he turned them all down.

"Then Samuel asked Father if he had any more sons. When told him his youngest was out with the sheep, the prophet insisted he send for me, and he delayed the sacrifices until I got there. As soon as I arrived, Samuel took the horn of holy oil and anointed my head. From that day to this, the Lord has been with me in a strange way. God enabled me to kill the lion and the bear—and the giant. And it's through him I've been able to conquer the Philistines. The people praises me, but it is the Lord who deserves the praises."

What did Samuel say the Lord anointed you for?"

"He didn't say."

"Do you know?"

"I'm beginning to suspect."

"You are the man God has chosen to take my father's kingdom?"

"I believe God has appointed me to lead Israel," whispered David humbly.

"And my father believes it—doesn't he?"

"I'm sure he suspects; why else would he want to kill me?"

"But if God has given you the kingdom, father should know he cannot prevent your having it."

"That's what I keep telling myself, but when I saw those javelins coming my way, I felt like the Lord gave me enough sense to dodge."

"Oh, David! I'm frightened! I thought Father's madness caused him to attack you. But he will never let you take his throne—not while he's alive."

"I know."

"David! You wouldn't?"

"No, my darling. I would never harm the king. Not because he's your father, but because he's the anointed of the Lord. I will never lift my hand against the Lord's anointed.

"Then how do you plan to get the kingdom?"

"I don't. As far as I'm concerned, the Lord gave the kingdom to your father, and he can take it away from him. And if God wants me to have it, he will give it to me in his own good time."

Michal was silent so long in the thick darkness, David thought she had fallen asleep. Then in a subdued, almost reverent voice she said, "Now I think I understand."

"Understand what?"

"Why God took the kingdom from my father and gave it you."

"Oh?"

"You really love God, don't you? Your religion is not reserved for sacrifices and feast days; you live it every day."

"I try. Michal, you see, religion is like weight: A hundred pounds carried in a sack in a sack on a man's back—or as excess fat—is a painful burden. But carried on the inside as bone, sinew, and muscle it is a priceless advantage. Your father's religion is all excess baggage carried on the outside. If it does not destroy him, it is certainly no help. And the responsibilities of leading God's people simply cannot be carried without God's help."

Again Michal was silent. Then in a husky, reverent whisper she asked, "David, what is God like?"

"God is like a friend who sticks closer than a brother. He is like the sun: He warms us, lights our pathways, and nourishes everything that feeds, clothes, and shelters us. He is like a shield: He protects us from our enemies. He is like water: He cleanses and refreshes us. He is like bread:

He nourishes and sustains us." David paused. "Shall I go on, my dear? I could sing God's praises all the night long."

"No, my love, but I get the idea. Your God sounds so wonderful; I wish he were my God, too."

"Isn't he your God, my darling? He wants to be."

"No." There was another long pause. "My religion is like my father's; it's all on the outside. I've never thought of God unless I wanted something—or was in trouble. It never occurred to me he was with me all the time. Mercy!" She giggled. "I must mend my ways."

Chapter 8

It was as if a page had turned in the household of Saul. As soon as the celebrations of the marriages of the king's daughters' were over, Saul arranged for the consummation of the long contracted marriage between Jonathan and Adena, the daughter of Saul's sister. Adena combined the dark beauty of Merab with Michal's sharp wit and quick energy, so Ahinoam was comforted in the absence of her daughters.

When Adena presented Saul with his first grandson before the year was out, she won her father-in-law's heart also. And little Mephibosheth was the pride and joy of the palace.

Merab also was expecting a baby. Ahinoam felt she could not leave Adena and the new baby in the hands of the servants, so she sent Michal to Mehola to look after Merab. If Merab was overjoyed to see her sister, she concealed it well.

"Why didn't Mother come?" she greeted Michal angrily.

Michal was so shocked at her sister's ravaged beauty, she could scarcely speak. Merab's flawless ivory skin was a mass of hideous brown splotches. Her dainty waistline had assumed barrel-like proportions. "She—she wanted to come, Merab—was all ready. But Adena had her baby yesterday; and—well—Mother couldn't leave her."

"Pray why not? Is Jonathan's wife more important to Mother than her own daughter?"

"But Merab, Mother plans to come as soon as Adena is able to be up. She hopes to be here before your baby comes."

"Hopes? Ha! If Adena can spare her? With my luck she probably won't get here at all. Sables—ugh! What on earth make girls foolish enough to want to get married?"

"Oh, Merab!" Michal was as surprised at her sister's bitter words as she was at her ravished appearance. Motherhood only made Adena more beautiful. Jonathan declared she looked like a fruit tree in full bloom.

Merab was almost unrecognizable. Michal was so disconcerted at the ruin of her sister's face and figure, she forgot her own discomfort.

Mehola was a day's journey from Gibeah, and Michal was sick from the rocking of the camel's back. The heat and the dust was almost unbearable. She felt she was coated with desert sand, but Merab did not offer her guest food or drink, or water to wash away the grime of the long journey. Michal was grateful her servants had gone to the servants' quarters where she trusted they were being made comfortable.

Merab seemed to be working herself up into an emotional state similar to their father's temper tantrums. In an effort to distract her, Michal inquired about Adriel.

"He's supposed to be out chasing Philistines with David. You mean you didn't know?" Merab continued without waiting for an answer. "Men have all the fun while women stay home and have babies!"

"Why, Merab! And here I am—green with envy. You and Adena both having babies, and me without even a prospect."

"Ha! You don't know how lucky you are." Merab cast an envious glance at Michal's trim figure. "In addition to ruining my digestion and my waistline, look at my face! It looks as if I had fallen into a pile of fresh cow dung. No wonder Adriel went off to war. I know he hates the sight of me. But it's all his fault. I told him I didn't want children-not now anyway. With all these wars, and the world in such turmoil, who wants children? He said he didn't care if I had one child or a dozen—that was my problem."

"You mean you don't want any children?"

"No I don't! Just look at me! How would you like to look like this?"

"I wouldn't care what I looked like if I could give David a son.
He tells me not to worry, when I'm a little older—"

"Was Jonathan's baby a boy?" interrupted Merab.
Michal nodded.

"With my luck I'm sure to have a girl. If it's a boy I shall certainly have no more children. Marriage may be fun for men, but all a woman gets out of it is a lot of hard work, having to put up with a man's nonsense, and a baby every year. God forbid!"

"But men being the way they are, how can you be sure you will have no more children?"

"Adriel can get a concubine—or a dozen for all I care—as long as he leaves me alone."

Michal gazed pityingly at her sister. Merab interpreted her sister's gaze correctly. "Don't tell me you enjoy sleeping with a man! Even you couldn't be that big a fool."

"But Merab, the marital relationship is a spiritual communion. It is the ultimate expression of love between husband and wife—"

"Oh don't give me that tripe! It's a disgusting process, and you know it!"

"Speak for yourself, my dear sister; speak for yourself."

Merab's pessimistic prediction failed to materialize. The daughter she feared turned out to be two sons. But even two fine, fat, healthy baby boys failed to mollify the new mother. Ahinoam did not arrive; Adriel was still away, and Merab found numerous other causes for complaint.

Michal secured two wet nurses for the twins, an excellent nurse for Merab, and kept the household running without a problem. All of which Merab seemingly ignored. True, her labor had been long and difficult, and there was no one to sympathize with her but Michal. Adriel's family and the servants tired of her complaints—real and imagined—long ago.

Adriel's mother insisted Merab had no milk for her babies because her hot temper dried it up. The wet nurses were most dependable, but Merab demanded her sister personally supervise each feeding. Michal took the babies to bed with her in a room so far removed from Merab the babies' cries could not disturb her.

Some nights Michal got almost no sleep at all. But she loved the twins so much, she wondered if she could have loved them more if they were her very own. And in spite of her weariness, caring for them was a joy; she could hardly bear the thought of leaving them. It was her first experience with babies, and they were an endless source of wonder and delight.

Michal remained in Mehola a full month. But when Adriel returned with word David was back in Gibeah, she knew she must return home immediately. With obvious but unexpressed regret, Merab let her go.

Chapter 9

When Michal arrived home she found David ready to flee. Her most impassioned pleas failed to dissuade him.

"It's no use, Michal. Jonathan told me your father has commanded everyone in the palace to kill me—even Jonathan. He won't, of course; but I wouldn't dare turn my back on Ishbosheth, and I'm not sure about the other two. I'm going to slip out as soon as it gets dark. Thank heaven there is no moon."

"If you must go, David, take me with you—please; I don't want to live without you."

"I wish I could, my darling, but I wouldn't dare. Your father would hunt us down for sure, and kill us both."

"Why is it you are not afraid of giants or thousands of Philistines, yet you flee for your life from my father?"

"It's quite simple, my dear. I can kill the Philistines. I cannot kill your father."

"Well I wish—."

"Don't say it, Michal. Your father is the Lord's anointed; we must let God deal with him."

There was a rapid knock at the door. David leaped to his feet, but was arrested by Jonathans voice outside. Quickly he unbolted the door.

After a hasty greeting for his sister, Jonathan addressed his brother-in-law. "Hurry, David, before some assassin tries to collect the bounty Father has placed on your head. He's in a terrible state tonight; I can't reason with him at all. But you hide in that cave beside Father's target range tomorrow. I'm going to talk with him while we practice. If I can persuade him to be sensible I'll let you know. If I can't, you must get out of Gibeah at once; he has every villain in the city laying for you."

Jonathan turned to Michal. "Quick, pack some food for David. If won't be safe to show himself to anyone. Every rascal in the kingdom will be out to collect the bounty. And even his best friends will be afraid to help him for fear of the king's wrath."

Jonathan's face softened at the stricken look in his sister's eyes. "I'm sorry, little sister; I know this isn't much of a homecoming. But I'll do the best I can. I must go now before Father misses me and suspects where I've gone."

Without another word, Jonathan slipped out into the night. In a few minutes David, too, melted into the darkness, and Michal was alone.

The next day dawned bright and beautiful. Jonathan did his best to make his father's target practice a pleasant experience. When the king seemed relaxed and in a better mood, Jonathan brought the conversation around to his friend.

"Why, Father, are you so determined to have David killed? He never did you any harm. On the contrary he has done everything in his power to please you. He has played his harp at your command; he risked his life to kill the giant your entire army quailed before; and the Philistines he left alive, he has scared clear out of Israel. You have never had a more profitable servant. How can you sin against this innocent man to slay him without a cause?"

"You are right, my son, and I'm sorry. I'll rescind the order immediately. You know I've not been myself lately. But, I'll swear, as the Lord lives, David shall not be slain."

So Saul returned to the palace, and Jonathan hurried to David's hiding place to tell him the good news. But David had heard the conversation, and came out to meet his friend.

There was rejoicing in David's household! Whatever reservations Michal might have about her father's change of heart, she did not voice them. And David, who always lived one day at a time, played his harp while his wife recounted her visit with Merab.

David's only comment was, "Poor Adriel."

"What do you mean 'Poor Adriel?' Wouldn't you like to have two fine sons?"

"I'd love it. But not if Merab was their mother. I don't see how you two could be sisters."

Michal smiled appreciatingly. "Oh David, I want a baby! Every time you go out to battle, I think I could stand it so much better if only I had your sons she doesn't even want, and I have none when I want one so much. Why doesn't God give me children?"

"Give him time, dear! Give him time. After all you are little more than a child. God has promised me many sons. Be patient; once the babies start coming, you may be more anxious to get them stopped."

Through all her remaining years, Michal looked back on the next few months as the happiest period of her life. David went back to the palace and played for Saul as he had on his first visit there. He romped with Jonathan's small son, and promised to look after him in the absence of his father.

For the first time David took Michal to Bethlehem to visit his parents. He obviously enjoyed displaying her fresh young beauty before his tall, handsome brothers. The whole city turned out to honor their returning hero. They praised him for courage in slaying the giant, and delivering Israel from the Philistines.

A man less humble than David would have been overcome with pride. But other than entertaining his young nephews with a few tales of his war exploits, David spent most of his time playing his harp and singing psalms for his mother. With deep regret, Michal and David mounted their camels to return to Gibeah.

"Oh David, why can't we stay here?" Michal pleaded. "It's so pleasant and peaceful. No crowds. No noise. No dirt. Even the sky seems bluer, and I knew the grass is greener. Let Father get someone else to fight his battles. He has Jonathan and Abner; they are good men. He doesn't need you."

"Of course he doesn't, Michal. And I want to stay here much more than you do. There is nothing in the world I would like better than spending my life in Bethlehem, leading my sheep in the green pastures and beside the still waters. Just the thought of it restores my soul."

"Then why can't we stay?"

"Because God has destined me to slay his enemies. You don't think I enjoy all the killing I've been doing, do you? I don't fight for your father; I fight for the Lord. I will have to keep on fighting until God gives Israel rest from her enemies. I keep hoping every battle will be the last. I had much rather play my harp, sing—and make love to my wife—than fight. But unless you want to be a slave, my pretty princess, as long as the heathen keep attacking us, I must fight."

On their way back to the palace, the travelers went by to visit Merab and Adriel. Michal wanted to see how the twins were doing, and she wanted David to see her precious nephews.

To Michal's dismay, she found Merab great with child again. And her condition had not improved her disposition.

The twins were already walking. Their father was certain he had the finest sons in the kingdom. The boys were fascinated with their Uncle David. It was difficult for them to be still for a moment, yet they sat in rapt enchantment while David placed his harp.

Because Merab was so indisposed, the visitors departed earlier than they had anticipated, but not before Merab exacted a promise from Michal to return for her confinement. Pity, envy, and condemnation for her sister struggled for mastery of Michal's heart. David suggested she save her pity for Adriel and the babies.

Chapter 10

By the time David and Michal sighted the watchtower, they know all was not well in Gibeah. The tower was crowded with watchers instead of the usual lone sentry. When the watchers sighted David's party, they swarmed down the tower like ants. Soon a runner sped over the horizon toward the travelers.

"Make haste, my captain," panted the messenger. "All the tribes of the Philistines have banded together and are marching toward Gibeah. They vow to avenge their fallen leader, the giant who you slew. The soldiers of Gibeah are massed; they only await your leadership. And runners have been dispatched to all the cities of Israel."

Before the runner finished his message, David leaped lightly to the ground, and forced his camel to kneel. Quickly, he remounted the beast, and beckoned the panting messenger to get on behind him. Pulling the animal to its feet, David coaxed the plodding desert steed into a gallop, and the caravan raced toward the city.

While David collected his weapons of war, and prepared to lead the army into battle, Michal tagged disconsolately at his heels.

"War! Always war," she lamented. "Why can't civilized people find better ways of settling their differences than sending their finest young men out to kill each other?"

"My wise little princess is not the first woman to ask that question, and you probably won't be the last. But I don't have the answer. War is not romantic as so many young men think before the try it. Fighting may bring honor to a few, but to the majority it brings dirt, danger, dysentery, and death. War is not glory; it's grueling toll. It's trying to sleep on the ground in the freezing rain, or marching all day under a blistering sun. It's a burning hell where hunger tramps with a tireless tread, and death awaits at the end of the road."

"Then why can't civilized people—?"

"There's your answer, my love; civilized people could find a better way. They wouldn't even have to be civilized. If all people would obey God, there would never be another war. But as long as men allow envy, hate, and greet to rule their lives, there will be wars. And as long as we are attacked, we must defend ourselves—or do you want to be some Philistine's slave? But you don't need to worry about that, my love; they would never put you on the slave block—even if you are the most beautiful woman in all Israel."

Michal blushed modestly, but she straightened her tired shoulders, and lifted her drooping chin to its usual proud angle.

"They wouldn't sell you, my dear; the wife of David and daughter of Saul would be roasted on Dagon's altar."

Michal shivered.

"How would you like that?"

"Not much." Michal tried to smile. "Please be careful, darling, and I know God will protect you. I shall pray night and day for your safe return."

"Thank you, my princess. But you see why I must go. And it might comfort you to remember I am probably safer fighting Philistines that I am in your father's court."

"I know, darling, and I'm so sorry. But I still want you to come back as soon as your possibly can. I loved you so much."

"And I love you," whispered David, as he bent to kiss his wife goodbye. "But I must hurry. We want to intercept the Philistines as quickly as possible. They will plunder, torture, and kill every step of the way."

"It is almost night now," protested Michal. "And you are tired and hungry. When will you eat or sleep?"

"If we don't stop the Philistines, none of us will be eating or sleeping for long."

"Wait, David! Please—I'll only be a moment," Michal cried as she dashed back into the house.

David nervously adjusted his sword, and shifted his shield to a more comfortable position. It was scarcely a minute, however, until Michal returned. She pushed a leather bag into his hands.

"It's only bread and cheese, and parched corn, but at least you won't starve tonight. I was so worried about your having to go, I forgot you had to eat. I'm sure God will take care of you, but I think we should give him all the help we can. So don't you take any foolish chances."

"Thank you, my love. I promise not to tempt God."

David kissed his wife's uplifted lips again, and hastened away in the gathering dusk to join his forces waiting at the city gates.

Chapter 11

Every runner from the battlefield brought a favorable report. David was scoring the greatest victories since the slaying of Goliath; he was slaughtering the Philistines in even greater numbers. Every captive Israelite had been set free, and David was sacking the cities of the Philistines for spoil to restore the plunder taken by the invading hordes.

But as each glowing accounts of David's exploits reached Gibeah, Saul becomes more morose. Carefully, the king inquired of the messengers as to the deeds of his own sons, Jonathan, Abinadab, and Melchishua, who accompanied David into battle.

Every messenger assured the king his sons were well, but they ascribed the victories to David. By the time the Philistines were vanquished, and the soldiers of Israel had returned to their homes once more, the evil spirit was again in full possession of the king.

Michal delayed her husband with every tactic her cunning young mind could devise, but in the afternoon of the day following his return to Gibeah, David reluctantly announced he must return to the palace, he deliberately arrived after night to avoid meeting the king until Jonathan had opportunity to evaluate his father's mood; his report was not encouraging.

David brought home ten mules loaded with spoil from Ashdod. There were gold and silver, rare jewels, and fine raiment. But his wife scarcely glanced at the booty; she had eyes only for her husband.

Michal hastened home from Mehola as soon as she learned David was coming. (Merab and Adriel had another baby boy.) She arrived to Gibeah only slightly ahead of the army. The whole city was buzzing with gossip about Saul's foul mood, and tittering about his unseemly jealousy. There was a growing rumor David would be the next king. The elders who witnessed Samuel's slaying of old king Agag, and heard him denounce

Saul, were discreetly inquiring and searching for the "neighbor" to whom God promised the kingdom.

What neighbor did Saul have who was better than David? Who would make a stronger king than the handsome Bethlehemite who behaved himself so wisely and well? All his victories and the honors heaped upon him—including marrying the king's daughter, had not changed the humble shepherd lad. David still played his harp for the crowds, sang his beautiful songs, and reverently attended all religious services. Where could Israel find a more Godly ruler? From the humblest to the greatest, the people adored him.

Michal killed the fatted calf for her victorious captain, and decorated the house with garlands for a hero's welcome, She was happiest, however, after their friends and the servants were all gone, and she was alone with her husband.

David never talked of his exploits on the battlefield, and Michal knew better than to enquire. When they were alone together, he usually played on his harp and harp and sang his latest psalms for his greatest admirer and most constructive critic. Michal lacked her husband's poetic zeal and religious fervor, but her good common sense and realistic approach to life was superior to his. David was a dreamer and his wife was a realist, a combination guaranteed to make heaven or hell of a marriage; it all depended on the mixture.

In the midst of battle, David had composed another psalm. He could hardly wait for the last servant to depart, to sing it for Michal. While he tuned his harp, she reclined on cushions at his feet. Weary as the conquering hero was, he could not retire until his wife had heard his new song.

The bright smile on Michal's face belied her burdened heart. She was filled with dire forebodings for their future. How would her husband react to the message she must give him before he faced her father again?

Michal was determined, however, nothing should spoil David's first night at home. All unpleasantness could wait until tomorrow. So she smiled encouragingly in all the right places as her husband sang, and repressed her resentment that he always sang about his love for God, and never of his love for her.

"In the Lord put I my trust," David sang.

"If I know my father, the Lord is going to need a little help," thought Michal dourly, but she smiled as sweetly as ever.

"How say you to my soul, flee as a bird to your mountains, "the song continued.

"You'll need a mountain, my love, and a big one to hide you from the king's wrath," Michal reflected.

> For, lo, the wicked bend their bow, they make ready their
> arrow upon the string that may privily shoot at the
> upright in heart.
> If the foundations be destroyed, what can the righteous do?
> The Lord is in the holy temple, the Lord's throne is in
> heaven: his eyelids try, the children of men.
> The Lord tries the righteous, but the wicked and him that
> loves violence his soul hates.
> Upon the wicked he shall rain snares, fire and brimstone,
> and an horrible tempest; this shall be the portion of
> their cup.
> For the righteous Lord loves righteousness; his countenance
> beholds the upright."

When David finished his song, he waited expectantly for his wife's acclaim. She was forced to stifle a prayer for God to hasten the fire and brimstone before she could speak.

"It's beautiful, darling. Simply beautiful! It's a shame you can't share your lovely psalms with the whole wide world. Your goodness, purity, and faith shine through them all."

David frowned. "It's not my goodness, heaven forbid! That I want to shine through my psalms; it's God's goodness I sing about. You didn't see that?"

"Of course, dear, but you see—I'm not a very objective listener. People usually hear what they listen for, and I must admit I listen for the beauty and goodness of the pure soul of my dear husband that shines through every psalm you write."

"I know you do," sighed David, not at all mollified. "And that's what worries me. I want you to look to God, lean on his promises, and trust him. God will sustain you. I might let you down, but God never will."

Michal arose from her pillows, gently took David's harp from his hands, laid it aside, and curled up in his lap. "I can't imagine my kind husband failing me—ever. Do you know you are the first person in my whole life who has treated me with respect, trusted me, and loved me for what I am—not who I am? Do you have any idea how much that means to me?"

"Yes, my darling, I do," David relented instantly. "Have you forgotten that my father did not even bother to include me among his sons when Samuel called him to the sacrifices? And my brothers ordered me off the battlefield minutes before I killed the giant. How many people love me for myself? You—and my mother. All others love me for what I can do for them.

"But it's because I love you so much I want you to love God. I can't bear the thought of being forever separated from you. It's torture to leave you when I go to war, and I fight the harder knowing I'm protecting you. Life is so short, and eternity is so long, I want you to love God supremely, so I can sing to you throughout the endless ages—where there will be no more wars and no more sad goodbyes."

"Not only the psalms you write, my love, are beautiful; everything you say is beautiful."

David gazed into the trusting brown eyes fixed on his face with such worshipful devotion. He sighed in exasperation, but he crushed her to his heart, picked her up in his powerful arms, and carried her to the bedroom.

When David was home, Michal always dismissed the servants, with instructions not to return until she called for them. She carefully closed them. She carefully closed the heavy curtains so the house would remain cool and dark.

The sun was shining before she waked the next morning; her weary husband still slept beside her. She wanted to get up and prepare his breakfast, but she knew how unpleasant it was to wake to an empty bed.

While she waited quietly for David to stir, Michal meditated on the best way and time to break the news to him. He must hear from her the rapidly spreading rumor that God had chosen him to supplant her father as king of Israel. Surely her husband would not think she had betrayed his confidence; she would have guarded his secret with her life. Apparently, the elders circulated the story of Samuel's pronounced judgment on Saul, and the people guessed the identity of the promised ruler because God's favor so obviously rested upon David.

Suddenly, Michal noticed her husband's even breathing had changed. She turned her head to find his adoring gaze fastened upon her.

"Do you have any idea what it's like," he asked as he gathered her into his arms, "to wake up in a soft bed beside a lovely woman after months on the battlefield?"

Michal smiled as she thanked God for the presence of mind to remain in bed.

"It is unfortunate the psalmists rhapsody only about the glory and honor of war. Why don't they sing about the stench of the blood, sweat, and unburied dead?

"Oh, forgive me, dear," whispered David contritely, as his wife stiffened in his arms. "I didn't seem to be morbid. But after months of sleeping—if I was lucky—on the hard ground, this heavenly bed and angelic bedmate has made me maudlin.

"From waking up in a tiny tent crowded with unwashed bodies reeking of stale sweat, to this," he gestured to include Michal and the festively garlanded room, "is enough to turn a man's head."

Michal decided it was not the proper time to give her husband bad news.

In spite of all his wife's stalling, the time came when David insisted he must report to the king. And Michal knew she dared not let him go unwarned.

"David," she hesitated while she tightened her arms around his neck.

"Yes?"

"There's something I have to tell you before you get to the palace. And I do hope you won't—. Surely you must know—," Michal stammered.

"What is it, my love? Haven't we always been able to tell each other everything?"

"Oh, yes, David. And that's what I love most about you. But I love you so much I had rather die than have you lose faith in me."

"Then I promise I won't lose faith in you, because I want you to live. So remember, I promise never, never to lose faith in you. How can you tell me?"

David's teasing words and trusting smile partially restored Michal's confidence. She blurted out the story quickly before doubt overwhelmed her again. "Oh, David, everybody in the city is talking about your being king of Israel in place of my father—and I didn't tell them—I didn't!"

"For a moment, David looked stunned. Then pushing his wife away from him, he threw back his head and laughed in obvious relief. "Is that all? You poor child. I already knew that. The rumor probably started when

I killed Goliath; it has grown with every victory God has given me. You didn't really think I would suspect you of betraying me, did you?"

"I know I couldn't bear it if you did," whispered Michal as she crept back into his arms. "You are my life. I'll never, never betray you, and I would not want to live if you didn't trust me. Promise me now, whatever may come between us, you will never doubt I'm on your side, and somewhere I'll be waiting for your return."

"A promise like that, my darling, should bring a man back from hell itself. With you and God on my side, what do I have to fear?"

"Well—for a start—there's King Saul."

"David laughed ruefully. "As usual, you're right. The devil, I may can handle; Saul, I'm not so sure, but I promise to try."

Chapter 12

David stood respectfully in the presence of his sovereign, and gave a detailed report of his victory over the Philistines. He attributed all the credit possible to Saul's sons, to Abner and the other captains, and took as little as possible for himself.

Saul accepted the report stoically, and made all the right responses. The malevolent gleam in the king's eyes, however, made the hair prickle on the warrior's neck.

His duty discharged, David took his accustomed seat by the window, and softly strummed on his harp. He appeared perfectly at ease, but was careful to keep the king within his range of vision. At the height of the first crescendo of Saul's favorite tune, David saw the king's hand reaching for the javelin by his side.

The spear was scarcely in the air when David bolted out the open window beside him. The weapon pierced the wall still warm from the pressure of the musician's body.

Saul screamed in maniacal frenzy, "Get him! Catch him! Kill him! Don't let my enemy get away."

The palace guard stumbled over each other in utter confusion as David fled.

It was a chagrinned and discouraged man who burst into the house he left so bravely little more than an hour earlier. When thousands of Philistines failed to do in more than two years of unrelenting effort, Saul accomplished in as many minutes: The mighty David fled for his life.

Michal quizzed her husband for every detail of his unfortunate encounter with her father. It was not a matter of curiosity but expediency: She dared not underestimate the threat of the king's destructive mood.

"Please don't be discouraged, darling," Michal pleaded. "We knew this could happen. If you can't fight my father, then we must run away."

"You know I cannot fight the Lord's anointed," David replied dully. "If God has chosen me to rule Israel, then he must give it to me; I will not lift a finger to take it."

"All right. If that's the way you want it, then that's the way it has to be. Quick! Let's get a few things together and get out of here.

"Where will we go? No one in all Israel would dare give us refuge; Saul would kill them."

"Why, David! With all the friends you have? How can you say a thing like that? Everyone loves you."

"Oh, yes! They love me—as long as I'm in the king's good graces. But they will never risk their lives to protect me."

"Pray, why not? Have you not risked your life many times to protect them?"

"But that's in the past; this is present danger, and that makes all the difference."

"Then we will find a mountain or a cave to hide in. You will not stay here and be killed. I don't care where we go as long as we go together. Hurry. I know my father; we've no time to lose."

In minutes, Michal had packed a few changes of clothes and provisions for their journey. David packed as much of the gold and silver as he thought they could carry, a good supply of spears, his bow and arrows, and his sword. He could not take his armor, but he would feel undressed without his sword.

Michal did not even give a backward glance at the house where she had been so happy, as she stepped boldly out the door. David, at her heels, saw her go rigid. Quietly, she stepped back inside and closed the door. Her face was white with fear.

"What is it?" David whispered. "What's wrong?"

"We're too late. The palace guards are crouching behind the shrubbery; they'll kill you the minute you step out the door. We'll have to wait until dark. The window above the back stairs is big enough for you to get through. We'll make a rope to let you down by—."

"What about? You can't stay here; your father would kill you if you were to help me escape."

"Oh, he won't hurt me; I know how to manage him—"

"If you had seen his eyes this afternoon, you would know he is capable of anything. He looked as if Satan was in full control; it was a terrible sight."

"He must be in a state to send the palace guard on such a shameful mission. Phalti is your greatest admirer in all the palace. And he has always been extra nice to me. He will stall as long as long as he can. But if they don't get you by morning, I'm sure Father will demand they come in after you. You must leave tonight."

"Not without you, my love—."

"But, David, it's like you said before, I would only slow you down, and we might both be killed. I'll stay here and stall them as long as possible, then you will have the whole night to get away. I can join you later. I'll go to Merab's or something. She's having another baby, you know, so I'll have a good excuse. Now, hurry! Let's get a rope made."

Michal collected her strongest sheets, and deftly bound them into a sturdy rope. "Take as much gold as you can, your weapons and all the food you can carry," she urged. "But I'm sure you will have to walk. Father will have the stables guarded, I know. That's the first order he gives when he wants to trap someone. A man on foot is usually easy to catch, but I'm sure your God will deliver you if you only do your best."

"Isn't he your God, too, Michal?"

"I don't know. My God has always been a stern and rigid Judge in some far-off heaven. Your God seems to be a friend who walks and talks with you."

"That he does, my love, and he'll walk with you if you will only get on the right road."

I'll try, darling; I really will, but first I must get you off. I think it's dark enough now they can't see you, but must be gone before the moon comes up."

A thorough search of the house failed to reveal anything strong enough to sustain David's weight while he went down the rope. Michal insisted on trying the rope around her own body, while she braced herself against the window frame. Reluctantly, David agreed. The mighty warrior looked back on the night's experiences as unique in more ways than one: It was the only time he ever entrusted his life into the hands of another human being.

When David was girt for his journey, Michal persuaded him to leave his heavy sword behind. "It will slow you down tonight, and you can always get another. "And what good is one sword against all the men my father will send after you? Your bow and your sling will be more practical."

For one brief moment, David held his wife close to his heart. "Take care of yourself, my darling. Don't anger your father. Tell him anything—tell him I threatened to kill you; he can't hate me any more than he does already. I'll pray every day that God will protect you."

"Don't worry about me; I can take care of myself."

"I'm sure you can or I wouldn't leave you; but, don't underestimate your father. I'll send for you as soon as I possibly can. You'll wait?"

"I'll wait," Michal whispered, "till death do us part."

David kissed his wife as if he could never let her go. Then without another word, he dropped the light rope to the ground, slipped silently through the window, carefully inched his way to the bottom. When the rope went slack, Michal drew it swiftly up, and listened for footfalls in the darkness. For what seemed like an eternity, she strained her ears for the slightest sound. She heard nothing.

At last she turned from the window and began to untie the sheets. Smoothing them carefully, she replaced them in the cupboard. Then she carried the stately image a zealous admirer had carved of David, and placed it in his bed. She put a pillow of goat's hair for his bolster, and drew the sheet up over it.

Chapter 13

The dreaded summons came with the first ray of dawn. Michal opened the door to a red-faced, apologetic Phaltiel.

"I'm sorry, my princess; your father demands we bring David to the palace immediately."

Michal's sleepy eyes widened with surprise and astonishment. "Whatever for? Even though he was not feeling well, my husband reported to the king yesterday. He has been ill in bed since then. Come," she motioned toward the bedroom, and tiptoed ahead of the soldiers. "He is sleeping at last; surely you are aware of the pressures your captain has endured. Does he not deserve a rest?"

"Of course, my lady; we are not here by choice. We'll tell the king; perhaps he will let the captain sleep until he wakes."

Like whipped dogs the soldiers retreated.

"They have more faith in the king's generosity than I do," Michal muttered to the closed door. But she was grateful for every minute she could delay the patrol she knew would be sent in search of David the moment his absence was discovered.

The sun was scarcely up when the soldiers returned. Guilt and fear struggled for control of their usually stolid faces. Michal was dressed and waiting when they knocked.

"I'm so sorry, my princess," said Phaltiel with obvious sincerity. "Your father says, if David will not get up, we are to carry him to the palace on his bed."

Michal breathed a sigh of resignation, and stood aside for the soldiers to enter. She did not follow them to observe their reactions to her deception but stood resolutely by the door. She cringed slightly exclamations of dismay, but she did not move.

Phaltiel dashed back to the door. "What have you done, little princess?" In his distress, the big captain lapsed into the title of endearment so long reserved for the king's younger daughter. "Your father may kill you! We have to tell him."

"No you don't: you can let me tell him. If he learns how easily you were deceived he may kill every one of you. Let me explain it to my father."

"My pleasure, my lady. Let's go."

Michal ran ahead of the soldiers when the group arrived at the palace. She fell on her face before her father's throne, and wept. "David ran away; I couldn't stop him—"

"Why have you deceived me so," Saul demanded, "and sent away my enemy that he has escaped?"

"But what could I do, Father? As soon as the soldiers left the house, David jumped up and ran. When I tried to stop him, he said, 'Let me go; why should I kill?' How could I hold him? Surely you do not think a lone woman could accomplish what the whole Philistine army has not been able to do."

"No—I suppose not," admitted Saul in disgust. Then he turned to the soldiers. "After him! He can't have gone far. Bring him to me at once."

Gratefully the soldiers fled.

It was two days before the search party returned. They reported David was in Ramah with Samuel. They feared to attempt to take the fugitive from the prophet.

Saul dispatched messengers immediately to return David to Gibeah.

The messengers returned two days later with a strange tale of being endowed by the Lord with the gift of prophecy. They found David with Samuel, all right; but the spirit of God descended upon them, and forbade them to touch David.

Saul was angry, but he sent yet other messengers with a stern command to bring David to him at once. But again the messengers returned with the same tale of having been touched by the hand of God, and restrained from capturing David.

The third time Saul sent messengers, and they returned with the same result, the king flew into a rage. After expressing his utter contempt for his "worthless" servants, he departed for Ramah himself.

But before Saul reached the city of David's refuge, the Spirit of God descended upon him also. He began to praise God, and tell of the wonderful blessings promised to them that love him and keep his commandments.

The servants were all amazed.

When the king's party reached Ramah, Saul stripped off his royal robes, prostrated himself before Samuel, praised God, and told of his wonderful works. The haughty monarch who left his throne on a mission of self-righteous vengeance, spent all day and night prostrate on the floor, babbling incoherently about the goodness of God.

While Saul was restrained by the Spirit, David fled back to Gibeah. Fearing to enter the walled city, lest he be trapped by Saul's servants, the fugitive gave a gold coin to a blind beggar, and asked him to tell Jonathan a friend awaited him outside the city gates.

The king's son went immediately to seek the friend he loved more than his own soul.

When David stood before Jonathan, he cried. "What have I done? What is my iniquity? And what is my sin before your father that he seeks my life?"

Jonathan was appalled. "God forbid, David; you shall not die. My father will do nothing either or small without telling me. If evil is intended toward you, why should my father hide it from me? It is not true."

Sadly, David disagreed with his beloved friend. "Your father certainly knows you love me. He has probably said, 'Don't tell Jonathan, lest he be grieved.' But as God lives and as you live, there is but a step between me and death."

"I believe you," said Jonathan sorrowfully. "What do you want me to do?"

"First, you see about Michal. It broke my heart to leave her at the mercy of her father, but there seemed to be no other way."

Jonathan laughed. "Don't you worry about that sly little fox; she can take care of herself anywhere. She is as scheming as our father, and twice as clever."

"I pray you are right, but you will look after her for me?"

"Let's put it this way: If she needs any help I can provide, I promise to supply it. Will that do?"

"That will do fine," David smiled. "Thank you, my brother. Tell my wife I am well, and I'll send for her as soon as I possibly can. I long to see her, but I dare not enter the city, and she must not come out lest your father's spies follow her to trap me."

"I shall deliver your message to my sister, but I'm sure you are mistaken concerning your danger."

"We shall see," said David resolutely. "Tomorrow is the new moon, and I should not fail to sit by the king at the feast. But let me go and hide myself in the field until the third day at noon. If your father asks about me, you say, 'David earnestly asked my permission to run to Bethlehem, for there is a yearly sacrifice there for all the family.' If he says 'that's all right,' then I will return to my home in peace. But if he is very angry, then you can be sure he is still determined to kill me."

"I'll do it," Jonathan promised. "But you will soon find you have nothing to fear."

"That's all I ask. Remember, we have sworn before God to be true to each other. However, if you find any iniquity in me, slay me yourself; why wait for your father to do it?"

"I know there is no iniquity in you, my brother. And if I knew of any evil my father was plotting against you, don't you think I'd tell you?"

"Yes, I believe you would. But how do you plan to get word to me if your father is still angry?"

"Come, let's go out to our archery fields."

When the two young men reached the great boulders, Jonathan lifted his voice in prayer: "Oh Lord God of Israel, when I have sounded my father out tomorrow, or the next day, and all is well for David, and I bring him not word, your curse be upon me. But if my father is plotting evil against, I will show it to him, and send him away in peace. And may God be with him as he has been with my father."

Jonathan turned to David. "I want you to promise me you will not only spare my life, and show mercy to me while I live, but you will show kindness to my family and my sons forever. Some day the Lord will destroy all your enemies from the face of the earth, and you shall reign supreme.

"I know God loves you, and he will make you king of Israel in my place. And I understand—because I love you, too. I pray, in that day, you will remember me and my house. Will you promise?"

"I promise," David took solemn oath.

"Thank you, my brother, and I know you will keep your promise even as I shall keep mine. Tomorrow, you will surely be missed at the feast of the new moon, because your place will be vacant. You wait three days, then come to the rock Ezel, and hide behind it like you did before. I will shoot three arrows beside the rock as though I were shooting at a target. And I will send a boy to retrieve the arrows. If I say to the lad, 'behold, the arrows are on this side of you, get them,' then you come out; everything is all right. But if I say to the young man, 'behold, the arrows are beyond,' flee, and the Lord go with you."

"Thank you, Jonathan; I'll be here."

"And regarding our covenant, may the Lord watch between you and me forever."

Chapter 14

So David hid himself the rocks. And when the new moon arose, the king sat down at the feast prepared for him and his captains. Saul sat at the head of the table as usual. Jonathan gave his place on the left side to Abner, and David's place on the king's right was empty.

Saul said nothing, but he looked speculatively at the empty chair. When the second day came, and David was still absent, the king said to Jonathan, "where is David? Why is he not here—either yesterday or today? Has something befallen him? Perhaps he is unclean."

Jonathan answered the king respectfully: "David earnestly asked leave of me to go to Bethlehem. He said, 'Let me go, I beg of you, for our family has a sacrifice in the city, and my brother has commanded me to be there. And if I have found favor in your eyes, let me get away, I beg of you, and see my family'."

Never had anyone seen the king so angry. His face livid with rage, he screamed at Jonathan: "You are as perverse and rebellious as your mother. Don't you think I know you have chosen to give the son of Jesse your place, and your choice will cut off the house of Saul forever? As long as that sheepherder lives upon the earth, you shall not be established, nor your kingdom. Now—I demand you bring him to me, for shall surely die."

"Please—Father, Why should David be killed? What has he done?"

For answer, Saul snatched the javelin beside him, and hurled it with all his might at his son.

Jonathan leaped from the table; he appeared almost as angry as his father, as he strode from the banquet hall. David was right; the king was determined to slay him. Grief for his friend, and shame for his father struggled for preeminence in his troubled heart.

At his son's unprecedented defiance, Saul went berserk. He raged and screamed in frustration. "First, God deserted me! Well—who needs him?

Then Samuel turned his back on me. I'll hew him down like he hewed old King Agag! My own wife defies me—says I shan't have a harem. I'll show her! Abner! Find the most beautiful young virgin in all Israel, and bring her to my bed."

"I'm sorry, my lord," said Abner in a daring effort to quiet the raging monarch. The most beautiful girl in Israel is my Rizpah, and she is already betrothed to me—"

"Bring her! Bring her! And be quick about "Saul shrieked.

"But my lord—" Saul snatched another javelin from the wall, and hurled it at Abner. The captain fled.

"My own house is crawling with serpents bent on my destruction. I'll show them there is still a king in Israel. Michal did this; she brought my enemy into my house. Phalti, bring her here and slay her at my feet."

"The big captain's face blanched beneath his tan. "May it please my lord—?"

"Nothing will please your lord except the blood of his enemies flowing before him. Be off! Bring me the son of Jesse's wife. If I can't slay him, I'll slay her." Saul reached for another javelin, and Phalti fled.

Phaltiel knew could never harm the princess, but he hastened to her house as quickly as his powerful legs could carry him. He wanted to warn the princess of her danger, and help her escape her father's wrath.

Michal received the news stoically; she refused to run—even when the captain offered to go with her. "It would be useless, Phalti; my father would find us and kill both of us. Let us hasten to the palace. If he thinks we are obeying him, perhaps it will quiet him enough we can reason with him."

"Little princess, you've seen your father possessed of evil spirits before, but never like this. It's as if he is Satan himself. No one can reason with him. Even Jonathan and Abner failed. So what can we do?"

"We can try," said Michal grimly. "Let's go."

All the way to the palace, Phalti pleaded with the king's daughter to run away. "Your father has demanded I slay you at his feet; you know I cannot do that. When I refuse, he will kill us both. At least we have a chance if we run away."

"And why can you not kill me, Phalti? Surely you have killed many people in war; why not me?"

"How can you ask such a question? Haven't I known you and guarded you since you were in swaddling clothes? How could I possibly kill you?"

"Perhaps that's our way out," mused Michal. "Are you married, Phalti?"

"No, my princess. Why do you ask?"

Michal ignored his question. "Why are you not married?"

"Well—there are three very good reasons; two of them be obvious."

"Oh?"

"What woman would want to marry a man with a face like mine?"

"Don't you believe it! The goodness shining from your face is ample covering for your scars."

"You are very kind, little princess; but not everyone is so generous. And then there is the matter of a dowry. While other soldiers go to war and collect spoils, I must stay and guard the place, or watch over the king."

"I know. David says he thinks the men who go to war should share the spoils equally with the ones who stay behind to guard their homes and families."

"Your husband is a good man, and he will make a wise king some day—if he lives long enough."

"And the third reason?"

"The only woman I ever wanted to marry—was not available."

"Phalti—would you be willing to marry me?"

The captain was so shocked he stumbled and stammered before he could answer. "How could I marry you, little princess? You are already married to David."

Again, Michal ignored his question. "Why is my father so angry?"

"Because he hates David."

"And why does he want to kill me?"

"To hurt David."

"What would hurt David even worse than killing me?"

"Giving you to another man."

"Right! Now, could you perhaps suggest to the king you might be willing to be that man?"

A gleam of hope shone briefly in Phalti's eyes, but it was quickly quenched. "In his present state, your father probably would stoop so low, but then David would kill me."

"I'm not suggesting a real marriage, of course. But, it would satisfy my father until I could get away and join David."

Phalti was silent for a few minutes. "I'll do it, little princess, on two conditions."

"I'm not in much of a position to bargain, but say on."

"You are not to tell a living soul—except David—that it is not a real marriage; my men would laugh me out of Israel."

"Your secret and your honor will be safe with me, my captain. What else?"

"If David should—if anything should ever happen to David, you will become my wife."

"Why not? If I should lose David, nothing would matter to me anyway. Oh I'm sorry," Michal added hastily, as she observed Phalti's crestfallen face. "I did not mean that the way it sounded. I consider that as honorable a proposal as any man could make to another man's wife. And if I couldn't be David's wife, there is no man in the kingdom I admire more than you. Your patient devotion to my father has endeared you to us all. I could not bear to see you lose your life in a futile attempt to save mine. You do as I say, and we'll both survive."

"If there is anyone who can cope with your father, I'm sure you're the one. But you have never seen him like this before."

Chapter 15

Michal could hear her father raging before they entered the banquet hall. She ran and threw herself on the floor at his feet. "Oh, thank you, my father! I'm so grateful you have spared me a fate worse than death."

Saul was shocked into silence. He was obviously prepared to shout down his daughter's pleas for mercy. What was she thanking him for?

"I told your enemy," Michal continued quickly before the king could recover, "that he might as well kill me, because you would kill me anyway for letting him escape. He said he didn't besmirch his honor by giving me to another man. He said you would probably give me to the biggest and ugliest man in the kingdom. I told him he need not worry; I would kill myself first. I'm so grateful, Father, that you are saving me from the pain of killing myself."

"So the son of Jesse did not care if I killed you. But I must not soil his honor. Ugliest man in the kingdom? Aha!" Saul's fanatical glance swept across the frightened men. A few were literally cowering before his wrath. His gaze settled on the big, pock-marked captain standing behind his kneeling daughter.

"Phaltiel! Take that woman to your tent. If you let her kill herself, or run away, or run away, or escape you by any means whatsoever, I will hang you by the tendons of you heels until the vultures pick the flesh from your carcass. Do you understand?

"Yes, my lord."

"Take her now—at once!"

"Yes, my lord."

"No! No!" Michal screamed. She grasped the skirt of her father's robe. "Please kill me, Father! Have you no mercy?"

"Get this daughter of a perverse and rebellious woman out of here," screamed the king, "At once."

64

"Yes, my lord." Phalti grasped Michal roughly and jerked her to her feet.

"Please, Father, please!"

"Get her out! Shut her up!"

Phalti clasped his hand over Michal's mouth, picked her up as if she were a child, and carried her, kicking and struggling from the banquet hall.

Michal and Phalti kept up their little charade until they were safely inside the captain's tent. Michal immediately ceased her struggles, and the big man set her gently on her feet.

"I'm sorry, my princess. I hope I didn't hurt you. But I'm afraid we outsmarted ourselves this time."

"Perhaps. But at least we're still alive, and I like that. It may not be important to you, but I plan to do a lot of living yet."

Phalti's homely face lighted with pleasure in a way Michal had never seen. Then the pleased smile was eclipsed by apprehension. "But if you run away as you planned, Saul will kill me."

"Don't worry. My father is crafty, too. He knows I would never deliberately endanger your life. So—we must change our plans a little. As soon as it is safe to join David, we'll both go. I the meantime, I cannot live here in your tent alone with you—"

"Surely, my princess," interrupted Phalti, "you do not think your servant would take advantage of your unfortunate position?"

"No—I don't. But I do think men, and I have no intention of tempting you. So—we get you a wife."

"But I told you—"

"I know. No dowry. But David brought home ten mules laden with spoil. That should provide ample dowry, and a house big enough for your wife and me."

"But there's no one—"

"Now, Phalti, let's be practical. You need a wife to bear you sons. If you can't get the one you want, you take one you can get."

"But—perhaps—"

Michal interpreted his hesitancy correctly. "Perish the thought, my captain. Even if David should be slain, you would still need a wife to bear you sons. I'm—well—you see," Michal blushed modestly. "I am barren."

Shock and incredulity competed to David for mastery on Phalti's ugly, honest face.

"I have been married to David for more than three years; I have borne him no children."

"But you're so young. You have grown two or three inches since you married," Phalti protested. "Perhaps—"

"I'm past eighteen. Many women have borne three or four children by the time they are my age."

"But—perhaps David—"

"It could not be," said Michal firmly. "David says the Lord has promised him many sons."

"But—how—?"

"He will simply have to do I'm asking you to do: Take another wife."

"But Michal," Phalti pleaded, humbly unaware he had called the princess by her name. "I don't want another wife. You are the only woman I ever wanted. If I have you—" "You will take someone else," interrupted Michal stubbornly, "We live in a practical world. If we are to survive, we must be practical, too. But it's sweet of you to say that," she added softly.

Phalti said nothing, but his dark, homely face looked pained.

"I'm sorry, Phalti; I don't mean to scold. But we are in this together; if we are to survive, we must cooperate. Now, surely you have a friend—"

"Friend?"

"Yes. Friend. You don't have to be in love with a woman to have a good marriage, but you do need to be friends. Fortunately, David and I are friends and lovers, too. You remember how much in love Adriel and Merab were? But they weren't friends; now they are practically enemies. You don't want that."

"I don't want—." Phalti lapsed into a gloomy silence.

"I know," Michal sympathized, "and I don't want to deceive my father, leave my home, or hurt David. Can you imagine how my husband will feel when he hears my father has given me away like a common slave? I pray he will not try to come here and kill you. I'm sure that's what my father expects him to do, and he'll have spies lying in wait for him.

"My greatest fear, however, is that David will go out and take to wife the first woman he sees—or worse—take a half dozen. I hope and pray my husband will trust me without hearing of my father's shameful conduct, but whatever hurt and shame we must endure, I want us to stay alive. God has plans for David, and—I hope—for me.

"Now, about that friend?"

"Well," Phalti relented slightly, "I do have a cousin."

"Good! You enquire about the dowry, and we'll start looking for a house. I'd rather go back to our house, but I fear my father would never permit it."

Before Phalti could leave the tent, a messenger arrived from the palace. His surprise to see Michal and the captain on apparently good terms was as ill concealed as his delight in giving orders to the big captain.

"The king has given you all that pertains to David. He commands you lay wait for him in his own house. When he returns, you are to slay him, and bring his head to the palace. You are to move into David's house before nightfall," the messenger added arrogantly.

Michal began to wail so loudly, Phalti was startled.

"Tell the king his wish is my command. We shall go there at once,"

Phalti shouted above Michal's cries. Then turning to the weeping princess, he yelled, "silence, woman!"

Michal choked her sobs, and the messenger departed swelling with importance. "So the house is taken care of," she whispered, when the man was out of hearing. Perhaps God has not deserted us after all.

"Now for that cousin."

Chapter 16

A strange household retired in David's house that night. Phalti's cousin, Adah, daughter of Hanun, was a big, raw-boned, shy, country girl. She was obviously delighted with the sudden turn of events in her hitherto dull existence. She could scarcely believe the good fortune that had befallen her and her family.

Phalti took one of the mules laden with spoil from Ashdod for a dowry. Adah's father insisted the mule was ample dowry for his daughter. Marriage with her esteemed cousin was an honor to the humble herdsman' house.

But Phalti was adamant that Hanun accept, in addition to the coveted mule, the changes of raiment for the family, a talent of silver, and one hundred gold coins.

It was undreamed-of wealth for the poor shepherd. He was grateful to have one less mouth to feed, and elated that his daughter would dwell in the capital city.

Adah was overawed at the thought of living in the same house with the princess. Phalti merely explained Michal's fall from her father's favor, and his own "unhappy duty" as jailer-husband. Under the circumstances, Adah readily understood Michal's grief for her banished husband, and her willingness to allow Phalti's newest wife the privilege of sharing his bed.

Adah was accustomed to long hours of gleaning in the fields under the broiling sun, and caring for her younger brothers and sisters. She insisted the household duties would be her pleasure, and Michal's wish was her command.

The princess was grateful for Phalti's wise choice in a wife. The girl was humble and helpful without being subservient. And her willingness to work enabled them to eliminate servants, who might be spies for the king. Only Leah, Michal's handmaid remained.

If Adah was annoyed at the unusual arrangements of the household, she concealed it well. She was unfailingly cheerful and cooperative. Her sense of humor, and the love and loyalty she manifested for her new family took of the sting out of Michal's confinement.

The princess insisted there would be no more formalities or rank in the household: Phalti and Adah were simply to address her as Michal. Having been disowned and disowned and banished by the king, Michal declared he was no longer her father, and she would never again address him as such.

"But, my lady," Adah hushed as the princess as the princess frowned. "Michal," she said timidly.

"That's better."

"But, regardless of the way the king treats you, he is still your father, and the only one you will ever have. God said 'honor your parents,' and he did not say provided they're honorable. I'm sorry, my—Michal," Adah continued apologetically; "I don't mean to scold. I know your father has been cruel, but he is a sick man; you know that. You need to love him for your own sake. If you cannot forgive your father, and love him, how can you pray? You know you want to pray for hus—for David," she stammered.

"And supposing I cannot forgive the king?"

"Then," Adah said timidly, "you need to pray for yourself."

Michal bit her lip, but she said nothing.

"Please don't be angry; I don't mean to criticize. I only want you to be happy."

Michal smiled. "I'm not angry, Adah; I know you mean well. And I'm happy to have you to comfort me."

Phalti was obviously pleased with the situation in his household. It was equally apparent that Michal was his first love. Adah accepted this as a matter of course, but it grieved the princess' heart.

Chapter 17

On the morning of the third day of the feast, Jonathan had gone early to the field at the appointed time to meet David; he took a little lad with him. And he said to the lad, "Run, find now the arrows which I shoot." And as the boy ran, he shot an arrow beyond him.

When the lad reached the place where the arrow fell, Jonathan cried after him, "Is not the arrow beyond you? Make haste, hurry, don't stay."

The boy gathered the arrows, and hastily returned to his master. But he knew nothing of his part in the drama being enacted; only Jonathan and David were aware of the tragedy of the moment.

Jonathan gave his bow and arrows to his servant, and sent him back to the city. As soon as the boy was out of sight, David arose out of his hiding place the south, fell on his face on the ground. He bowed himself three times, then Jonathan lifted him up. The two men embraced and wept unashamed on each other's shoulders, but David wept unashamed on each other's shoulders, but David wept louder than Jonathan.

And Jonathan said, "Go in peace, my brother. My father is indeed determined to kill you; there is nothing more we can do. Inasmuch as we have both sworn in the name of the Lord saying: The Lord be between you and me, and between your children forever. Hasten now, and may God go with you."

So David fled for his life, and Jonathan returning to the city to face his father's wrath.

David went to Nob, the city of the priests, to see Ahimelech. But the priest's suspicions were aroused.

"What are you doing out here alone? Where is your sword and band of soldiers?

"The king sent me on a secret mission. My servants are supposed to meet me at an appointed place. I need some food. I'd like to have at least five loaves of bread, but I'll take whatever you have to spare."

"But I have no common bread here, only the hallowed bread. However, if the young men have purified themselves," the priest hesitated.

"We have been on the road for three days, so the young men cannot be contaminated. And the bread is just bread after all, even if it was sanctified on the alter."

So the priest gave David the hallowed bread he had removed from the altar when he replaced it with the fresh bread. But there was in the house of God that day a servant of Saul, Doeg, an Edomite. He was chief of the king's herdsmen.

The Edomite said nothing, but he eyed David covertly. David forced himself to continue his conversation with the priest as if nothing were amiss.

"Ahimelech, do you have a spear or sword here? I came off without any weapons because the king's business demanded haste."

"The sword of Goliath the Philistine, whom you slew in the valley of Elah, is here. It is wrapped in a cloth behind the ephod. If you want it, take it; there is none other here.

"There is none other like it; give it to me."

So David fled from Nob, the city of the priests, for fear of Saul, and sought refuge with Achish the king of Gath of the Philistines.

And the servants of Achish asked him, "Is not this David the king of the land? Did the Israelites not sing about him as they danced in their victories over us? Did they not say, 'Saul has slain his thousands, and David his ten thousands'?"

And David heard these words, and he was sore afraid of the king of Gath. So he changed his behavior, and pretended to be mad. He clawed aimlessly at the doors of the palace gates, and drooled into his beard.

Then Achish said to his servants: "This man is mad. Why have you brought him to me? Don't I have trouble enough without a mad man on my hands? Get him out of my house."

So David fled from Gath, and escaped to a huge cave near Adullam. And when his brothers and all his father's house heard about his misfortunes, they joined him in his cave. For they, too, feared the king's wrath.

When the story of David's banishment was noised abroad, all his friends in distress, and everyone in debt, and everyone discontented gathered themselves unto their champion. And there were with him about four hundred men.

Then David went down to Mizpeh of Moab, and said to the king of Moab, "Let my father and my mother, I beg of you, find sanctuary with you until I know what God will do for me." And David brought his parents to the king of Moab, and they dwelt there as long as David was hiding in the cave.

The prophet Gad heard of David's plight, and went down to see him. "Don't stay in this cave," said Gad. "Get out of here and go into the land of Judah, and seek refuge there."

So David obeyed the voice of the prophet; he went down to Judah, and camped in the forest of Hareth.

When Saul heard David was out of hiding, and many men followed him, he complained bitterly. He had not returned to the palace, but was camped under a tree in Ramah. He was still girt for battle, with his spear in his hand, and his servants gathered around him awaiting his orders.

Then Saul said to his waiting servants, "Now listen, you Benjamites, will the son of Jesse give everyone of you fields and vineyards, and make you all captains of thousands, and captains of hundreds? Why have you all conspired against me? Why would none of you tell me my own son had made a league with my enemy? Are none of you sorry for me? Why didn't you tell me my son had conspired with servant against me, and my enemies lie in wait for me this day?"

Then Doeg the Edomite, which had been made chief of servants of Saul, said, "I saw the son of Jesse coming to Nob to Ahimelech, the son of Ahitub. And the priest enquired of the Lord for David, and gave him food, and the sword of Goliath the Philistine."

Angrily, Saul summoned Ahimelech, and commanded him to bring with him all his father's house, the priests of Nob. And they all came and stood before the king.

And Saul demanded of Ahimelech, saying, "Why have you conspired against me, you and you and the son of Jesse, in that you have given him bread, and a sword? And why did you enquire of the Lord for him so he could rise against me, and hide from me as he is doing right now?"

"And who is so faithful among all the king's servants as David? Is he not your son-in-law? Does he not go at your bidding? Is he not honorable in your house?" Ahimelech questioned Saul in honest amazement. "David came to me and asked my help in discharging the business of the king; it was then humbly enquired of the Lord for him.

"Please, my lord king," Ahimelech humbly begged, "do not blame me nor my father's house, for we are all your servants. If David has displeased you, we knew nothing at all about it."

But the evil spirit possessed Saul completely, and he raged at the innocent priest. "David is no longer my son-in-law; he is my enemy. He seeks my life, and you have helped him try to kill me! You have armed, fed him, and guided him. You shall die, Ahimelech! You and all your father's house shall be slain!"

The king turned to the foot soldiers who surrounded him. "Fall on the priests of the Lord, and slay them—every one! You must do it because they are in league with David. They knew where he was, and they didn't tell me."

But the soldiers feared the Lord more than they feared the king. They dared not lift their swords against the Lord's priests, so they stood still, mute with fear.

Livid with rage, Saul turned to Doeg, the Edomite who neither feared God nor respected men. "Kill them!" he screamed; "I command you—kill them!"

Gleefully, the Edomite fell upon the unarmed, gentle, helpless, righteous men. He obviously enjoyed his bloody butchery; before he stopped, eighty-five priests, still clad in their once-white linen ephods lay bleeding on the ground.

Even that bloody shambles did not satisfy the wrath of Saul, nor the lust of Doeg; rather it seemed with the edge of the sword every man, woman, and child—even the tiny infants. Then he fell on the cattle, the sheep, and the beasts of burden. The Godless Edomite did not stop his bloody carnage until every living thing in Nob was dead.

Mute with fear, and sick with revulsion, Saul's servant meekly followed him back to Gibeah. Drunk with blood, and swelled with pride, the evil Doeg preened himself at the head of the column.

When the foot soldiers returned to their homes that night, a pall fell over Gibeah. In hushed whispers, the people discussed the massacre at Nob, and speculated on the dire consequences.

Chapter 18

Phalti was unusually quiet when he came home at the end of the day Saul returned to Gibeah. His only comment in response to Michal's questions was the king was back at the palace. Aware the captain was concealing something, Michal's first thought was, of course, of David.

"Did the king find David?" She asked fearfully.

"No, Michal; David is still safe. I promise you that."

"What then? What is wrong?"

"The king is so completely possessed of the evil spirit, I tremble at what he may do next. He is determined to slay David; I fear the captain cannot elude him forever." Phalti explained patiently.

"God will protect David," said Adah shyly. "Has he not promised him the kingdom?"

"How do you know that?" asked Michal quickly.

Adah shrugged. "Doesn't everybody? Has God not given David victory over Saul in encounter? Why else is the king so angry with his loyal captain? David has done no wrong."

"Thank you, Adah," said Michal gratefully; but she watched Phalti covertly, and when he returned to his duties at the palace on the morrow, she asked Adah to talk with the neighbors. She was certain Phalti knew more than he was willing to tell his womenfolk.

For the first time, Adah failed to do Michal's bidding with alacrity. "If there is something my husband does not wish me to know, I could not possibly seek to learn it," Adah demurred.

"Well, bless you, my dear," said Michal ironically; "I fear I'm not so conscientious. If Phalti is hiding something, I must know what it is. If you won't go the neighbors, I will."

Adah sighed regretfully. "Phalti said if you were determined to know, I was to tell you."

"Tell me what?"

"You are sure you want to know?"

What? Know what? Adah, quit stalling! What did Phalti tell you he didn't tell me?"

Oh, it was nothing like that, believe me; he didn't want to hurt you, that was all."

Michal had to smile. I'm not jealous, Adah; don't let that trouble you. But I must know what's wrong. Now, tell me."

Fear and compassion fought for mastery in Adah's honest face. "The king has destroyed the city of Nob."

"The city of the priests? Oh, Adah, he wouldn't dare! Not even Saul would do that! No king could possibly get by with it; God will kill him—for sure."

"Did you ever hear of a king daring to take a woman from her husband before? And his own daughter at that? The king is mad, I tell you; he will do anything. Everyone is terrified—except Doug. That vicious butcher did the dirty work. May God have mercy on Israel!"

"Well, Saul won't have any mercy on us; you can depend on that. How far will God let him go? And when God's wrath does fall on him, will any of us escape? Why did the soldiers tolerate Saul and Doeg slaughtering the priests? There was at least a hundred men there; why didn't they interfere?"

"Surely you remember how skillful your father is with a sword. No one except David would dare stand up to him, and David won't lift a hand against him."

"Yes, I know; the 'Lord's anointed,' he says. Well, that will make no difference to the Philistines. God can always send his old enemies after Saul; without David to fight his battles, he won't last long, Michal added with a touch of vengeance.

"But if Saul goes, what about Israel?" asked Adah.

"When Saul goes, David will be king, and Israel will be safe."

"And what about you?"

"When David is king, he will send for me; and you can have Phalti all to yourself."

Adah smiled. "I shall pray God will hasten David's victory." Then she blushed and stammered, "I'm sorry; I didn't mean—"

"Don't apologize, Adah. I'm glad you love Phalti enough to want me out of the way—"

"Oh, but you are not in the way; we love you."

"Thank you. And I love both of you; but, you see, David is my husband, and I love him more than anyone in all the world."

"I know you two fell in love, and then got married. Do you think it possible for people to get married, and then fall in love?" asked Adah wistfully.

"Not only possible, but practical; it happens all the time. There is Jonathan and Adena; they had never seen each other before they were married, and after three years, they are very much in love. Then there is Merab and Adriel; they were madly in love, and now they are not even friends. Being the right person is far more important than marrying the right person."

"And Merab so beautiful, too," said Adah, her voice tinged with envy.

"Have you seen her lately?" asked Michal dryly.

"Not since she married,"

That's what I thought. Marriage does not agree with Merab. But I'm not blaming Adriel," Michal added hastily. "I fear Merab would not be happy with any man. Y sister has not yet discovered she must first learn to be happy with herself."

Phalti brought a bit more cheerful news from the palace the following day. One man did escape the massacre at Nob. Abiathar, one of the sons of Ahimelech, fled the ravished city and joined David and his band of "outlaws."

David, however, was reported almost beside himself with grief. He felt he had brought about the slaughter of the priests.

Michal had not wept for herself, the priests, or their families; but her tears flowed in sympathy for her tender-hearted husband. Adah comforted the princess as a mother would comfort a child.

"Oh God," she prayed, "please deliver us—and soon."

Chapter 19

A band of marauding Philistines attacked Keilah, and were robbing the threshing floors. Unless they could be repulsed, there would be no food for winter, and the people who survived the raiders would be left to starve.

The men of Keilah sent messengers to David. Therefore, David enquired of the Lord, saying, "Shall I go and smite these Philistines?"

And the Lord said to David, "Go, and smite the Philistines, and save Keilah."

But when David's men heard of his plans, they were afraid; they said, "If we live in fear of our lives her in Judah, how dangerous will it be in Keilah against the armies of the Philistines?"

Then David enquired of the Lord again. And the Lord answered him and said, "Arise, go down to Keilah, for I will deliver the Philistines into your hand." So David and his men went to Keilah, and fought with the Philistines, and captured their cattle, and smote them with a great slaughter. So David saved the people of Keilah.

When Abiathar followed David to Keilah, he carried a linen ephod with him so he could perform his priestly duties, and seek guidance for David and his men.

But when Saul heard David was in Keilah, he said, "God has delivered him into my hands. He trapped himself by entering into a city with gates and bars." So Saul called the men of Israel together to go to war against David in Keilah.

When David learned about Saul's plot against him, he asked Abiathar the priest to put on his ephod, and come and pray with him. Then David said, "O Lord God of Israel, I have heard Saul is coming to Keilah to destroy the city because I am here. Will the men of Keilah deliver me up to Saul? Will Saul come down? I have sought always to serve my Lord. Now I pray, My Lord God, tell your servant what to do."

And the Lord said, He will come down."

Then David said, "Will the men of Keilah deliver me and my men into the hand of Saul?"

And the Lord said, "They will deliver you up."

So David and his men, who numbered about six hundred, arose and fled into the wilderness, near Ziph, and remained there in the mountain strongholds.

When Saul heard David had escaped from Keilah, he pursued the fugitives into the wilderness and searched for them every day. But God protected David and his men.

While David and his band were eluding Saul in the tree-covered mountain wilderness, Jonathan slipped away from his father's camp, and went in search of his beloved friend that he might strengthen and encourage him. When David saw his brother-in-law coming, he ran to meet him, embraced him, and they rejoiced together.

And Jonathan said, "Don't be afraid, David; my father shall never find you. One day you will be king over Israel, and I will be next to you, and my father knows it."

"Only the promises of God sustains me," said David. "I don't know why he would have me go through all this persecution, but I'm sure he will give me peace, and the kingdom in his own good time. I pray daily for patience; the problem is, of course, I want God to give me patience *right now*. But, tell me, how is Michal?"

Jonathan hesitated. It was evident no one had told David what had befallen his wife. Was it better he hear the news from his friend, or should Jonathan risk his not hearing it at all? Apparently, the fugitive had about all the troubles he could handle at the present.

She is well—as well as she could be under the circumstances," replied Jonathan honestly. And she sends her love."

"Praise God," said David humbly. "And would you give her this for me? He withdrew a tiny parchment scroll from his knapsack.

So the friends renewed their covenant before God, and David stayed in his hiding place. Jonathan returned to his father's camp, convinced him of the futility of pursuing David in the dense forests on the cavernous mountains, and persuaded the king to go back home.

Jonathan went immediately to deliver David's message to Michal, and to give her the comforting news the army failed to find her husband. However temporary it might be, she would be encouraged to know the pursuit of David had been discontinued.

Michael received the news with joy, and gratefully accepted the scroll from her husband. She could hardly wait for her brother to leave before she untied the scroll.

Another psalm! She threw it to the floor in disappointment and disgust. Why couldn't her husband think of anything but God! She wanted a personal message—some assurance of his love, and that he missed her. It was only after much persuasion from Adah she picked up the scroll and began to read:

> Hold not thy peace, O God of my praise;
> For the mouth of the wicked and the mouth of the deceitful are
>   opened against me; they have spoken against me with a
>   lying tongue.
> They compassed me about also with words of hatred; and fought
>   against me without a cause.
> For my love they are my adversaries, but I give myself unto prayer.
> And they have rewarded me evil for good, and hatred for my love.
> Set thou a wicked man over him, and let Satan stand at his right
>   hand.
> When he shall be judged, let him be condemned, and let his prayer
>   become sin.
> Let his days be few, and let another take his office.

Michael stopped reading, and visibly shivered. Chill bumps raised on her bare arms.

"Oh, how beautiful," said Adah in honest admiration. And how wonderful you can read. Would you—do you suppose I could learn to read?"

Of course," said Michal absently.

Both women were silent, but Michal read no more. After a while she rolled up the scroll, and placed it in a large earthen jar along with many others.

Did I say something wrong?" asked Adah timidly.

Michal tried to smile. "No. But David's song is so true; he has been rewarded evil for good. He brought so much joy and happiness to the palace. He never did anyone any harm. Yet he must seek refuge in the caves of the rocks, and he hunted down like an animal. Now, apparently he is praying for God to avenge him, and God always answers his prayers.

"Oh, Adah, you should hear David pray. He simply asks God, 'Shall I go, or shall I stay?' and God answers him. When he wrote in his song, 'Let his days be few, and let another take his office,' I know he was talking about Israel's wicked king, and I know God will grant his request. But how will God do it? And what will happen to Israel? To all of us?

I don't know," said Adah quietly. "But I do know God does all things well, and however he does it will be all right!"

"I wish I had your faith," said Michal; but there was more irony than desire in her tone.

Michal's apprehension was amply justified. Phalti came home earlier than usual. The Zithites had sent a messenger to Saul saying that David was hiding in the woods in the hill of Hachilah, on the south side of Jeshimon. Saul commanded all his soldiers to be ready to march at dawn.

"What will you do if you encounter David?" asked Michal when she learned Phalti was to accompany Saul.

"If Saul is not present, I will send him away in peace."

"But what if others watch, and tell Saul?

"There is probably not a member of the palace guard who would not do the same—perhaps not a single Israelite."

"But what if Doeg, or some other heathen is there?"

"Then I shall go with David. He is the man God has chosen to be our king; I will not lift my hand against him."

The smile on the face of the woman he loved was balm to Phalti's troubled heart

Chapter 20

When Saul's forces reached Ziph, David's men had fled to the wilderness of Maon. Saul ordered his men after them in hot pursuit.

David fled in haste from the army of Saul. For a while the fugitives managed to keep far enough ahead of Saul's army to stay on the opposite side of the mountain, but eventually, Saul divided his superior forces and sent them on both sides of the mountain in different directions, and David was caught between them.

When David's men were surrounded, and capture seemed certain, a messenger arrived for Saul; The Philistines had invaded Israel again. Reluctantly, Saul abandoned his quest for vengeance, and went back to defend his kingdom.

So David fled from Maon, and went and dwelt in the strongholds of Engedi.

As soon as Saul returned to Gibeah from driving out the Philistines, there was a message awaiting him that David was hiding the wilderness of Engedi. So Saul took three thousand of the most valiant warriors in all Israel, and went to seek David and his men on the rocks of the wild goats.

When they came to the sheepcotes at the foot of the mountain, they found a huge cave. They had traveled far, and Saul was weary. At Phalti's insistence, the king went into the cool, dark cave to take a nap.

Now David and his men were hiding in that cave. At the sound of the approaching army, the fugitives crouched among the boulders at the sides of the cave.

Saul and his men were skylighted against the entrance; the men in hiding could watch their every move. When Saul went to sleep, David's men began to whisper to their captain: "Remember the time you told us the Lord promised to deliver your enemy into your hand, so you could do to him whatever you pleased? Well, now's your chance."

So David arose and crept silently to the side of the sleeping monarch. With Goliath's sword, he cut off a portion of the skirt of Saul's robe. When he returned to his men, they rebuked their leader for not having cut off his enemy's head.

But David's conscience smote him for having defiled the king's garment, and he said to his men, "The Lord forbid I should do this thing to my master, the Lord's anointed, to stretch forth my hand against him, for he is still the anointed of the Lord."

So David restrained his servants, and suffered them not to rise against Saul. And Saul arose from his sleep, and left the cave. After he had gone on his way, David followed him at a safe distance. When the army crossed the deep valley to the other side of the mountain, David cried after Saul: "My Lord the king!"

When Saul looked back David stooped with his face to the earth; he bowed himself, and said to Saul, "Why do you listen to other men's words, saying David is your enemy? Remember, this day your own eyes have seen how the Lord delivered you into my hand in the cave. Many of my men insisted I kill you, but I spared your life, and I told my men I would not lift my hand against my lord because he is the Lord's anointed.

"If you doubt your servant's word, my father, look; her is the skirt of your robe in my hand. I could have killed you when I cut off your garment. Does this not prove to you there is neither evil nor transgression in my heart? I have never sinned against you, yet you hunt me down like an animal to take my life.

"The Lord judge between us, and may the Lord avenge me of you, by my hand shall not be upon you. According to the ancient proverb, 'Wickedness proceeds from the wicked,' but I will not lift my hand against my Lord's anointed.

"Whom is the king of Israel pursuing? Are you chasing a dead dog? Or a flea?

Let, therefore, the Lord be our judge, decide which of us is in the right, plead my cause, and delver me out of your hand."

When David finished speaking, Saul said, "Is it really your voice, my son David?" And Saul lifted up his voice and wept. And he said to David, "You are more righteous than I, because you have rewarded me good, whereas I have rewarded you evil. And you have proved to me this day that you bear me no ill, when the Lord delivered me into your hand, and you did not kill me.

If a man encounter an enemy, will he let him walk away? May the Lord reward you good for what you have done for me this day.

"And now I must confess I know you shall surely be king, and the kingdom of Israel shall grow great and powerful under your leadership.

"Will you swear to me now before the Lord that you will not cut off my children after me, and you will not destroy my name out of my father's house?"

"Need you ask, my father? Have I every done any harm to you or any member of your family? You know I love Jonathan as my own soul. And surely you do not question my lover for Michal. And Ahinoam has been like a mother to . . . ."

"Yes, yes, I know," Saul interrupted, and he turned and went home.

But David did not go home. In spite of the pleas of his tired, hungry men, they retreated further into the mountain wilderness.

"Why can't we go home?" his men pleaded. We are without food, and where will we find shelter in these mountains? Saul is gone, and he promised not to harm us ever again."

David laughed "Any man who is willing to gamble his life on Saul's word is free to go back."

Silently the men trudged on up the trudged on up the mountain.

Chapter 21

Samuel, the first prophet after Moses, the last of the judges, the only man ever to be prophet, priest, and judge in Israel was dead. All Israel gathered together to mourn him. He was buried at his home in Ramah.

Dressed in the rags of a beggar, his beard untrimmed, and his hair unkempt, David went to Ramah to lament Samuel. Regardless of the danger involved, he was determined to pay his last respects to his beloved friend and protector.

As he stood with the other ragged poor, and watched the stately procession pass by, David's heart pained him that he could not be marching with the king's sons and captains. Saul strode haughtily at the head of the procession.

"The bloody butcher," muttered a toothless old beggar at David's side.

"May God hasten the day when Saul is overthrown, and David is our king," whispered another.

The old man spoke again: "Just as well he gave his daughter to another man; who would want a queen from Saul's bloody house?"

The hair began to prickle on the back of David's neck. He shuffled over against the speaker. "What about Saul's daughter?"

"Gave her to another man, he did; biggest, ugliest soldier in Gibeah."

"Surely you jest," said David. "Not even a can take a woman from her husband."

"Would a man who would slaughter God's priests. Let man's laws stop him? The man is mad, utterly mad, I tell you. He took Abner's betrothed, too—for his concubine! Mark my words, Abner will have his vengeance; he is not so scrupulous as David about the Lord's anointed."

"You are sure?" asked David fearfully.

"Sure? Of course, I'm sure. Everybody knows it. Where have you been?"

David clutched his rags about him, shrunk away from the crowd, and fled to the wilderness of Paran where his men awaited him.

David's men observed their captain's sad countenance and they said, "He grieves for Samuel." So they subdued their usual high spirits in deference to his grief.

But, happy or grieved, a man must; the men reminded David of their need from their need for provision.

There lived near by in Carmel, a rich herdsman by the name of Nabal. So David sent out ten young men and said, "Get up to Carmel, and go to Nabal, and greet his in my name. And this shall you say to our rich neighbor, 'Peace to you, and to your house, and may God bless all that you have.

"'Now I have heard that you are shearing your sheep. Remember we guarded your flocks all the time they were in Carmel. There was not one lamb missing from among them. Ask your servants; they will tell you of our service to you. Therefore, let my servants find favor in your sight, for we come in need. Give, I beg of you, whatsoever you feel our service has been worth to you, to your servants and to your son, David."

So David's servants went and spoke to Nabal all the words of David.

But Nabal answered David's servants, and said, "Who is David? Who is this son of Jesse? There are many runaway servants now days. Shall I take my bread and drink, and the meat I have prepared for my shearers, and give it to strangers I know nothing about?"

So the young men returned and returned and told David all that Nabal said.

And David said to his men, "Gird on his sword also, and there went up with David about four hundred men, and two hundred stayed by their stuff.

But one of the shearers told Abigail, Nabal's wife, saying, "Behold, David sent messengers out of the wilderness to salute our master, and he railed on them. But David's men were very good to us; we were not hurt, neither missed we anything as long as they were with us in the pastures.

"They were a wall to us both day and night. As long as were with them keeping the sheep, neither robbers nor wolves came near us. Now we appeal to you; tell us what to do, for evil against our master, and against our master, and against all his household, because he is such a son of Satan that no man can reason with him."

Then Abigail made haste, and took two hundred loaves of bread, two bottles of wine, five dressed sheep, five measures of parched corn, one hundred clusters of raisins, and two hundred cakes of figs, and laid them on mules. And she said to her servants, "Go on ahead, and I will follow you." But she did not tell her husband, Nabal.

And Abigail mounted a mule, and rode out to meet David. As she came down a narrow mountain pass, David and his men came to meet her.

Now David had said to his men, "Surely in vain have I kept all this fellow had in the wilderness, so that he lost; and he has requited me evil for good. I shall go down to Nabal's came, and wipe out every man in his household."

And when Abigail saw David, she hastily lighted off her mule, fell before David on her face, and bowed herself to the ground. As she fell at his feet, she said, "Upon me, my lord, upon me let this iniquity be. Let your handmaid, I beg of you, speak; and listen to my plea.

"Please, my lord, I beg of you, pay no attention to this wicked ungrateful man, Nabal. For as his name is, so is he. Nabal is his name and he is a fool, but I did not see your messengers. Now, therefore, my lord, for God's and for your own sake, seeing the Lord has withheld you from bloodshed, and from avenging yourself with your own hand upon your enemies, let Nabal be as others who will seek evil to my lord.

"Now take, I beg of you, this blessing which your handmaid has brought unto my lord, and let it be given unto the young men that follow you.

"Forgive, I pray, the trespass of this your handmaid. God will certainly establish my lord's house because you fight the battles of the Lord, and evil has never found in you in your life.

"Yet a man dares to pursue you, and try to kill you. But the life of my lord is ordained to be a part of the plan of God, and the lives of your enemies shall the Lord sling out as you would sling a rock from the middle of your sling.

"And may it be, when the Lord has accomplished his plan for your life, and has given you all the good things he has promised you, and has made you ruler over Israel, that you shall suffer no grief or heartache over needless bloodshed, or having avenged yourself. But when the Lord has given victory to my lord, remember, I pray, your handmaid."

And David said to Abigail, "Blessed be the Lord God of Israel, who sent you to meet me. Thank God for your advice, and may he richly bless you for preventing me from shedding blood this day, and from taking vengeance into my own hand. I know vengeance belongs to God, and he will repay.

"For I swear, as the Lord God of Israel lives, who has held me back from hurting you, except you had hastened to meet me, surely there would not have been left to Nabal a man to see the light of another day."

So David accepted the gifts from Abigail, and told her to go in peace to her house "Rest assured that I have obeyed your ad monition, and have accepted you as a friend."

When Abigail returned home a great feast was in progress in her house, and Nabal was very drunk. So she decided to tell him nothing of her activities until morning.

But when morning and Abigail told her husband of her husband of her encounter with David, and of the gifts she had given him, Nabal became so furiously angry that he fell senseless to the ground. After lying like a stone for about ten days, the Lord smote him, and he died.

When David heard that Nabal was dead, he said, "Blessed be the Lord who has avenged me of Nabal, and has kept me from the sin wreaking vengeance upon him. For the Lord has returned the wickedness of Nabal upon his own head."

So David sent messengers to commune with Abigail, and to ask her to be his wife. When the servants arrived in Carmel, and delivered David's message, Abigail arose and bowed herself on her face to the earth, and said, "Behold, let your handmaid be a servant to was the feet of the servants of my lord."

And Abigail hurriedly arose, and accompanied by five or handmaids, she mounted a mule, and went with the messengers of David, and became his wife.

But David did not find in Abigail the joy and fellowship he had enjoyed with Michal. So Kenaz, David's armorbearer said to his master, "I have a sister, a beautiful maiden who lives in Jezereel. Let me, I pray, bring my sister to be wife to my lord.

So David also took Ahinoam of Jezereel, and both Abigail and Ahinoam were wives to David. But Michal still lived in his heart.

Chapter 22

It was a strange household which dwelt in David's house in Gibeah. Phalti and Adah showed every kindness to Michal, but she remained virtually a prisoner in her own home. She refused to go near the palace, communicate with the family, which she felt had cast her out as an unprofitable slave. Only Jonathan dared defy his father's wrath to visit Michal, and carry her news from David. A pall of grief and fear hung over the once-happy home of the king of Israel.

Michal took more pleasure in the psalms Jonathan brought her than she did in his assurance that Saul had vowed not to hunt David again. You notice David is still in hiding," she observed skeptically. "Apparently, he doesn't believe the king either."

"I know," Jonathan apologized in a tone of despair. "Father is so confused and inconsistent; no one knows what to believe—or do. If only he could be reconciled to the will of God, and surrender the kingdom to David, we could all live in peace."

"But you know as well as I do he will never do that."

"I fear you're right, Michal; but what can I do?"

"Do what David is doing, I suppose: wait for God to work it out."

"But our situations are quite; David must increase which means I must decrease. I love, too. I want to live to see my sons become men. If Father would relinquish the kingdom the king to David—"

"But you know very well he won't—not while he's alive."

"I know," agreed Jonathan with bitter sadness. "And when he goes, we will probably all go. My lovely wife. My precious children. Oh, Michal! God is cruel!"

"God, Jonathan? Or Saul?" Michal asked softly.

Michal's brothers had all taken wives, and there were four new babies in the palace. But the joy Ahinoam, Saul's wife, might have found in her son's three babies was marred by the presence of the fourth child. Little

Armoni was the son of Rizpah, Saul's concubine, the beautiful maiden who had been betrothed to Abner.

Ahinoam grieved for herself far less than she grieved for Michal and Rizpah, and for their youth that was wasted, away from the men they loved. But most of all Saul's queen grieved for Israel, torn by the foolishness of a mad king, and for David, the innocent victim of Saul's madness.

With thanksgiving, Michal received the messengers from Adriel that Merab was expecting another child, and presence was urgently needed. Adriel sent a writ, signed with the king's seal, giving Michal permission to Mehola.

As great as Michal's relief at leaving Gibeah, was her wrath at being according the treatment of a slave by the king. She would have gladly foregone her pleasure in leaving the oppressed city, and deprived Merab of the comfort of her presence in Mehola, for the satisfaction of defying the king. But Adah was near confinement, and Michal wanted to leave her alone with Phalti. Perhaps their experience of parenthood without her constant presence might bring them into the marital relationship Michal so wanted them to have.

Merab's bitterness seemed to increase with the birth of each new baby. The fact that she had presented her husband her husband with fourth fine son, did dispel her blank mood.

"Oh, Merab," rebuked," rebuked Michal, "if only I could have David, and could give him sons, I would not complain about anything in all the world."

"That's easy for you to say," Merab lashed out angrily. "You still have your figure, and all the looks you ever had. But look at me!" I look like a witch. Babies ugh! Well, I wish they were yours instead of mine. You are most welcome to every one of them."

"Merab, please! Don't say such things. David says we should be careful what we pray for, because God answers prayer."

"God does not answer my prayers. I've prayed and prayed not to have any more children. I'd rather be dead than be nothing but a brood mare. Why bring sons into the world only to have them slaughtered to appease the greedy whims of some selfish monarch? I'm about to agree with our father; I think God is dead."

"Saul may be your father; he is no longer mine! And the god he taught us about may be dead—perhaps he never lived—but David's God is very much alive, and I want to know him."

"I don't care about anybody's god. I only want to quit having babies, and to get my figure and my looks back." Merab looked with open envy at her younger sister. "I almost wish I had been barren like you."

Michal reeled as from a blow. "What do you mean, 'barren like me?'"

"Well, aren't you? You have had two husbands and no babies. The servants told me Phalti's other wife was having a baby. And Adriel says David has taken two new wives, and they are both with child. If you are not barren, what do you know that you are not telling me?"

Merab was so engrossed with her destructive gossip, she was unaware of the effect on her sister until she saw that her face was ashen, and her brown eyes resembled the eyes of a doe with an arrow through its heart.

"Well, for heaven's sake, Michal; don't tell me you didn't know David had married again. What did you expect? You have another husband, don't you?"

Michal did not answer, but she struggled desperately for composure. Jonathan knew. And Phalti must have known, too. They were trying to be kind to her, but the cruel truth would have been much easier to take if it had come from either of them. Had David heard of her marriage to Phalti? But surely he must know the situation was not of her own choosing. Death was her only alternative, and she was not nearly ready to die. She was not master of her own fate—nor was she protested by God's Spirit as David was. How could he do such a thing? Had he not sworn never to lose faith in her? Had he not promised to send to send for her? To wait?

Michal had devised numerous schemes to elude her without endangering Phalti. She could have managed-but the messengers never came. She had begged Phalti to take her and Adah, and join David's band of "outlaws" but he had always had a plausible excuse. Had he known about David's wives all along?

In her hour of agony, Michal grasped the one straw of comfort: David had taken *two* wives; if he had found joy in the first, would he have taken the second?

"Michal? Are you all right?" Merab manifested the first spark of concern she had ever shown for her sister. Or was it irritation?

"I'm quite all right," said Michal evenly. "After all, David has been gone for more than a year. And men being men, you know," she shrugged. "Mercy! It's almost morning; you go to sleep, and I must look after the baby. You have such precious babies, Merab; I, too, wish they were mine."

Chapter 23

Michal tried to remember the psalms David sent her? Had there been any hint of other women in them? She could hardly wait to get home to read them more carefully. The fact he only sang of his love for God, and failed to include her, or send any personal message had enraged her until she had paid very little attention to his missives.

Merab's three little boys, in addition to the new baby, kept Michal going night and day. The boys basked in the attention their aunt gave them, and the twins never tired of hearing her tell of the exploits of their uncle David.

Merab's spirits, however, failed to improve along with her body. All of Michal's efforts to cheer her met with little success.

"What's to rejoice about?" she asked sourly, when her sister encouraged her to smile, and to get back into her pretty dresses. "When I'm delivered of one baby, it only makes room for another one. What's the use? Adriel thinks because I have servants to wait on me, I should not complain. Well, the servants don't have the babies! And when the boys get hurt or into a fight, they think they have to have to have their mother."

"I'm so sorry, Merab, that you don't enjoy being a wife and mother. You don't have to enjoy it, you know; but once you get married, you do have to do it.'

"If girls only knew what they were getting into, they would not be so anxious to get married. Oh, how I'd like to tell them a thing or two!"

"Save your breath, Merab," Michal said lightly, in attempt to soothe her angry sister. "How much good would it have done if someone had tried to determined you were to get married? And then there are girls who enjoy being married—they love being wives and mothers."

"Well! They can have it! I was simply young and foolish; I had no idea what marriage was like."

"Why didn't you? Didn't you see the problems our mother had? And she had <u>six</u> babies. Her mother had <u>fourteen</u>—"

"Oh, Michal, hush! That's different. Anyway, I don't care what anybody else does; I'm not going to have any more babies. I'll—I'll die first!"

"Careful, Merab. You don't really mean that."

"Don't I though? You wait and see. I've already told Adriel: <u>no more babies!</u> He thinks I jest, too. He'll find out. I told him he could take another wife—or a dozen for all I care. And do you know what that big brute said."

"He probably said one wife was enough for him," Michal bantered.

Merab began to bristle.

"I'm sorry, Merab; I didn't mean to be ugly. But you have to admit you have not made your husband very happy or comfortable. And those are the things men usually marry for."

"Well! What about me? Do you think he has made me happy or comfortable?"

Michal sighed. "My dear sister. Be realistic. This is a man's world. Not many men ever stop to think about their wives comfort or happiness. And if they do, few of them care. A man can bellow like a bull if he gets a thorn in his finger, but a woman is supposed to suffer quietly through the agonies of childbirth, lest she disturb her lord and master. That's the way things are, Merab; and wise women accept it."

"You can accept it if you want to; I won't. Why should a woman suffer in silence to bring male children into the world to be slaughtered on some battlefield?"

"I couldn't agree more, and I don't want my sons sacrificed to the lust, greed, or vengeance of any king. But the only way we will ever get these conditions is <u>through</u> our men—not by spitting them. And the only way to get a husband interested in your welfare is to make every effort to show an interest in his. David is—was always as interested in my welfare as I was in his."

"Phalti is also interested in his wives' welfare, is he?"

"Phalti is very good to Adah."

"Isn't he your husband, too?"

"David is my husband," Michal said in a tone that even Merab knew closed the subject.

When little Ahimaaz was a month old, Michal prepared to return to Gibeah. Adriel was voluble in his appreciation of her services. "I declare,

Michal, I don't know what we would do without you. When you start having your family, you must let us return the favor. But you had better get busy; we are already way ahead of you."

"We are as far ahead of you as we are going to get," Merab said in acid tones. She was obviously embarrassed at Adriel for bringing up such an indelicate subject. But Michal smiled in honest appreciation.

"Thank you, Adriel. I won't let you forget. Only hope I can have sons as fine as yours. It has been my pleasure to care for them. I wish we lived close together so I could see them every day."

"So do I," said Adriel wistfully; you are a born mother, Michal. I pray you shall have many sons."

"Thank you, Adriel; that's the nicest thing anyone ever said to me."

"Merab was so shocked at the pleased expression on Michal's face, she let her ride away without another word.

Chapter 24

When Michal arrived home, she could scarcely take time to show proper appreciation for Phalti and Adah's new baby, she was so anxious to analyze the psalms David had sent her. But the baby was a girl, so little Rachel must have extra attention lest the new parents' shame be increased.

"Oh, Adah! She's beautiful. Who knows? She may be a queen some day." Michal was so effusive, the new parents began to look a little less guilty.

"Well, she is sweet," Adah admitted, "but we wanted a boy, of course."

"A boy! Oh, for heaven's sake! Who wants boys? They may end up unburied on some bloody battlefield. Girls, you can keep."

Before Michal finished admiring his daughter, even Phalti was looking at his little girl with open admiration. And his obvious pleasure in having the princess back was intensified.

At her first opportunity, Michal took David's psalms from the earthen jar, and picked out all the ones he sent in the past year. The one Jonathan brought from Ziph after David cut off Saul's skirt was surely written about the time he took the first wife:

> Save me, O God, by thy name, and judge me by thy strength.
> Hear my prayer, O God; give ear to the words of my mouth.
> For strangers are risen up against me, and oppressors seek after my
>   soul; they have not set God before them.
> Behold, God is my helper; the Lord is with them that uphold
>   my soul.
> He shall reward evil unto my enemies; cut them off in thy truth.
> I will freely sacrifice unto thee; I will praise thy name, O Lord;
>   for it is good.

For he has delivered me out of all trouble; and my eye has seen
    his desire upon my enemies.

There was surely nothing in that song about women. She tried another:

Deliver me, O Lord, from the evil man; pressure me from the
    violent man
Nothing here.
In thee, O Lord, do I put my trust; let me never be ashamed;
    deliver me in thy righteous.
Same stuff; she tried the next one.
Help, O Lord, for the Godly man ceases; for the faithful fail
    from the children of men . . . .
The wicked walk on every side, when the vilest
Men are exalted.

Michal read every word of the psalms, but could find no evidence of any interest in women. She replaced them in the jar with a sigh of relief.

It was just as well she forgot that David did not write about her in his psalms either—not even in the early days of their marriage. And there was never any doubt in her mind that he was very interested in her.

The loneliness, the waiting, and the constant fear that the king might find David was wearing Michal down. She desperately tried to rest secure in the belief that God promised David the kingdom. If he had, surely no one could destroy him. David believed it, she knew. Yet he fled in fear from Saul. It was all so confusing. If God was going to make David king why didn't he hurry up about it? They she repented the thought; she knew David would never sit on the through in Gibeah as long as the king or one of his sons was alive.

Why couldn't Saul bow to the will of God? Or better yet, why could he not have obeyed God, and kept his throne? Then she and David could have lived out to attempt to live out their lives in domestic tranquility in Bethlehem.

Getting to be a queen in an attempt to earn the respect of her brothers and sister no longer mattered to Michal. She would be perfectly happy with her own little home and family if she could share it with the man she loved. Let her father keep the kingdom.

But then, if God had not anointed David king, he would never have come to the palace, and she would never have met him. Spiritual things seemed to be beyond her understanding. Perhaps David was right after all in letting God solve his problems. Scheming as she was, Michal could think of no way out of her painful dilemma.

Phalti reported to the palace as usual the following morning, but he returned shortly. Ziphite messengers had arrived at the palace, with the assurance they could lead Saul directly to David's hiding place in the hills of Hachilah near Jeshimon.

Saul and three thousand of his chosen warriors were to leave immediately; Phalti was to accompany them.

"I'm sorry, Michal," he said with genuine regret in his voice. But Jonathan and I will do our best to warn David; I'm sure no harm will come to him."

"David's God will warn him," Michal said firmly. "But how foolish for three thousand men to be forced to leave their homes, their families, and their work to go trailing after a man who never did any of them any harm."

"True. And I do hope David realizes only the king is to blame; if he doesn't, it may go hard with some of us when David becomes king."

Chapter 25

When Saul and his three thousand chosen men reached the wilderness of Ziph, they pitched camp in the hill of Hachilah. The fugitives saw them the army coming while the troops were still a long way off. David sent out spies who reported the invaders were indeed Saul's most valiant warriors, led by the king himself.

So David crept down to the camp, and observed the place where the king lay. Abner, the captain of Saul's army lay in the trench with the king, and the men were pitched all around them.

Then David returned to his own camp, and called aside his most audacious followers: Ahimelech the Hittite, and Abishai the son of Zeruiah, David's sister, brother to Joab.

"I'm going to try to slip into Saul's camp and taunt him again. Perhaps I can make him so ashamed of himself he will go away without fighting us as he did the last time."

"Why don't you kill him?" asked Ahimelech, "so we can all go home."

"I can't. Saul is still the Lord's anointed; if I should lift my hand against him, I would lose God's favor, too. To be in God's will, we must remain in obedience to him. My God will take care of Saul in his own good time. In the meantime, we must wait."

"I'll go with you, Uncle David, said Abishai.

So David and Abishai slipped down to the camp under the cover of darkness, and stole in among the sleeping soldiers to the place where the king lay asleep in the trench. Abner and the palace guard lay all around him. The royal spear, which had been hurled at David so many times, was stuck into the ground beside Saul's pillow.

"Please, Uncle David," pleaded Abishai, "God has delivered your enemy into your hand. If you won't kill him, let me, I pray, smite him with this spear, and I will not need to smite him the second time."

"No, Abishai; you must not destroy him, for who can stretch forth his hand against the Lord's anointed, and be guiltless? As sure as the Lord lives, God will smite him; or his day will come to die; or he will perish in battle.

"The Lord forbid that I should lift my hand against the Lord's anointed. But take his spear, and his cruse of water, and let's get out of here."

So David took the spear and the cruse of water from Saul's pillow, and they slipped away between the soldiers, and no man saw them come or go. No one waked because a deep sleep from the Lord had fallen upon them.

Then David went over to the other side, and stood on top of a hill afar off, a great space being between them. He cried to Saul's army, especially to Abner, saying: "Won't you answer me, Abner?"

Then Abner answered, saying: "Who are you that cries unto the king?"

And David said: "Are you not a valiant man, Abner? Who in all Israel is as brave as Abner the son of Ner? Why, then have not kept a better watch over your Lord the king? For there went in among you a man who wanted to kill your master. You have been negligent in your duty. As sure as God lives, you should be put to death for failing to keep a proper watch over your king, the Lord's anointed."

And David held the spear and cruse of water aloft, and said: "See the spear and cruse that was beside the king's pillow?"

Saul recognized David's voice, and said: "Is it your voice I hear, my son David?"

"It is my voice indeed, my lord, O king. Why does my lord pursue his servant? What have I done? What evil have you ever charged against me? Now, therefore, I pray, let my lord the king listen to the words of his most faithful: If the Lord has sent you out against me, let me pay for my sin. But if some man has set you against me, may he be cursed of the Lord; for I have driven out from my home may he be cursed of the Lord; for I have been driven out from my home and my people, and have been forced to dwell among the heathen.

"Now, I pray, slay me not in God's presence. Is it not a waste for the king of Israel and his bravest men to come out after a flea, or to hunt a partridge in the mountains?"

Then Saul cried, "You are right, my son David; I have sinned. Come home, and I promise I will never again do you any harm, because my life was precious in your sight today. I confess I have played the fool, and have sinned exceedingly."

And David answered: "Here is the king's spear! Let one of the young men come over and get it. May the Lord judge every man according to his righteousness and his faithfulness. The Lord knows he delivered you into my hand today, and I would not lift my hand against his anointed. And as your life was precious in my eyes, may my life be precious in the sight of the Lord, and may he deliver me out of all tribulation."

"May you be blessed of the Lord, my son David. I know you will do great things, and David went back to his camp.

"So you were right again," Abishai admitted joyfully. "Now that Saul has sworn never to harm you, Uncle David, we can al go back to our homes."

"Don't be deceived, my dear nephew, by the king's pretty speeches. I know that if I stay here, I shall surely die one day at the hand of Saul. The best thing I can do is to speedily escape into the land of the Philistines. When Saul cannot find me anywhere in all the coasts of Israel, he will despair of searching for me, and I shall escape his murderous hands."

Chapter 26

So David, with his six hundred mighty warriors, their wives and their children, fled the land of their fathers, and begged refuge among the Philistines, their traditional enemies. And Achish, the king of Gath, gave the refugees sanctuary.

And David lived under the protection of Achish, at Gath, he and his men and their households. David took with him his two wives, Ahinoam the Jezreelitess, and Abigail the Carmelitess, Nabal's wife.

When Saul heard David had escaped to Gath, he dared not pursue him there; so, reluctantly, he went home.

After a few months, David said to Achish: "If I have found favor in your sight, let me, I pray, find a place in some town in your country, that I may have for a home. Why should your humble servant dwell in the royal city with the king?"

So Achish gave Ziklag to David, and, the city belonged to the kings of Judah from that day forward.

For a full year and four months, David lived with the Philistines. And he and his men invaded cities of the Geshurites, and the Gezrites, and the Amalekites; all were ancient enemies of Israel, which Joshua had failed to expel from the promised land. When David smote the cities, he left nothing alive except the sheep, oxen, mules, and camels, which he took, together with other spoil, and returned to Achish.

And when Achish asked, "Where have you raided today?"

David said, "Against the south of Judah, and against the south of the Kenites."

And because David saved neither man nor woman alive to bring tidings to Gath, Achish believed David. And Achish said, "David has made his people Israel utterly to abhor him; therefore he shall be my servant forever."

And Achish took great delight in the rich booty David brought him, and insisted the Israelites keep a generous portion for themselves. So David and his men grew rich while they lived in Ziklag; they built up the city, and fortified it.

After years of privation in the wilderness, while hiding from Saul, the fugitive reveled in being the hunters instead of the hunted. But David's men knew their master was no marauder; he was merely rooting out the enemies of Israel in preparation for the day when he would be Israel's king. So the men fought valiantly, with covetous eyes on high positions in the royal army, when their leader became ruler of the land.

Chapter 27

Michal rejoiced when she learned David had escaped into Philistia. Saul would not dare seek his son-in-law among his ancient enemies. And any danger David encountered there would be small compared to his peril in his own country.

No God-fearing man in all Israel would lift his hand against David, because everyone knew he was the Lord's anointed for their future king. There were, however, many heathen in the land, who feared neither God nor man; they would gladly hunt him down for the price Saul had placed on his innocent head.

But as the months stretched into a year, with no word from David, the waiting became almost unbearable. Michal was actually relieved when messengers came from Adriel asking her to return to Mehola. It seemed that Merab was having another baby after all.

Adah was also nearing her second confinement; so it was a convenient time for Michal to absent herself from the household. She felt the servants could adequately minister to Adah's needs, and she surely needed her husband to herself.

In spite of Merab's complaints, and oft-repeated threats, Michal was appalled at her sister's appearance. Even though she was great with child, Merab was as gaunt, hollow cheeked, and emaciated as if she were in the midst of famine. She was scarcely a shadow of her former beautiful self.

It was impossible for Michal to hide her alarm. "Merab! What on earth—? Are you not well?"

"Of course I'm not well! I'm having another baby, or had you not noticed?"

"Is that all—I mean, we-ll, having babies is not a sickness. Adah is having another baby, and she is in the best of health."

"Is that all? "Having babies is not a sickness! Best of health," mimicked Merab. "How would you know? All right, so I have not eaten. Well, I have not felt like eating. I may as well starve to death as kill myself having babies."

Michal could not believe her ears. Surely her sister would not deliberately starve to death. What about the four babies she already had? Michal went in search of Adriel.

Merab's husband was in despair. "We have done all we know how to do. Our physician has done everything in his power. She has simply refused to eat."

"But why?"

Adriel shrugged hopelessly. "She insists she had rather starve than have another baby. But the baby is almost here; there is nothing I can do now."

"Suppose you agreed that she have no more babies?"

"I finally did, It's better to have half a wife than none at all, I suppose. But if she loved me—."

"Oh, Adriel! Haven't you learned by now? Merab loves only Merab."

Adriel smiled grimly. "Are you sure you two are sisters?"

Michal tried to smile, too. "Our mother insists on it."

"Now I know why David refused to marry her: He knew her better than I did. But she was so beautiful," Adriel added wistfully.

"There are a few qualities more desirable in wives than beauty," Michal observed ironically.

"So I have discovered," said Adriel bitterly. "Now fortunate was David to marry a woman with beauty, brains, compassion, <u>and</u> common sense," he added.

Michal searched her brother-in-law's face for irony or innuendo. Apparently, there was neither; evidently the statement was intended as a compliment. "Thank you, Adriel," she said humbly.

Whether Michal's encouragement or Adriel's promise wrought the miracle was debatable, but Merab began to eat. And she even became almost pleasant. The ten days before little Aiah's birth was the most companionable time Michal ever spent with her sister. Outside of a few cutting remarks about barren women, and harems, Merab was quite civil. Her cheeks began to fill out, and she ordered her servants to prepare her best clothes in anticipation of the time she would look "decent" again.

To the amazement of the household, little Aiah arrived as fat and healthy as his four older brothers at birth. It should have been a time for feasting and celebrating. But there was no rejoicing in Adriel's household: Merab was dead.

The sister Michal had loved all her life with a devotion akin to worship, was gone. Though Merab never expressed such sentiments, Michal knew her sister trusted her, depended on her, and enjoyed having her there. She had allowed no one else to care for her newborn babies, and she and her husband had obviously felt more secure when the children were in her care than their own.

Michal could not imagine the world without her beloved sister. No one was more aware of Merab's egotism and than her sister, but it never diminished her devotion. That was simply Merab, and she loved her. Love covered Merab's shortcomings for Michal even as it had for Adriel.

Chapter 28

The house of Saul came to Mehola to lament Merab. And she was buried in the family burying ground of Barzillai.

It was the first time in more than two years Michal had seen any of her family except Jonathan. Ahinoam clung to her youngest child, and wept on her neck. Saul looked at his only living daughter with tender longing; Michal held her head high, gazed straight ahead.

When the burial was over, and the mourners had gone, Michal stayed to look after the baby. The children clung to her, and Adriel seemed to find such comfort in her presence, she dreaded leaving. She tried to console him as he grieved for Merab, and decried the five tumultuous years of their marriage.

"But look at your five precious sons, Adriel; there are men who would give a king's ransom for such a heritage. Would that I might be so blessed."

"But my sons need a mother," Adriel lamented. "I want now to ask a petition of you, my sister; I pray you will not say me nay."

And Michal said: "Say on."

"You know I am in Gibeah with Saul almost say much as I am here in Mehola. I cannot care for my sons, nor can I rest easy leaving them here with servants. Would you, my sister, take my children? If you will be their mother, they shall be your sons. I will, of course, provide their food and raiment. But I'm asking you to give them that which they need most: a mother's love."

And so Michal brought up Merab's sons for Adriel the son of Barzillai the Meholathite.

There was no more boredom in Michal's household. The twins, Joel and Joab, were motion. It was difficult to stop them long enough to eat or sleep. Little Shamah was usually right behind them. Ahimaaz preferred to stay by Michal's side while she ministered to baby Aiah.

If Phalti and Adah were upset by the sudden additions to their household, they concealed it well. Adah insisted Michal send the wet nurse back to Mehola, and allow her to feed the baby. She declared she had more than enough milk for her new baby girl. So little Rebekah and grew fat side by side.

Young Rachel was overwhelmed by her five new "brothers," but delighted with all the attention they gave her.

Michal bloomed under the warmth of love the boys heaped upon her. Her naturally affectionate nature starved during the two sterile years since David fled, and she was cut off from the family she adored all her life. Her beloved nephews were balm to her wounded spirit, and helped to fill the vacuum left by the loss of her loved ones.

"I always knew you'd make a wonderful mother," said Phalti wistfully. He cheerfully assumed the role of father to the little boys, and was so patient and helpful, Michal was touchingly grateful.

"You're a good husband and father, Phalti; I'm sorry you and Adah have to be burdened with six extra people in your home."

Phalti looked pained. "The privilege of taking care of my princess is my pleasure; and what she loves, I love." Then with ill—concealed yearning, as if emboldened by Michal's praise, he added, "I have tried to be patient, my little love; must you wait for David forever?"

Michal stiffened; it was as if a chill wind had blown away the warm current between them. "I must wait," she said firmly.

"And if he never comes for you?"

"He will come."

"How long will you wait?"

"Until he comes."

Phalti sighed. "And you know I yearn for you—even as you yearn for David?"

"I'm sorry, Phalti, I keep hoping Adah will fill the place in your heart you have for me; I never meant to hurt you. Perhaps I should go away; now that I have Merab's children, I'm sure the king would permit me to leave."

"Oh, no! Please, I'm not complaining. Forget what I said. Merely having you here is enough; I shall not ask for more."

So Michal's household settled into a kind of routine. It was something like a beehive, but a routine, nevertheless. Adriel came to visit his sons daily when he was in Gibeah, and once a month when he was a day's journey away at Mehola. He was always voluble in his appreciation of the good care his sons were obviously receiving. Their devotion to Michal was his mother.

Michal's sons filled her days with sunshine. They brought her the love and respect she had yearned for all her life. And they left her little time to grieve for her sister or yearn for her husband. She felt, however, as if she lived on top of a volcano. And she constantly listened for the rumblings that she hoped would precede the eruption.

Chapter 29

Again the Philistines gathered their armies together to make war against Israel. And King Achish said to David, "You know, of course, that you and your men must go out to the battle with me."

"You know what kind of warriors you servants are," David parried.

"I surely do," said Achish. Therefore, I will make you my bodyguard forever."

But David's men were distressed. "Surely, my lord, you do not expect us to go to war against our own people," said Abiathar, the priest.

"But what will Achish think if we refuse?" protested David. He thinks we have been raiding Israelites all this year. We cannot tell him no."

"We will not fight our own people," the men cried stubbornly.

"God would not have us fight us against Israel," David agreed; "nor would he have Achish slay us, so he will show us a way out. We have but to enquire of him, and follow his directions. He will provide our escape even as he has protected us from Saul these three years. So let not your hearts be troubled, neither let them be afraid. Wait on the Lord; be of good courage, and he will strengthen your hearts."

Saul destroyed all the wizards, and those with familiar spirits, out of the land. And he had slain God's priests with the sword of Doeg. Therefore, when Samuel died, the king had no one to guide him.

The Philistines gathered themselves together, and they came and pitched camp in Shunem. And Saul gathered all Israel together, and they pitched camp in Mt. Gilboa. Jonathan, Abinadab, and Melchishua went with their father. Ishbosheth remained in Gibeah to attend the affairs of state. Adriel took over David's command, and Phalti and his palace guard brought up the rear.

When the king saw all the hosts of the Philistines, he was sore afraid, and his heart fainted within him. But when he enquired of the Lord, he got no answer—neither by dreams, nor by Urim, nor by the prophets.

Then in desperation, Saul said to his servants, "Seek me a woman with a familiar spirit, that I may enquire of her."

And Adriel said, "I have heard there is a woman with a familiar spirit at Endor. But she is reported to be a very wise and crafty woman. She is loved and respected by her friends and neighbors, and avoided by her enemies. If she is as wise as she is reputed to be, she surely will not talk with my lord the king, lest she lose her life."

So Saul disguised himself: He lay aside his royal robes, and put on ordinary raiment. He went, and his two most trusted servants, Phalti and Adriel went with him, and they came to the woman by night.

When they entered the tiny hovel, the king said, "I beg of you, divine for me by the familiar spirit, and bring up for me, the man whom I shall name."

But the woman was wary, and she questioned him carefully: "Surely, you know what Saul has done, how he cut off those with familiar spirits, and the wizards out of the land. Why, then do you lay a snare for me to get killed?"

And Saul swore to the woman, by the Lord, saying, "As sure as the Lord lives, you shall not by harmed for this."

Finally the woman said, "Well, whom do you want me to bring up."

"Bring up Samuel, "Saul replied.

"Why, my lord," asked Adriel, "do you call for? Did he ever speak a comfortable word to you? He often rebuked you, but did he ever praise you?"

"True, my son, Samuel never praised me, but he always told me the truth. His guidance came from God, and I must have guidance."

So the woman put on a voluminous black robe, and covered her head with a heavy black veil. Then she lighted a bowl of incense on the small table in the center of the earthen floor of the tiny room. As the room filled with the fragrant smoke, the woman began a prayerful chant in a strange tongue.

To the witch's surprise and dismay, Samuel rose from the earthen floor, and stood before her in the clouds of smoke. She cried out to the king in terror: "Why have you deceived me? You are Saul!"

"Don't be afraid," said Saul soothingly; just tell me what you saw."

"I saw a ghost coming up out of the ground!"

"What does the ghost look like?"

"An old man, and he is covered with a mantle."

Saul, believing it was Samuel, stooped with his face to the earth, and bowed himself before the prophet.

"Why have you disturbed me by bringing me back to earth?" Samuel asked Saul.

"Because I'm in terrible trouble. The Philistines have invaded us again. But God has departed from me. He won't answer me either by the prophets or by dreams, so I have to have me what to do."

"What good will it do to ask me? I speak for God; since the Lord has departed from you and become your enemy, how can I help? Didn't I tell you the Lord had rent the kingdom out of your hand and given it to David? There is nothing you or I either can do about it now. Because you would not obey the commandments of God to destroy his enemies, he has given the kingdom to a man who will.

"And because of your disobedience, the army of Israel will fall before the Philistines tomorrow, and you and your sons will be slain."

Then Saul fell flat on the ground in terror because of Samuel's message. He was paralyzed with fear, and He was faint with hunger, because had eaten nothing all day.

Even the witch had compassion on the king when she saw how frightened he was. "Please, my lord, your handmaid obeyed your command, and I risked my life to do so. Now won't you listen to me? Let me prepare you something to eat so you have strength to sustain you as you go out to face whatever lies before you."

"Why should I eat? What difference does it make now? All is lost."

Then Phalti pleaded with the king: "I beg of you, my lord, listen to this wise woman's advice. You need something to eat."

"My father can face whatever we must endure better if he will eat," said Adriel. "Starving yourself will not help you, nor will it change what God has already determined to do."

So Saul arose from the earth, and his servants insisted he rest on the bed until the food was ready.

The woman had a fat calf in the house; hastily she killed and dressed the calf, baked unleavened bread, and brought the food to Saul and his servants. They ate, thanked the woman, and went out into the night to return to the doomed army of Israel.

Chapter 30

The Philistines gathered all their armies at Aphek, while the Israelites encamped by a fountain in Jezreel. And the lords of the Philistines passed in review by hundreds and by thousands. But David and his men brought up the rear with Achish.

"What are these Hebrews doing here?" asked the princes of the Philistines.

"This is David," said Achish. "He was indeed once servant to Saul, king of Israel, but he has been with me all these years, and I have found no fault in him since the time he sought refuge with me from the wrath of Saul, to this good day."

But the princes of the Philistines were angry, and they said to Achish: "Make this fellow go back to his appointed place. He must not go down to the battle with us, lest in battle he join our adversaries. How could he better reconcile himself to his master than with the heads of our men? Is not this the same David of whom the Israelites sang one to another in their dances, saying, 'Saul has slain his thousands, and David his ten thousands?' Those 'thousands' he slew were Philistines; he shall not go with us."

So Achish called David and said, "As surely as the Lord lives, you have been upright, and your going out and coming in with me in my army has been good. I have found no evil in you since the time you came to me until this day. Nevertheless, the lords are not in favor of your going with me. Therefore, I want you to return now in peace to your city, so we won't displease the lords of the Philistines."

"But what have I done?" protested David. "What fault have you found in your servant that I may not go and fight against the enemies of my lord the king?"

"I know," said Achish consoling, "that you are as good in my sight as an angel of God. Notwithstanding, the princes of the Philistines have said:

'He shall not go out with us to battle.' Therefore, you get up early in the morning; take all the Israelites with you, and as soon as it is light enough to see, you leave."

So David and his men obeyed the voice of Achish. As soon as it was light, they departed for Philistia. And the Philistines went on up to Jezreel.

As David and his men marched back to Ziklag, David said to Abiathar the priest, "Now do you see how much better it is to do the best you can with your problems, and leave the solutions to God? If we had refused to go up to battle against Israel with Achish, he would have put us all to the sword. Now that he thinks we wanted to fight for him, he loves us more than ever."

"But suppose the princes had not objected," asked Abiathar skeptically, "What would you have done then?"

"God would have provided another way out. Remember? He led us to go, and where the Spirit of God leads, the grace of God always provides."

An all of David's men lifted up their voices in praise of their master's and faith.

"Give your praises to God," said David sternly. "I but followed where he led."

After three days of hard marching, David and his men arrived in Ziklag. But the Amalekites had invaded the south, and razed Ziklag to the ground.

When David and his tired and hungry men found their homes burned, and their wives, and their sons, and their daughters gone; they lifted up their voices and wept until they had no more power to weep.

David's two wives, Abigail and Ahinoam, were gone, too: and David was as grief-stricken as the others, yet they talked of stoning him. However, David encouraged himself in the Lord his God. In the midst of his grief, he poured out his soul in prayer and praise to his Creator:

> "How long will you forget me, O Lord? Forever?
> How long will you hide your face from me?
> How long shall I take counsel in my soul,
>   having sorrow in my heart daily?
> How long shall my enemy be exalted over me?
> Consider and hear me, O Lord my God; lighten
>   my eyes, lest I sleep the sleep of death;

Lest my enemy say, 'I have prevailed against him;
And those that trouble me rejoice when I'm hurt.
But I have trusted in your mercy;
My heart shall rejoice in your salvation.
I will sing always unto my Lord,
Because he has blessed me so bountifully."

When David finished his song, he said to Abiathar, "Bring the ephod, and we will ask the Lord what he wants us to do."

And David asked the Lord, "Shall I pursue after this band of marauders? Shall I overtake them?"

And the Lord answered him: "Pursue, for you shall surely overtake them, and without fail recover all."

So David went, he and the six hundred men that were with him, and came to the brook Besor, where two hundred of his men who were too faint to travel were left behind. But David and four hundred men hastened on in pursuit of the vandals.

The pursuers found a sick Egyptians slave abandoned in a field, and they brought him before David. The man had been without bread or water for three days and nights. The Israelites piled their captive with food and drink, and when he revived, David questioned him.

"Where do you come from, and to whom do you belong?"

"I am a young man from Egypt, slave to an Amalekite. When I fell sick three days ago, my master left me here. We invaded the south of the Cherethites, and we burned Ziklag with fire."

"Could you take us to your master's company?

"If you will swear to me by your God that you will not kill me, nor deliver me to my master, I will take you to his company."

David granted the young man's requests, and he led the Israelites to his master's camp.

When David stood on the hill overlooking the enemy stronghold, it looked as if the Amalekites were spread abroad upon the face of the whole earth. They were eating, drinking, dancing, and making merry because of the spoil they had taken out of the land of the Philistines, and of Judah.

David and his men fell upon the drunken revelers at twilight, and the battle lasted until the evening of the next day. The only Amalekites who escaped were four hundred young men who fled on camels.

So the Israelites recovered all their enemies had carried away, and David rescued his two wives. Every man recovered his wife, his children, and his possessions: nothing was missing.

And David took also the flocks and herds the Amalekites had captured. As they drove the cattle before them back to Ziklag, David said, "This is our spoil."

When the company came to the two hundred men they left fainting beside the brook Besor, David greeted them warmly. "But the selfish, greedy men in David's victorious army said, "Because they did not go with us we will not give them any of the spoil we captured. Let each man take his wife and his children, and go home."

"No! You shall not do this," said David. "Listen, my brothers; it was the Lord who gave us victory and this spoil. He preserved us, and delivered our enemies into our hands. No one shall listen to you in this matter, but he that went down to battle shall listen to you alike with these who kept watch over our possessions."

And so it became a law in Israel that the soldier shared the spoil he captured with the man who stayed behind and kept the home fires burning.

When David returned to Ziklag, he sent a portion of the spoil to all the elders of Judah, and to his friends there, saying, "Behold a present for you of the spoil of the enemies of the Lord." And he sent gifts to Hebron, and to all the places where he and his men had found refuge from the wrath of Saul.

Chapter 31

While David and his men were fighting the Amalekites, the armies of Israel clashed in a mighty battle with the Philistines in Mt. Gilboa. But without David to lead them, the hearts of the men of Israel quailed without them and they fled before the Philistines.

And the Philistines followed hard upon Saul and his sons. They slew Jonathan, Abinadab, and Melchishua.

Having been forewarned by the woman of Endor, when Phalti and Adriel saw the battle was lost, they slipped away. Amid the noise, the tumult, and the confusion of the battle, they mounted camels, and fled to Gibeah. But Saul refused to flee. With fatalistic courage, fought to his death. He fell beside the bodies of his fallen sons.

As the battle went sore against the king, the archers hit him, and he knew he was mortally wounded. "Draw your sword," he begged his armorbearer," and thrust me through the heart, lest these heathen come and abuse me before they slay me."

But his armorbearer refused, because he was afraid to lift his hand against the Lord's anointed. So Saul took his own sword, and fell upon it. And when his armorbearer saw the king was dead, he fell likewise on his sword, and died with his master.

So Saul, the mighty warrior, who, under God's leadership had so valiantly delivered Israel many times, bereft of God, died ingloriously by his own hand. The king's three sons, his armorbearer, and all his men who could not escape, died that same day together.

And the Israelites who were across the valley from Mt. Gilboa, and the ones on the other side of Jordan saw the remnant of Saul's army was in flight, and heard the king and his sons were dead. Immediately, they forsook their cities and fled. The Philistines followed hard upon the fleeing Israelites, and when the heathens came upon the empty cities of the Children of God, they moved in and dwelt in them.

The day following the great battle, the Philistines went out to strip the slain. And when they found Saul, and his three fallen sons, they cut off the king's once proud and haughty head, and stripped him of his giant armor. They sent their grisly trophies on a tour of Philistia, and displayed them in the temples of their idol gods for all the people to see.

When the tour was completed, the Philistines placed the suit of brazen armor in the temple of Ashtaroth, and they fastened the king's mutilated body to the wall of the temple of Bethshan.

But when the inhabitants of Jabesh-gilead heard what the Philistines had done to the king of Israel, the valiant men arose, and the traveled all night to reach Bethshan. There they took the body of Saul, and the bodies of his sons from the heathen temple, returned them to Jabesh-gilead, and cremated them. Then they buried the bone under a tree in Jabesh, and fasted and mourned seven days for their fallen leaders.

When Phalti and Adriel fled from the battle, the returned to Gibeah. As soon as they reported the destruction of Saul and his army to Ishbosheth, they hastened to Michal. As gently as possible, Phalti broke the news of the tragic defeat of the armies of Israel at Mt. Gilboa, and the death of the king and his sons.

"Not Jonathan?" cried Michal. "Surely not Jon?"

"He died bravely," Phalti assured her. "Many Philistines fell at his feet."

Momentarily, Michal dropped her proud black head, and the only tears Phalti ever saw her shed, coursed her taut, pale cheeks. Then she took one deep breath, raised her tear-wet face, and started giving order: "Phalti, get the camels ready; pack as much food gold as possible. Adriel, go to the palace; get my mother and my brothers' wives and children ready to flee. Adah, help me get the children together. Pack a change of clothes for them. Call the servants; we've no time to lose."

"But where will we go? Asked Phalti. "The army is defeated; the Philistines are not behind us—"

"We will cross the Jordan," said Michal firmly. The Philistines are not likely to follow us there. David will come and rescue us eventually, but we must survive until he comes."

At the mention of David's name, a veiled look covered Phalti's face; nevertheless, he did Michal's bidding without further questions. The others, too, hastened to follow her instructions as if relieved to have someone tell them what to do.

Soon, Michal with Merab's five sons, Adah with her two daughters, and Phalti and four handmaids were mounted on camels, and speeding toward the palace. But ere they reached the palace compound, they met Adriel. He was carrying Mephibosheth, Jonathan's eldest son in his arms; the child was screaming in pain and terror. Hildah, Adena's handmaid, and Rizpah, Saul's concubine, ran behind them, with Rizpah's two sons in their arms.

"Where is my mother?" shouted Michal above Mephibosheth's cries.

"I'm sorry," panted Adriel, "but I could not persuade her to come. I failed to convince her the king and sons were dead. And she insists if they were dead, there would be no reason for her to remain alive. I can't seem to convince anyone," he added hopelessly; "they are all sure Saul's army is invincible."

"With David leading it, it was, said Michal tonelessly. "But Adena? Where is Adena? Could she not persuade Mother to flee? And where are the other boys' wives and their children? Where is Ishbosheth? He is responsible for the king's household."

"I'm sorry," repeated Adriel; "I did my best. Ishbosheth ran as soon as we told him what happened; he is probably half way to the Jordan by now. The women assured me Saul and his sons could not be defeated, and that no Philistine would dare come near Gibeah. I did persuade Rizpah to come, and Hildah stole Mephibosheth away; but she dropped him on the stairs. He fell down those stone steps; I fear both his ankles are broken."

Michal swept a worried glance over the ten small children in her care, and looked back toward the palace. Suddenly there was a cry from behind them: "The Philistines are coming!"

"Hurry!" Michal motioned to Adriel, Rizpah, and Hildah to mount the already-kneeling camels. Without a backward glance, she led her little band of refugees toward the Jordan River, and safety.

PART TWO

Chapter 32

Not knowing Saul and his sons were dead, David rested two in Ziklag after he returned from the slaughter of the Amalekites. And on the evening of the third day, a man came out from the camp of Saul, with his clothes torn, and dirt on his head. And he came to David, and fell to the earth before him, and bowed his face to the ground.

"Where do you come from?" David asked his grieving visitor.

"I am escaped out of the camp of Israel," said the man humbly.

"How did the battle go?" asked David eagerly; "tell me."

"The Israelites fled from the battle. Many of them are wounded, and many are dead. And Saul and Jonathan his son are dead also."

With pain and unbelief, David asked, "How do you know Saul and Jonathan are dead?"

"I happened to be passing by Mt. Gilboa, and I saw Saul fleeing before the chariots and horsemen of the Philistines. There was a spear thrust between the chinks in his armor. When I went to him, he asked me who I was. I told him I was an Amalekite, and he begged me to kill him. He said he was mortally wounded, but he could not die, and he did not want to be taken alive by the Philistines.

"So I stood upon the king's body, and I slew him with my sword, because I was sure he could not live with that spear thrust through him. And I took the crown from his head, and have brought them here to my lord, David."

Then David took hold of his clothes, and rent them from his body, and the men who were with him did likewise. And they mourned, and wept, and fasted until the sun went down, for Saul and for Jonathan his son, and for all the people of the Lord, and for the house of Israel.

And when David could control his grief, he said to the young man, "Who are you? And where do you come from? What do you know about the king's wife, and his daughter?"

"I am the son of a stranger, an Amalekite," replied his visitor. "And I know nothing more or less about the king's family."

"Why were you not afraid to stretch forth hand against the Lord's anointed?" demanded David.

And the Amalekite, still amazed that David grieved for the bitter enemy who had hunted him down like a dog, said: "But why is my lord wroth? It was your God who took the kingdom from Saul, and gave it into your hand. I thought to have been rewarded—and you censure me?"

"God did indeed curse Saul, and rend the kingdom from his hand, but he did not tell me I could do either. How dare an uncircumcised Amalekite lift hand against God's anointed?"

And David called one of his young warriors, and commanded him to slay the stranger. "Your blood be upon your own head," said David angrily. "For with your own mouth you have testified that you have slain the Lord's anointed."

Then David took his harp, and out of a heart of grief and sorrow, he sang this lamentation:

> "The beauty of Israel is slain upon the high places.
> How are the mighty fallen!
> Tell it not in Gath; publish it not in Askelon.
> Lest the daughters of the Philistines rejoice,
> Lest the daughters of the uncircumcised triumph.
> You mountains of Gilboa, let there be no dew,
> Neither let. There be rain upon you, nor fields of
>   fruits.
> For there the shield of the mighty has been
>   vilely cast away,
> The shield of Saul, as if he had not been anointed
>   with holy oil.
> From the blood of the slain, from the weight of
>   the mighty,
> The bow of Jonathan turned not back,
> And the sword of Saul returned not empty.
> Saul and Jonathan were lovely and pleasant
>   in their lives,
> And in the their death they were not divided.
> They were swifter than eagles;

They were stronger than lions.
You daughters of Israel, weep over Saul,
Who clothed you in scarlet, and with other
    delights,
Who put ornaments of gold upon your apparel.
How are the mighty fallen in the midst of
    the battle!
Oh Jonathan, you were slain in your prime.
I am distressed for you, my brother
    Jonathan.
Very pleasant have you been unto me;
Your love to me was wonderful, passing
    the love of women.
How are the mighty fallen, and the weapons
    of war perished!"

And when the period of mourning for Saul was passed, David enquired of the Lord, saying, "What shall I do? Shall I go up to any of the cities of Judah?"

And the Lord said, "Go up."

"Where shall I go, Lord?"

"Unto Hebron."

So David went to Hebron. He took his two wives, Abigail and Ahinoam; and he took every man who followed him, and his household. And they dwelt in the cities of Hebron.

Eventually, the men of Judah came and besought David that he might be their new leader. And David told the elders of Judah that Samuel had anointed David king over all the house of Judah.

Then they told David the men of Jabesh Gilead had rescued the bodies of Saul and his sons, and buried them in Jabesh. So David sent messengers to the men of Jabesh-Gilead, and said to: "May the Lord bless you for the kindness in honoring your king.

"Therefore, may God strengthen your hands, and give you courage to bear the death of your master.

"Because they had no leader, the house of Judah has appointed me king over them."

But before the men of Jabesh-Gilead could respond to David's subtle invitation, Abner the son of Ner, the cousin of king Saul, who had been captain of his armies, took Ishbosheth, Saul's only remaining son, and proclaimed him king over all Israel.

So Ishbosheth began to reign over Israel in Mahanaim, but the house of Judah followed David.

Chapter 33

The sun was sliding behind the distant horizon when Michal led her frightened little band through the gates of Gibeah toward safety beyond the Jordan river. Without a backward glance, she urged her plodding camel into his fastest gait; the others followed suit.

The cries of the frightened children, and the plopping of the padded fest of the desert animals, were the only sounds that broke the stillness on the lonely road to Jericho. The darkness came with one swift stride, and the refugees were forced to slow their camels to a walk.

The little column advanced two abreast. Each adult carried a child. Michal and Adriel led the way. The five-year-old twins, by virtue of their seniority, rode with them; Joab with Michal, and Joel with his father. Phalti and Adah followed; Phalti carried little Rachel, and Adah carried baby Rebekah.

Behind them came Rizpah, Saul's concubine, with her baby Mephibosheth in her arms. Her little Armoni was securely strapped to the saddle of the pack camel, led by Phalti. They were followed by Hildah, Adena's handmaid, carrying Mephibosheth, Jonathan's son, who had manfully stifled his cries. Lean, Michal's handmaid, carried Shamah, Adriel's son, and rode beside Hildah.

Last came Adriel's two youngest sons, little Aiah and his nurse, Ruah; and Adah's handmaid, Zilpah, carrying Ahimaaz.

The narrow road wound like a dim tunnel between the rocks and boulders ahead of the travelers. It took constant urging from the drivers to keep the plodding camels moving. The infants had been lulled to sleep by the steady rocking gait of their steeds, and the older children soon quieted in the reassuring arms of their elders.

Suddenly on the wings of the hot desert breeze the smell of smoke wafted to the refugees. "Wait," cried Michal, as she jerked her camel's head, and turned to look back toward Gibeah.

The caravan halted. Mephibosheth's muted whimpers were barely audible above the camel's labored breathing. No other sound broke the silence of the black, desert night.

A faint glow appeared in the star-studded sky lighted by a tiny crescent moon. It puzzled Michal. She watched it and saw it grow brighter. The dark sky became pink and then dull red. Suddenly she saw a huge tongue of flame leap high toward the heavens. She raised up in her saddle; her already-thudding heart began a sickening bumping against her ribs.

The Philistines had come, and they were burning the city. The flames appeared to be toward the south side. The city gates! The people would be trapped within their own protecting walls. The refugees watched with horrified eyes as the flames shot higher and higher, and widened rapidly into a broad expanse of crimson sky.

The red horizon was hideous with lurid color. Except for the great swirls of black smoke that went twisting up to hang in billowing clouds above the flames, it looked like a sunrise out of time and place.

The fire spread northward with unbelievable rapidity. Soon the towers of the palace were silhouetted against the flames. Without a word, Michal turned her desert "ship" once more toward Jericho, and urged him into a lope. The others followed. The silence of the fugitives was eloquent testimony to the grief in their hearts for the beloved voices forever stilled, and the dear faces they never expected to see again on earth.

In less then an hour, the camels slowed to their usual plodding gate, and refused to move any faster. But even at a walk, the sturdy animals covered many weary miles. To the tired and hungry travelers, it seemed they had gone halfway around the world.

Eventually, the silence was broken when Hildah urged her camel up beside Michal's mount. "Please, my lady, can't we rest a while? I can't bear to watch little Mephibosheth suffer any longer."

"Had you rather watch him die?" asked Michal coldly, with no attempt to slow her animal's pace. "Can't you imagine what the Philistines would do with the crown prince if they caught him? And with all who carried him away?"

"But couldn't we rest a little while?" pleaded Hildah. "At least long enough to bandage the child's swollen ankles?"

"I'm sorry," said Michal with a touch of compassion in her voice, "but we cannot stop until we reach Jericho. There must be food and shelter available when all these babies wake up. We dare not let tomorrow's sun catch us out here on the desert."

"Michal is right," agreed Adriel. "We cannot expose the babies to the broiling sun; we must reach Jericho by morning."

Another hour passed silently except for the plop-plop of the plodding camels. Then came a dull thud and a sharp cry from Joel. The caravan halted. Adriel leaped to the ground, and picked up his crying son.

"What happened?" asked Michal.

"I must have gone to sleep," said Adriel contritely. "Joel fell off."

Phalti was quick to defend Adriel. "Neither of us had any sleep last night, and only an hour or two the night before."

Michal commanded her camel to kneel. "Here, Adriel, take Joab." When the sleeping child had been transferred to the arms of his father, Michal lifted up the bottom of her skirt, caught the hem of her undergarment between her teeth, and tore. She handed the strip of cloth to Adriel, tore another, and handed it to Phalti. "Bind the children to your girdles, and yourselves to the saddles; then you can sleep."

"Who could sleep," asked Adah, "in such a horrible position?" She squirmed as far as the saddle and her sleeping baby would permit in an effort to relax cramped muscles, and limbs aching from their unaccustomed confinement.

"When you have been without sleep long enough, you can sleep anywhere," said Phalti, said Phalti, as he followed Michal's instructions.

"Would anyone else like a tether?" asked Michal.

"May I have one to bind Mephibosheth's ankles?" Hildah asked timidly.

Michal tore two more strips for Hildah.

"May I have one to bind my baby to the saddle, so I can rest my arms?" asked Rizpah.

Michal tore two more strips, and silently handed them to her father's concubine. Her sympathy and admiration for the beautiful and courageous girl, who had suffered more cruelly then herself, was too deep for words.

As a precautionary measure, Michal handed a strip of cloth to all the other adults, and insisted they bind themselves to their saddles to avoid further delaying accidents. Then she remounted her camel, and they plodded on toward Jericho.

The refugees drew near the ancient walled city at the break of day. In addition to being exhausted, hungry, sleepy, and aching in every muscle, the women were raw and bleeding from hard saddles.

But their visions of rest and shelter were soon dispelled: Jericho was preparing for a siege—the Philistines were coming.

Having seen what happened to Gibeah at the hands of the Philistines, the fugitives refused to enter the walled city. They watered their camels at the fountain outside the city gates, and replenished their own water supply.

"Please, my lady," begged Hildah, "can't we stop long enough to get a physician for Mephibosheth? His little feet and ankles are so black and swollen. If we don't get help, he may be left crippled for life."

"Better that he should be crippled than dead," said Michal stubbornly, but the harsh words were forced past a lump in her throat.

As the weary travelers plodded on around Jericho to the wilderness beyond, they met fruit vendors bringing in dates, raisins, and figs for the day's market. Michal purchased as much as they could carry, and they were all somewhat refreshed after breakfasting on the succulent fruit. But with the rising sun, the heat, the exhaustion, and the crying babies became unbearable.

Leaving the road, the little caravan pushed into the wilderness. Passing up several small, easily accessible caves, Phalti finally stumbled onto a large one completely shielded by a waterfall. Phalti led the little caravan single file through a narrow aperture behind the rushing water, and into the welcome seclusion of the cool, dimly lighted cave. At last they could rest.

The cave was at the end of a narrow canyon, protested on either side by sheer rock walls. It commanded a view of the entire valley below. They would be safe from a surprise attack, and two men should be able to stand off an army.

As soon as the camels were unloaded, Michal insisted Adriel and Phalti find a remote corner of the cave, and go to sleep. Then she turned her attention to Mephibosheth. From the soles of his feet to his knees, the flesh was black and swollen.

"Take him out and dip his swollen feet and legs into the cool stream," she told Hildah, "while I find some splints. I don't know if splints will help now, but at least they will prevent further injuries."

When the long-neglected babies had been bathed and changed, and everyone had feasted on bread, cheese, parched corn, dates, raisins, and figs, the women were all tired unto death, but the children were ready to play.

"Find a place for your beds," said Michal, "and I will look after the children."

"Oh, no," protested Hildah. "Mephibosheth needs me; let me keep watch."

"But Mephibosheth is asleep at last," observed Adah, "so let me look after the children."

"I was able to sleep a little last night," Rizpah assured Michal, "so I beg of you, let me take the first watch."

The handmaids offered their services also. Michal searched the faces of all the exhausted but willing women. The granite dependability she sensed in the face of the beautiful young woman, whose young and beauty had been sacrificed on the altar of her father's madness, determined her choice. She was certain the children would be safest in the hands of Rizpah.

Chapter 34

So David began to reign over Judah in Hebron, and Ishbosheth began to reign over the other tribes of Israel in Mahanaim. And Joab the son of Zeruiah, David's sister, led the army of David, while Abner, Saul's cousin, led Ishbosheth's army.

Joab and the servants of David went out and encamped by the pool of Gibeon. And Abner with the remnant of Saul's army came and encamped on the other side of the pool.

And Abner said, "Why should we slay each other? We are brothers. Let us choose twelve men from each of the armies, and let them wrestle. Which ever group can overcome the other, we will declare the victor, and we will all abide by that decision."

"That is fine with me; let them wrestle," said Joab.

So Abner and Joab went back to their men, and told them of the decision their captains had reached. Abner chose twelve mighty warriors from the tribe of Benjamin, and Joab chose twelve of David's bravest warriors.

And the men caught everyone his fellow by his head, and thrust his sword in his opponent's side. So twenty-four of the mightiest warriors of the children of Israel died by the pool of Gibeon.

As soon as the men fell, their fellows rushed upon each other, and there was a very sore battle that day. Eventually, Abner was beaten; he and the army of Israel fled before the men of Judah, the servants of David.

Three sons of Zeruiah, David's sister, were there: Joab, Abishai, and Asahel. And Asahel who was as fleet of foot as a wild deer, was determined to punish Abner for his deceitfulness, and for leading an army against David, whom God had anointed king of all Israel.

So Asahel pursued Abner. He paid no head to the other fleeing men but pursued the captain only.

Then Abner looked behind him, and said, "Are you Asahel?"

"I am."

"Then you catch one of my men and take his sword; I refuse to fight an unarmed man."

But Asahel paid no head; he continued to follow Abner.

"Please, Asahel, quit chasing me. Why should I kill you? If I strike you down unarmed, how shall I justify myself to your brother, Joab?"

Asahel refused to turn aside, however, or to slack his pace in his pursuit of Abner. So Abner raised his spear and pushed it backward to look as if Asahel had run into the spear while pursuing Abner too close.

And the spear pierced Asahel's heart, and came out behind him; he fell dead on the spot.

As the servants of David caught up with Asahel who was running far ahead of them, they stopped beside his bleeding body, and stood still in grief and respect. But Joab and Abishai continued to pursue Abner; they were determined to avenge their brother's death. And, eventually, the others followed.

Just before the sun went down, the men of Judah came to the hill of Ammah, that lies before Giah in the wilderness of Gibeon. And the routed Israelites gathered themselves together behind Abner into a troop again, and they stood on top of the hill above the men of Judah.

Then Abner called to Joab, and said, "Shall the sword devour forever? Don't you know our fighting will only lead to more bitterness? How long will it be before you command your men to quit following their brothers?"

And Joab said, "As sure as God lives, if you had not spoken, I would have sent my sent my men out again in the morning to hunt you down. But you are right; brother should not fight brother."

So Joab blew his trumpet and his men gathered together to return home.

And Abner and his men walked all that night through the plain. They passed over the Jordan River, went through Bithron, and came at last, tired, wounded, and sore, to Mahanaim. They left 360 of their men dead on the battlefield by the pool of Gibeon.

When Joab gathered his men together, they picked up their wounded, and buried in the sepulcher of his father. Then Joab and his men walked all night, and came to Hebron at the break of day.

And all Hebron mourned for Asahel, but Joab swore vengeance against Abner.

Chapter 35

Phalti and Adriel slept until nightfall in the cool darkness of the cave. Then they arose, saddled two of the camels, packed their weapons and a little food, and went out under the cover of darkness to learn the fate of Israel. No amount of persuasion could stay them.

"Israel needs every man," said Phalti. "Two of her best warriors must not remain safe in a cave while Israel dies."

Only Michal made no effort to stop them.

"Israel will not die," she said with conviction. "Now that Saul is dead, David will deliver Israel from the hand of the Philistines."

"God will deliver Israel," said Adah. "But I'm sure he will use David," she said hastily.

"God needs every man," said Phalti, "so we must go."

The women and children huddled together in the chill darkness of the cave for warmth and security, but still they were cold, and the children were frightened. So Michal and Rizpah gathered sticks for a fire, and took watching it through the night. And they all slept securely, even Mephibosheth.

Life in the cave was not unpleasant. There was an abundance of clear, sparkling water. And Adah found plenty of herbs in the valley to supplement their dwindling food supply.

Michal decreed that no one talk of their misfortunes, but give thanks for their deliverance. She insisted it was only a matter of time until David came to rescue them. In the meantime, the children were not to be frightened or discouraged by any discussion of war, death, or absent loved ones. So except for Mephibosheth, the children played happily all day, and slept soundly on their beds of leaves at night.

Neither Michal nor Rizpah could conceal her joy that the tyrant who had oppressed them so cruelly was dead. That he had been father to

Michal, and husband to Rizpah did not change the injustices they suffered at his hands. But they discussed their new status only in private.

"Will you go back to Abner?" asked Michal.

"Would he want me after I have borne two sons for Saul?" Rizpah countered with a question of her own.

"Would you give up your sons?"

"Never."

Michal smiled encouragingly, and her admiration for the mother of her little half brothers increased.

"If Abner loves you, he can love your sons."

"And will you go back to David?"

"Of course. As soon as he comes for me." But Michal spoke with more confidence than conviction. She had heard nothing from her husband for so long, and everyone knew about David's two new wives.

"But what about Phalti?" asked Rizpah hesitantly.

"Phalti understands," said Michal, again with more hope than confidence.

"How fortunate that you have borne Phalti no children."

Michal said nothing.

"And still he seems to love you so much."

"Oh, Phalti loves Adah," said Michal quickly.

"You are very kind," said Rizpah admiringly. "But it is obvious Adah knows Phalti loves you best."

"I grew up as a child under Phalti's protection at the palace; he loves me as the daughter of his king."

Rizpah said nothing, but the wisdom and understanding in her big, dark eyes caught Michal to change the subject. "I'm anxious to get somewhere and find a physician for Mephibosheth. He does not complain, but I know his ankles are not healing properly. I would take one of the camels and try to get help for him, but Phalti said to wait; we might find only Philistines."

Seven days passed before Phalti and Adriel returned. The news they brought was a crushing blow to Michal and to Rizpah: Ishbosheth was king! Then Rizpah legally belonged to him. Revolution contorted the beautiful face that was beginning to regain a measure of serenity. And David would be unable to return for Michal without provoking yet another war.

"But why, Phalti, why? Ishbosheth knows God has given the kingdom to David," Michal protested.

"Your father knew it, too. That knowledge never stopped him, did it?"

"Ishbosheth has signed his own death warrant," Michal said vehemently.

"So did your father, but who could reason with him?"

"What will we do?" Michal spoke in a tone nearer despair than any Phalti had ever heard from her.

"We haven't much choice. Ishbosheth has set up his palace in Mahanaim. He has ordered all troops to report for duty. Even if we were willing to abandon our homeland, every road will be guarded. Adriel and I must go back, and we have to take our families along."

Without another word, Michal began packing their meager belongings; the others joined her. Soon the little caravan was winding its way out of the safety of the cave that had sheltered them from man, beasts, and the elements. Even the children looked back with sighs of regret as they left their peaceful little sanctuary in the wilderness, and wended their way back to the world of strife.

Chapter 36

So there was a long war between the house of Saul and the house of Saul and the house of David. But David waxed stronger and stronger, and the house of Saul waxed weaker and weaker.

Michal heard nothing from David directly, but all Israel heard reports of Judah's popular new king. In the palace at Hebron, Ahinoam the Jezreelitess bore David his firstborn son, Amnon. His second son, Chileab, was born to Abigail the wife of Nabal the Carmelite.

David also took to wife Maacah the daughter of Talmar, king of Geshur, and she bore him a third son whose name was Absalom. Then David married another wife, Haggith, who bore him a fourth son, Adonijah. He also married Abital who bore his fifth son, Shephatiah; and he married Eglah who bore his sixth son, Ithream.

Every time Michal heard of a new wife or child David had acquired, it was like a knife in her heart. She thought of all the hopes and dreams and her young husband had shared, and the plans they had made for their children.

But as the years passed and no word came from her husband, Michal began to wonderful if David really had forgotten her, and all the plans they had made for a glorious Israel. Surely Judah's clever new king could devise some way to rescue her if he really wanted her. She was forced to admit, however, that Ishbosheth kept a closer guard over her than Saul ever had, and Abner took obvious delight in being her jailer. Michal suspected Abner did only that which pleased him; he was the real power in Israel, and Saul's son was but a tool in the hands of the captain of his army.

But Saul's daughter had little time to grieve. Merab's five sons kept her busy night and day. She also acquired Jonathan's son, Mephibosheth. With father, brothers and sisters gone, the little lad and his nurse made their home with Michal. And Hildah's fears had been justified: Mephibosheth was lame on both his feet.

Ishbosheth claimed his legal right to Rizpah, and she and her two sons had been forced to go and live with the new king and his wife, Sarah, and their two daughters. Rizpah visited Michal occasionally; her hopelessness and resignation was pathetic.

"Do you ever see Abner?" Michal asked on one of Rizpah's infrequent visits.

"Yes," said Rizpah dull, but the question seemed to kindle a spark of interest in her tragic eyes.

"If Abner is as strong as everyone seems to think he is, why does he not take you away?"

"It would mean an open break with the king. Abner does not feel he can afford that—not yet. And what do you hear free David?"

Michal knew Rizpah had closed the subject. "All I've heard lately," she said bitterly, "is that he has more wives and more children. "Of course," she added hastily, "we must remember the king of Judah has responsibilities we are not aware of. And I know he cannot come for me without provoking more war with Israel. David had always fought only in self-defense against Israel, I'm glad he has not changed."

It was a loyal speech, and sounded convincing, but Rizpah looked at her so searchingly that Michal, too, changed the subject.

"Well, we may not have our men," said Michal defensively, but at least we have our boys. And they are growing up to be such fine young men. We are celebrating Joab and Joel's twelfth birthday next month. Now I wish Merab could see them now."

The sun had already set when Phalti came in from work. "I never knew from one day to the next if I will have a palace to guard," he complained to Michal. "How I wish you and I could run away from it all."

"And would you leave Adah and the two sweet daughters and the sons she has given you?"

"For you, my dear, I would gladly leave the whole wide world." Phalti smiled, then more seriously he reminded her, "You will soon be thirty years old; surely you do not want to go childless through life."

"But I am not childless," protested Michal. "I could not love my sons more if I had borne them. And I'm sure they love me as much as if I given them life."

"Perhaps. But you are such a vibrant, living person, surely you can't be happy to be only the mother of another woman's sons."

"I can't be happy unless I bear sons for David," declared Michal with stubborn zeal. "But if I cannot have his sons, I shall be satisfied with the sons I have; they will be my comfort in my old age."

Phalti sighed with resignation, and went from his unsatisfactory home to his unsatisfactory work.

In less than an hour the following morning, Phalti was back home. He left his post only in dire emergencies, so Michal knew there was trouble even before she saw his ashen face.

"What now?" she asked fearfully.

"All hell has broken loose in the palace; only God knows where we will go from here."

"What happened?"

"Send the children out," said Phalti.

Adah took the children to their quarters. The big captain, who had not quailed before Saul nor all the cruel hordes of Philistine army, was visibly shaking.

"Phalti, what on earth?" Michal asked as soon as the children were out of hearing.

"Ishbosheth caught Abner coming out of Rizpah's room this morning. It was obvious he had spent the night there, but, when the accused him he blew up. 'Am I a dog?' Abner screamed. 'Haven't I shielded the house of Saul against the house of Judah? Could I not have delivered you into the hand of David anytime I chose? How dare you charge me with fault concerning this woman? Was she not mine before your father took her?'

"Then Abner reminded Ishbosheth that God had given the kingdom to David, and he assured the king he was going to do likewise. He said, 'I will translate the kingdom from the house of Saul, and set up the throne of David over Israel from Dan to Beersheba.'"

"What did Ishbosheth say?"

"Not a word. He knows he has no power in Israel. Abner has ruled all these seven years since Saul's death. When Abner leaves, Ishbosheth is finished, and he knows it only too well."

"Will Abner really give the kingdom to David?"

"He will."

"Then why didn't he do it seven years ago?"

"He was so sure he could hold Israel. After all, David only had one tribe, and Abner held nine tribes. He saw no reason to fear David would gain control. But now he knows his cause is lost anyway. The incident this morning merely gave him an excuse to surrender without admitting he has been defeated.

"Apparently, he forgot that God gave all Israel to David," Michal said with biting irony. "But where will he go?"

"I'm sure he hopes to ingratiate himself with David by voluntarily handing him the kingdom. He probably thinks David will let him lead his armies. He was once David's captain, remember. He is a good leader, and David knows how forgiving David is."

"Oh, you can be sure Abner is looking out for Abner. But what about Ishbosheth?"

"David won't touch him, and Abner knows that, too. It's the wisest move our defeat captain could possibly make."

"Then why are you so distressed?"

"But what about you, my princess? What about you? All these years I have loved you, and patiently waited for you—always hoping you would learn to love me. Will you go now and be a part of a man's harem who has ignored you for ten years?"

"When David becomes king of all Israel, what choice will I have but to do his bidding?" Michal hedged.

"We could run away—leave Israel—go into Philistia—anywhere."

"You know the kind of warrior David is. Do you really think any king would defy to shield us?"

"Well—we could hide. We could go back to the cave where we hid from the Philistine; David would never find us there."

"Hide? With ten children?"

"But I cannot give you up," wailed Phalti."

Michal saw tears in the big soldier's eyes, and her heart was touched by his grief, but she could not reply.

"If David had sent for you years ago, I was prepared to lose you. But you have been mine much longer than you were his. I cannot bear to let you go."

"You've been wonderful, Phalti. No other man could have been so kind and generous. You took care of me when my own family turned me out. And I have given you nothing in return."

"Not so!" Phalti interrupted. "Your presence in my home has been manna to my soul. I could not have survived seeing you taken by another man. David, yes, but you loved him, and I had no hope of ever having you then. The passing years have made you mine. We've brought up our children together. David has six other wives. He no longer needs you; I do."

The love mingled with the pain in Phalti's eyes was more than Michal could bear. "If David sends for me, we both know I must go. If he does not send for me—I will be your wife."

The captain dropped to his knees at Michal's feet; he raised both her hands to lips and kissed them fervently. "I ask no more," he said gratefully. "I ask no more," he said gratefully. "I ask no more."

Michal's conscience prickled her. She knew she had made no concession whatever, because David would send for her. And the mere thought of reunion with her beloved husband wiped out all awareness of the good man kneeling so gratefully at her feet.

Chapter 37

So Abner said messengers to the king of Judah with an apology for his misconduct, and an acknowledgement that the kingdom of Israel belonged to David. "Make a league with me," said Abner, "and my hand shall be with you; I will deliver all Israel into your hands."

"I will make a league with you," said David, "on one condition: You shall not see my face except you first bring Michal, Saul's daughter. Bring me my wife when you come, then I will talk with you."

"Surely you jest," said the messengers. "You would jeopardize the peace of Israel for a woman? Is any woman so important?"

"This one is," said David, with no hint of apology. "I have nothing more to say until I get my wife."

"But she has a husband in Israel. And children—five—six—perhaps more."

David's face paled, and he was silent for a moment. Then he said stubbornly, "She is my wife. I wish no harm to her children or their father; leave them in Mahanaim. Michal is mine. Bring her to me or there will be no treaty with Israel, and the war will continue."

"But we have no authority to take a woman from her husband," insisted the messengers. And sorrowfully they returned to Israel.

David then sent messengers to Ishbosheth saying: "Deliver me my wife, Michal, whom I espoused to me for an hundred foreskins of the Philistines. And give me the kingdom which is mine from the Lord, and no harm will come to you. The house has never had cause to fear his servant David."

So Ishbosheth sent Abner to take Michal from Phalti, and escort her to Hebron. Hildah showed the captain in, and called for Michal.

"Do you come peaceably, cousin?" Michal asked.

"Peaceably," said Abner, but he grinned at her in a most irritating manner. "Your husband has sent for you."

"Oh?" Michal parried. "And why did he not come for me himself?"

Realizing he had been out-maneuvered, Abner dropped his familiar approach, and assumed his most military air. "The king of Judah requests your presence in Hebron immediately."

Michal's heart raced, but she continued to be wary. "And if I refuse the king's invitation?"

Abner retained his composure with difficulty. "David has agreed to discuss the peace and unity of Israel only after you have been returned to him. You are honored, my cousin," he said mockingly. This is the first time in all history the possession of a woman has been made an operative clause in a peace treaty between nations."

Abner waited expectantly for Michal's reaction. She returned his look with withering scorn. His short temper flared: "I may as well tell you, Ishbosheth has ordered me to take you to Hebron at once."

Michal bowed in cool disdain. "And, of course, you must take orders from your king," she said with biting iron. "When the king commands, we must all obey."

Abner refused to rise to her bait.

Michal bowed low in mock humility. "Could any sacrifice be too great for the peace of Israel? And my sons—do they go with me?"

"No."

Michal lower her eyelids to hide the pain she was determined not show. "Tell your lord and master I shall be ready within the hour," she said in the same mocking tone, her head high and her eyes dry.

"I don't know how I will tell Phalti goodbye," Michal confided to Adah. "But has loving service through the years will not let me go without seeing him. And there are so many instructions I need to give him about the boys. I'm sure David will send for my sons when I ask him, but first I must ask Adriel. Oh Adah, ten long years have I waited for this summons, and now that it has come, I can't seem to think of anything except that I will see David at last."

The twins ran to the palace to fetch Phalti. But Michal and her handmaid were already mounted on the camels when he arrived. She expected him grieve, but Michal was totally unprepared for his reaction.

The big captain ignored Abner and his band of soldiers; he ran straight to Michal with outstretched arms. "No! No! No!" he cried. "My little princess, you cannot leave me!" Tears rolled into his beard as he wept unashamed.

"She is the queen of Israel," said Abner haughtily. "She goes to assume her rightful position." He turned to his soldiers: "Forward march." And the caravan wended its way toward Hebron.

Matching his stride to the camel's ambling gait, Phalti walked beside Michal. "I cannot let you go," he pleaded. "Surely you must know how much I love you. Life holds nothing for me without you. I'll never again ask for anything more than your presence if you will only stay."

"Shhh," whispered Michal. "Don't give Abner the pleasure of seeing you suffer. I have to go. As you can see, David sent a band of soldiers after me. He refused to talk peace with Israel until I am returned to him. Ishbosheth ordered me to go. There is nothing either of us can do."

"But I cannot live without you. If you cannot stay with me, then I will go with you."

"I fear David would not allow you in Hebron. In fact, I doubt if Abner will permit you to continue with us. Then there is Adah and the children; you must go back!"

"But I can't go back. Where you go, I will go. I'll tell David I took care of you for him. You tell him how I saved you from the king's wrath. Ask him to let me be your bodyguard. The Queen must have guards. I've guarded you all your life. Where could he find one who would be more loyal—more trust worthy? You ask him, Michal; he'll do it for you." The courageous captain, who feared neither man her beast, wept like a child for his lost love.

"Please don't cry, Phalti. You go back home and look after our household. As soon as I reach Hebron, I'll ask David to send for all of you. He'll do it for me, I know. After all, Ishbosheth is finished. David knows what kind of men you and Adriel are. There is no reason for you not to serve David as you served Saul and his son."

"But what if David is angry with us for not coming over to him when Saul died?'

"Oh, you know David. He would forgive the devil himself if he said he was sorry. Don't you remember the beautiful song he wrote about Saul and Jonathan? And when I tell him how good you have been to me, there will be no problem; you'll see."

Michal and Phalti talked quietly, lest they be overheard. And Phalti assured Michal he would do her bidding, but he continued to weep as he walked swiftly to keep up with her plodding camel.

When the caravan reached Bahurum, Abner commanded a halt. While the men watered the camels, and refreshed themselves, he came back to Phalti and Michal. "Now, I have had enough of this nonsense, Captain. You know I have no choice in this matter. Michal has no choice. And you have no choice. The king has spoken, and, we must obey. You go back to Mahanaim—now! Return at once!"

Still weeping, Phalti turned back; and Michal rode on toward the south, without a backward glance.

Chapter 38

The journey to Hebron was turned for Michal. It was not the heat or the dust, the burning sun or the rocking camel; the discomforts she scarcely noticed. Her misery was entirely mental: What if she had changed beyond David's concept of her? True, her slender, girlish figure had merely filled out to more womanly curves, and there was no gray in her black hair or lines in her face, but ten years had probably wrought more changes than she could see.

What were David's six wives like? Would she be expected to share living quarters with them? Would they resent her as a part of the house of Saul, David's bitter enemy? Would she be respected as the first wife, or resented as a newcomer?

What about the children? Would David's firstborn son be the crown prince, or would the son she hoped to give him have that honor? Would he allow her to bring Merab's sons and Jonathan's lame Mephibosheth to the royal household?

Would David restore Adriel and Phalti to their places of honor at the palace? What would he do with Ishbosheth? Not that Michal particularly cared about the fate of her weak, cruel, stupid brother. The brutal injustices he had inflicted on her for the past seven years had wiped out any affection she ever felt for the last surviving member of her family.

One moment Michal was furious with Abner for the constant delays, and the next she wanted him to loiter indefinitely. Her primary goal of the last ten years would soon be reached—and where would she go from there? Would God grant her the children she ardently craved? Or was she barren as Merab had so cruelly suggested?

Surely the next few days would be most crucial of her life. She knew she could never return to the idyllic situation she and private household where she could avoid seeing David with other women and children, she could tolerate their existence.

Like a flash, Michal recalled Phalti's declaration of his love for her. Could she be happy merely to be near David? Could she be satisfied to serve her husband, ask nothing in return? Her stubborn heart rebelled at the thought, and she had to admit she could not. But she pushed such distasteful thoughts to the back of her mind.

In every city they passed through, Abner stopped and held communication with the elders of Israel. He reminded each of them that they sought for David to be king over them in past times.

"Now is the time to unite the kingdom under David," Abner insisted. "You know that the Lord has said: 'By the hand of my servant David I will save my people Israel out of the hand of the Philistines, and out of the hand of all their enemies.'"

All the men of Israel agreed with Abner, and he carried that word to David in Hebron. And David made a feast for Abner and the twenty men who were with him.

Michal's caravan arrived at the gates of Hebron in the late afternoon. They were met by two royal escorts: one to lead Abner and his twenty soldiers to the palace, and the other to take Michal and kinds of receptions. She was prepared to accept the possibility that David would not meet her. She even hoped he would not. She wanted time to wash away the grime and weariness of her long journey.

She was actually relieved that her husband was not at the city gates, yet there was also a faint twinge of disappointment. By the time they reached their destination, however, she convinced herself David understood her need for rest and a bath. He knew she wanted to be at her best on their first meeting.

The two soldiers escorted Michal and Leah to a huge complex on the hillside above the palace. It was a rambling, three-storied structure that appeared to have acquired many additions. The building was surrounded by a large courtyard, enclosed by a high, stone wall. Small children played happily under the trees in the compound. Three cradles, guarded by three nurses, reposed under a huge oak tree.

Michal tried not to see the resemblance to her beloved husband on the faces of the curious children who swarmed about her. She and her handmaid drew their heavy traveling veils about their faces, and followed their escorts up three flights of stairs to lavishly appointed, but isolated rooms on the rooftop.

Safe within the privacy of her quarters, Michal paused to examine her surroundings. The walls of the compound were covered with grapevines. One corner of the courtyard wall seemed to be composed of natural rocks, from which flowed a stream of clear, sparkling water. Several children romped in the shallow pool at the base of the spring.

She heard David had six sons. She counted four little girls. Well, of course! She should have known David probably had two daughters, too. But girls were simply not of sufficient importance to be mentioned.

"I wonder how far men would get without women," Michal remarked scornfully to Leah.

"What do you mean, my lady?" asked Leah.

"Nothing. Nothing at all. I was only thinking out loud."

In spite of weariness, apprehension of her uncertain future, Michal thrilled to the beauty of the city below her. It was situated in a fertile valley watered by numerous springs and walls. The high wall around Hebron looked as if it were impregnable. The city covered a large portion of the valley, and extended halfway up the hillside. The royal compound was not far from the city wall. The palace lay beneath the women's quartered on the first rise of the hill. Adjacent to the palace, another large building was under construction, but the workmen had apparently gone for the day.

When Michal turned to examine her rooms, she received the first encouragement of many years. Several trunks contained a royal wardrobe. The garments were exactly her size, and all in her favorite fabrics and colors. David had not forgotten her, and he even knew her size. Suddenly, life was sweet again.

Michal hurried through her bath. She arrayed herself in a sky-blue, velvet gown, David's favorite color, and lay down on her luxurious bed. She was anxious for David to come, yet she was so weary, she hoped to rest a little while before being reunited with her husband.

The sun was slipping behind the western horizon when a servant girl knocked at Michal's door. She carried a tray loaded with steaming roast beef, corn on the cob, brown bread, and fresh grapes. There was nothing she liked better. David remembered. Again her heart sang; her weariness was forgotten.

When the girl returned for the tray, she was accompanied by a messenger from the palace. The king had made a feast for Abner and his men. Affairs of state would require his attention into the night, so David would see her tomorrow. He also sent a note.

Michal was so sick with disappointment, she could scarcely unroll the parchment. Another psalm! Slowly she began to read:

> "Hear me when I call, O God of my righteousness:
> you have enlarged me when I was in distress; have
> mercy upon me, and hear my prayer.
> O you sons of men, how long will you turn my glory into
> Shame? How long will you love vanity, and seek after
> Leasing?
> But know that the Lord has set apart him that is
> Godly for himself: the Lord will hear when I call
> Unto him.
> Stand in awe, and sin not: commune with your own
> Heart upon your bed, and be still.
> There be many that say, Who will show us any good?
> Lord, lift up the light of your countenance upon
> Us.
> You have put gladness in my heart, more than in the
> Time that their corn and their wine increased.
> I will both lay me down in peace, and sleep: for you,
> Lord, only make me dwell in safety."

The seventh verse was underlined. It did not look to her as if she had put much gladness in his heart if he could not spare the time to see her after such a long absence. Slowly Michal removed her velvet gown, its beauty gone. Bitter tears stung her eyelids, but she refused to let them fall. So! Abner, who had fought David for seven years, was more important to him than his own wife he had not seen for ten.

Michal dismissed her handmaid, blew out the candle, and crept into bed in the cool darkness. Suddenly the strangeness of her surroundings, the absence of her children, and now David's defection, all to combine into one crushing blow. Scalding tears forced their way past her clenched eyelids and wet her pillow, but no sound escaped her lips.

The princess had endured injustices all her life without whining; she saw no reason to begin now. But for the first time she had no concept of what lay before her.

Chapter 39

David and his courtier communed with Abner until almost the break of day. But before the king of Judah and the captain of Israel's armies parted, all the details for the unity of the two warring kingdoms had been arranged. The people of God were to be reunited in peace; there would be no more bloodshed.

And David said to Abner: "Go tell Ishbosheth he is free to remain in the palace at Mahanaim, or anywhere else he chooses. I never did. The Lord is my inheritance; all I want is what he has given me."

"It is easy to see, my lord," said Abner humbly, "why God rent the kingdom from the hand of my master, Saul, and gave it to you. Not in all Israel have I found a man so gracious and so God-like as my lord David."

"Bless you, Abner; you are most kind. I rejoice that you are willing to bring peace to Israel; I never wanted it otherwise. How it grieved my soul that I could not convince Saul I meant him no harm. You know I never fought back at him; I merely tried to defend myself against his attacks."

"I know, my lord David. And I tried to convince Saul you could have wiped us out anytime had you chosen to do so. But you knew Saul even better than I did; he believed what he wanted to believe. If he had acknowledged you were innocent, he would have been forced to relinquish the kingdom to you; that he could not do, and live."

"How sad he could not see it was God who displeased with him—not his servant David. If he had been obedient to God, he could have kept the kingdom in the first place. And even after God anointed me king of Israel, Saul could have returned to his lands, and lived happily with his family. His unwillingness to admit his guilt, and accept God's chastisement, condemned his house to destruction."

"Jonathan tried to tell him all of that—over and over," Abner lamented.

"Israel lost a brave and mighty warrior in the death of Saul. We all lost a prince among princes in the death of Jonathan, and I lost my most loyal and beloved friend."

"I knew your true feelings until you reacted as you did to the death of Saul and his sons. It was then that you won the hearts of all our people. And we will be happy to welcome you as our king."

"Bless you, my lord David; I will try my best to see you never have cause to regret your decision."

"And bless you, my lord David. I must go now," said Abner rising, "and gather all Israel unto my lord the king that they may make a league with you, and you may reign over all your heart desires."

"Go in peace, my brother, and may God go with you."

"My! My! How Abner's tune change," said Abiathar, the priest. "Why didn't you ask him he fought you for seven years if he held you in such noble esteem?"

"That would have been pointless and unwise," said David. The past is gone; the men are dead. Raking the dead ashes of our mistakes will not wipe them out. We cannot change the shape of the past; we can only shape the future."

"Well spoken, my lord; but if the king is so forgiving, why did he stop construction on the palace for Saul's daughter, and cancel his plans to make her queen of Israel?"

"I did not know about her children when I asked for her return."

"But my lord David has other wives and children."

"That's different," said David stubbornly.

"Yes, quite different. Your wife was helpless when her father gave her to another man. My lord David was free to make his own choices."

"But you don't know Michal," said David defensively. "She could have wrapped Phalti around her little finger. He loved her from childhood; he would never have touched the hem of her garment without her consent."

"You knew she had a husband, and know God's law forbids a man taking back his wife after she has been wife to another man. If you can't accept her, why did you not leave her where she was?"

"I did not know she been wife to another man. If I had known about the children earlier, I would never have sent for her. But if I had relented later, it would have looked as if I feared Ishbosheth. Israel does not want a king who is weak. Michal is my wife; I shall keep her." David spoke with a finality that closed the subject, and returned to his bed.

Before David arose the next morning, his army, led by Joab, returned from pursuing an invading robber band. They brought with them a great spoil. When Joab heard that Abner had communed with the king, and had been sent away in peace, he was furious. He hastened to the palace to confront the king.

"What have you done?" asked David. "Abner actually came in here? Why have you sent him away? Are you sure he is already gone? You know Abner. You know very well he came here as a spy to find out what your plans are so he can destroy you."

"Patience, Joab; why must you be so suspicious? Abner came as a friend. The peace of Israel was the purpose of his visit. He has gone even now to even now to gather the tribes together to make a league with me. Why should I not let him go?"

Joab went out seething with anger, and sent messengers after Abner—in the king's name. The messengers overtook Abner at the well of Sirah, and brought him back to Hebron. Joab met them at the city gate. He asked to speak privately with Abner. When they were out of sight of the messengers, Joab suddenly plunged his sword under Abner's fifth rib. As the captain lay dying, Joab said, "I told you I'd make you pay for killing my brother, Asahel."

When David heard of Abner's death, he was grieved and angry, "I and my kingdom are innocent before the Lord of the blood of Abner," said the king. "Let the guilt rest on the head of Joab, and on all his father's house. Let there not fail from the house of Joab one that has an issue, or that is a leaper, or that is crippled, or that falls in battle, or that is hungry."

And David commanded Joab and that were with him to rend their clothes, dress themselves in sackcloth, and mourn before Abner. And king David himself followed the bier.

They buried Abner in Hebron; the king wept, and all the people wept with him. "How could Abner have died so foolishly? David lamented. "Your hands were not bound, Abner, nor were your feet in fetters. As a man falls before wicked men, so you fell."

When David's servants brought his evening meal, he refused to eat. "God do so to me, and more also if I taste bread, or anything else, until the sun goes down on this evil day."

And all the people took notice of David's righteous indignation, and it pleased them. But whatever the king did pleased the people. And the people of Judah, and all the people of Israel understood that it was not the will of the king to slay Abner.

And David said to his servants: "I want you to know that a prince and a great man has fallen this day in Israel. I feel weak today; though I am anointed of the Lord, these sons of Zeruiah have disobeyed and outwitted me. May the Lord reward this evil man according to his wickedness."

Michal had no word from David all day. But a servant told her of the treacherous death of Abner, and she watched the funeral procession from her window. Leah went down and gleaned the news from the household servants, but Michal remained in seclusion. She grieved at the manner in which her cousin met his death, and for Rizpah, but she could not lament his passing. She knew Abner was solely responsible for the seven years of bloody war between Judah and Israel, and she was not as forgiving as David.

Michal comforted herself in the silence from the palace. She understood David's position; his hospitality had been outraged, and Abner's death could destroy his long-sought peace with Israel. He would surely send for her tomorrow.

Chapter 40

When Ishbosheth heard of the death of Abner, he collapsed in hysterical fear. "What will I do! What will I do?" he cried to his servants. "Who will lead my army? Who will protect us from David? He has treacherously slain Abner; what is to keep him from killing us all?"

The servants of Ishbosheth were troubled, but no one offered to take Abner's place. The soldiers retired to their tents mumbling and complaining; the morning light found more than half of them gone. They had folded their tents in the night, and silently slipped away.

With no one to lead them, the army was in total disarray. The captains of the bands went from one captain's tent to another, but the only agreement they could reach was that they did not want to continue the senseless war with Judah. The men who had served with David admitted they preferred to follow him. Several gave vent to long-suppressed resentments. It seemed no one approved of fighting brother, yet as good as soldiers they battled for seven weary years.

Feelings ran high among the men; many openly condemned the fallen Abner. As anger boiled, tempers flared, and more men boldly packed their tents, and departed for their homes. But many were professional soldiers, and the army tents were the only homes they knew. There was nowhere to go.

Two Benjamites, captains of bands, who often denounced Israel's war against Judah, decided to take matters into their own hands. The men were brothers, Baanah and Nechab, sons of Rimmon, a Beerothite. In their plot against Judah Ishbosheth, they inquired of his servants as to the king's welfare. They learned he took a nap every day at noon, after he ate. It was the captains' custom to take wheat from the palace storehouse to feed their troops, so they could easily enter the king's house without arousing suspicion.

Baanah and Rechab walked boldly into the palace during the noonday heat, while the servants were resting after the noon meal. Ishbosheth was asleep on his bed. Baanah plunged a spear through the king's heart. Rechab cut off his head with one swift blow of his sword.

The traitorous captains wrapped the king's head in a goatskin, thrust it into a half-empty bag of wheat, and fled to their waiting camels. They hurried out of the city as fast as they could without attracting attention. When the reached the open plain, they urged their camels into a gallop. They did not stop when darkness fell, but rode all night; they arrived in Hebron before noon the next day.

Baanah and Rechab carried the head of their slain monarch to David and said to the king, "Behold the head of Ishbosheth, the son of Saul your enemy, who tried to kill you. The Lord has avenged my lord the king this day of Saul and of his seed."

And David said to Rechab and Baanah his brother, "As surely as the Lord lives, who has redeemed my soul out of all adversity, you shall die. When one told me he had slain Saul, thinking to have brought me good tidings, I took him and slew him in Ziklag. He thought I would give him a reward for his tidings. How much more, when wicked men have slain a righteous man in his own house upon his own bed, shall I not require his blood of your hands, and take you away from the earth?"

And David commanded his servants, and they slew the traitorous captains. They cut off their hands and their feet, and hung them up over the pool in Hebron as an example to evildoers. But the head of Ishbosheth they buried in the sepulcher of Abner in Hebron.

From her window in the women's quarters, Michal saw the turmoil at the palace below. She sent Leah to discover the reason.

It was a long while before the handmaid returned. When Leah entered the room, Michal's wrath at her delay was cooled by the look of sadness and compassion on her servant's face.

"I'm sorry, my lady, that I took so long. There was much confusion at the."

"What is wrong? Has something happened to David? Tell me!"

"Oh no, my lady," said Leah quickly. "The king is fine. It's—it's your brother."

"Ishbosheth? Don't tell me actually came to see David. He didn't come after me?" Michal asked apprehensive.

"Well, no—not really—you see—" Leah hesitated. "My lady, your brother is dead."

The blank curtain she always hid behind in times of grief, pain, sorrow, or fright came down over Michal's face. "It could and no other way," she said quietly. "What happened?"

"Do you remember Baanah and Rechab?"

"The troublemaking captains?"

Leah nodded.

"Of course."

"They killed your brother."

"But the palace guard? Where was Phalti?"

"There has been no word as yet from Mahanaim. The king has sent messengers to enquire of conditions there, and to offer his sympathy. He has slain the traitors."

"So he will not send for me again today."

"The king has many problems, my lady."

"Of course," said Michal absently, with her head bowed, but she scarcely heard.

"I'm so sorry, my lady; he was not much of a brother to you, but he was all the family you had left. I know it is sad to be all alone."

Michal raised her head, and her inscrutable brown eyes, without a trace of tears, gazed unseeingly at her faithful servant; a ghost of a smile relaxed the tension of her face. "Except for David, I have always been alone, and my family deprived me of him."

Chapter 41

After the death of Ishbosheth, all the tribes of Israel came to David in Hebron, and besought him to be their king. "We are your own flesh and blood," they pleaded, "and in times past, when Saul was king over us, it was you who led us out and brought victory to Israel. Did not the Lord commission you to feed his people Israel? Did he not make you captain over all Israel? We are Israelites, too."

So all the elders of Israel came to the king in Hebron. King David made a league with them before the Lord, and they anointed him king over all Israel. But the elders did not want the king to remain in Hebron. They insisted the palace should be more centrally located, preferably in neutral territory—land that was neither a part of Judah nor Israel.

Jebus was a strong walled city occupied by the by the Jebusites. Its position high above the Kidron valley was set in a small triangle bounded on the other two sides by the Tyropoean and Zedek valleys. The natural mountain defenses had been reinforced by solid rock walls high and thick. The gushing spring, Gihon, was located near, and its overflow had been diverted into the city. Because Jebus was considered impregnable, very few attempts had been made by the conquering Hebrews to drive the Jebusites out.

David was tired of bloodshed. Even if Jebus was a part of the Promised Land God had given Israel, he did not want to take it by force. But the city was centrally located and would make an ideal capital city, so in his efforts to appease both Judah and Israel, David and his men went to Jebus, and offered to buy the city. The inhabitants scorned the offer.

"Why, even the blind and the lame could defend our city against any invasion," they boasted. "So unless David can tame away our blind and lame he cannot come in here."

David wanted to take the city peaceably, but the insult to the armies of the Lord was not to be borne. Carefully he compassed the city. Around and around it he went, searching for any weakness in the walls that might enable them to make a breach. Eventually, he found a small gutter through which the spring, Gihon, overflowed through the city wall.

"The man," said David, "who can climb up to that gutter, go through it, and open the city gates, I will make chief captain of the armies of Israel."

Many men vied for the coveted position, but over Joab succeeded. Under the cover of darkness, the wily captain crept through the gutter, entered the sleeping city, slew the sentries, and opened the unguarded gates.

In a matter of hours the battle was over. Having always depended on their thick stone walls to protect them, the Jebusites maintained a weak army. Unprepared, and half asleep, they were no match for David's seasoned warriors lusting for vengeance.

So David took the mighty stronghold, and called it the city of David, the title by which it is known until this day. He sent his men back to Hebron with orders to move his palace treasures and his household to Jerusalem once. The king stayed in the city to supervise its evacuation and reconstruction. The captured Jebusites were allowed to remain as servants of Israel, or they were free to leave in peace. Many chose to remain.

When Michal heard the army was going to Jebus to secure the city for the new capital, she was glad. Now David would have time for her. But as she watched from her window, she saw the royal chariot leading the troops, and her heart sank. David was actually going away without a word to her. Something precious within her soul began to shrivel and die.

For all her seclusion, Michal kept up with the affairs in the women's quarters of the king's household. She knew David had not been near since she arrived, and none of his wives had visited the palace. Members of the royal household never made a move that was not know to their servants, and the servants gossiped freely. Leah kept her mistress well informed on all the activities in David's household, and the city.

Leah saw the army move out, and correctly interpreted the effect on her mistress. In an effort to cheer her, she said, "The unfinished building beside the palace for the daughter of Saul."

"Why was it not finished? There has been no work on it since we came," said Michal with her usual realism.

"No one seems to know," shrugged Leah. "Perhaps because the king decided to move his palace."

Michal pondered this latest of information. David selected a beautiful wardrobe for her, and started to build her a palace, yet she had received no direct word from him except the psalm on the night of her arrival. He could not be disappointed in her; he had not seen her. What made the king change his mind?

There was only one thing to do: When David returned, she would go to the palace and confront him. An open rejection, she could endure; the eternal suspense was killing her. Having decided on a definite course of action, Michal's spirits revived. Even if it was wrong, she had to do something.

Chapter 42

Runners kept Hebron informed of the progress at Jebus. The news of the conquest was received with mixed emotions. All Israel rejoiced that David had conquered their ancient enemy, who had defied the armies of God since Joshua let them across the Jordan. But the royal palace had brought fame and fortune to Hebron; the people were loath to see it go.

It was with excitement, however, if not joy, that the king's household made preparations to move to the new capital. Michal could no longer remain aloof from the other members of David's family. She dreaded meeting them for many reasons, but was sure she could manage it with David by her side. Without him, however, and with her position so uncertain, the meeting seemed intolerable.

Michal observed from her window that the women and children gathered in the compound every evening after the sun disappeared behind the mountain. During the long twilight, the children romped, and played games. Sometimes the mothers joined them, but usually they visited among themselves until the gathering darkness drove them inside.

Carefully, Michal selected a gown similar to the ones worn by other women in the compound. She arranged her hair as simply as possible, and left off all her jewelry. She had no idea whether the women would despise her as the daughter of David's enemy, or accord her the favored position of the first wife. She knew Leah could tell her exactly how the household felt about her, but she refused to listen to gossip about herself from the servants.

Michal noticed the oldest woman seemed to be the leader of the group. She frequently settled squabbles among the children, and apparently issued orders to the household servants. Michal did ask Leah if she knew her name. The handmaid quickly told her the woman's name was Abigail, and said she had graciously inquired or Michal's welfare many times.

This bit of unsolicited information warmed Michal's lonely heart, but she could not bring herself to ask for more. Leah was obviously bursting with desire to talk, but her mistress' silence restrained her.

Soon after the women gathered in the compound, Michal descended the stairs. The serenity of her countenance gave no clue to the turmoil within her soul, or the tight band around her heart. She walked directly to Abigail, and bowed low before her.

"I am Michal," she said simply. "I have waited long for the king to present me to his household, but apparently his many duties will not spare him the time. I decided to wait no longer to meet the lovely women David has asked to share his life."

"Bless you, my lady," replied Abigail, bowling graciously in return. "And welcome to our midst, Princess Michal."

Abigail's friendly tone, and her addition of princess to Michal's name, answered many unspoken questions for the newcomer. It was balm to her sore and troubled heart.

"My name is Abigail. And this is Ahinoam, the mother of the king's firstborn son. This is Princess Maacah, the daughter of Talmar, king of Geshur. This is Haggith, Abital, and Eglah."

Each of the women bowed graciously to Michal. They were all as beautiful and, charming as they had appeared from her window. Apparently, they accepted her simply as one of them, without awe or resentment. The tight band around her heart eased a bit more.

"I understand we will soon be leaving Hebron," said Michal quietly. "I wondered if there was any preparation I should be making."

"Not especially," said Abigail. "We are to be ready to leave as soon as the king commands. He will send for us when our homes are ready. But the servants will do the packing. If you have anything you'd rather not trust to their care, it would be wise to get it ready, but that's all."

The relaxed atmosphere of the garden, the friendly women, and the happy children made Michal wonder why she had so dread the encounter. With a sigh of relief, she looked about her at the madly racing youngsters. From her window, she had seen a little boy who resembled David so much she wanted a closer look at him.

Observing her interest, Abigail asked, "Would you like to meet the children?"

"I'd love too," said Michal, and was pleasantly surprised to realize her statement was true.

"Come, children," cried Abigail above their childish laughter. "Come and meet Princess Michal, your father's wife."

A few of the children were already gathered about the stranger. They seemed curious without being bold or bashful. The other children came immediately in response to Abigail's call.

Michal's gaze lingered on the charming little boy with the thick curly black hair like David's. Abigail observed her admiration, and called the child to her side. A little girl, who looked very much like the child to her side. A little girl, who looked very much like the boy, followed at his heels.

"This is Absalom," said Abigail warmly, "Princess Maacah's son, and his sister, Tamar."

"How are you, Absalom and Tamar," asked Michal.

"I'm fine, thank you," said Absalom. And his sister echoed his sentiments in a childish lisp.

Michal forced her attention from the two lovely children to the others who were crowding up to greet her. Suddenly the pent-up longing for children of her own, the homesickness for her nephews, and her loneliness and disappointments overwhelmed her. She dropped to her knees, and gathered the little ones into her arms. As she did so, their mothers took the newcomer to their hearts, and Michal was no longer a stranger.

Chapter 43

Michal's new living quarters in Jerusalem were located on a hillside above the palace similar to the ones in Hebron, but the were much more private. Each wife had her own separate house. All the houses were surrounded by a common stone wall, and in the center of the compound a long covered perch provided a central gathering place. There were cushioned couches and marble benches to provide ample seating for the royal family. Vines loaded with clusters of white and purple grapes covered the open sides of the porch to give it a cool seclusion. Date palms, fig, and olive trees dotted the grounds. And a stream of clear, sparkling water poured through an aperture in the compound wall. It resembled the spring in Hebron—even to the pool at the base. The children were delighted; each discovery was greeted with peals of happy laughter.

The wives were assigned to their quarters in the identical houses. The homes were arranged in a circle around the open porch. The first one on the right of the right of the gate to the compound had Michal's name on the door. The house on the left of the gate was Abigail's. On Michal's right was Princess Maacah. Apparently, David had placed his wives in proximity to the gate in the order he had married them. No one could complain of favoritism.

Michal's drooping spirits revived again. David did remember she was his first wife. But her longing to see him was mingled with resentment, and even dread.

On the day following the arrival of the royal household in Jerusalem, David planned a feast to welcome his family. Tables were set up on the porch, and steaming bowls of food were brought from the palace kitchen. The banquet was to begin as soon as the hot desert sun slipped behind the distant hills.

No amount of persuasion could prevail on Michal to attend. She could not meet her husband in the presence of his other wives and their children. Again she donned the blue velvet gown David had chosen for her, and lay down on her bed with a "headache."

Michal closed her windows, and pressed her hands to her ears to shut out jubilant sounds coming from the banquet tables. In spite of her efforts, ripples of laughter came to her above the soft strains of the harpists. She could visualize the progress of the feast by the sounds that reached her ears. When the laughter stopped, she knew the children had been sent to bed.

After an almost unendurable agony of waiting, the music ceased, and Michal knew the banquet was over. She resolved not to leave her room unless David came to her. But she could not endure the silence from the garden; she slipped quietly from her bed so Leah would not hear her, and crept to the window.

Cautiously, Michal peered through the curtains, and her heart sank: The king was leaving. At the gate, however, hesitated, then came directly toward her door. Forgetting to be cautious, Michal flew back to her bed. She was soothing her hair, and desperately trying to still her hammering heart when she heard a knock at the door. Leah, like the good servant she was, answered it immediately, but it seemed like ages to her anxious mistress.

"My lord the king," said Leah, bowing low. "Please come in."

"I understand my wife is ill; does she feel up to seeing me?"

"I can think of no medicine, my lord, that would do her so much good."

Michal reclined as attractively as possible on her pillows, but as David's footsteps drew near, her pounding heart seemed to pull her bold upright. And suddenly, framed in her doorway, was the husband she had last seen dangling on a rope from her bedroom window as he fled for his life. David, clad in his royal robes, stood tall and stalwart. He had matured with the passing years, and the maturity had greatly increased his charm.

The king stood silently in the candlelight, and looked at his wife with eyes so remote, it was almost as if he did not see her at all. But as they stared at each other across the years, his eyes began to soften until Michal saw once again shepherd lad she loved so dearly.

"You are even more beautiful then I remembered," he said almost to himself.

"And you look every inch a king."

David took one step toward her, and Michal sprang from her bed, and threw herself into his outstretched arms. The tears she had restrained for ten years spilled down her cheeks, and they both wept like children.

After the first shock of their joyous grief passed, David kissed away Michal's tears, picked her up in his arms, and carried her back to her bed. There he sat down, still cradling her in his arms like a child.

"My darling Michal! My little princess is really mine again. How could I have waited so long to claim you? Can you ever forgive me? My love! My own dear love. No man shall ever take you from me again." David crushed her against his heart until Michal thought her ribs would surely break.

"How I have missed you, my darling. You'll never know how I've suffered at the thoughts of what might be happening to you. The only was I survived was by committing you to God's care."

How do you think I've suffered?" whispered Michal against Michal against his ear. "The waiting, waiting, and not knowing if you remembered or cared."

David winced as from a blow. Slowly he relaxed his hold and held Michal back so he could look into her eyes. "But I told you I would send for you—."

"And I believed you," Michal interrupted; that's all that kept me alive."

"But you promised to wait—"

Suddenly there came an imperious knock on the door. David and Michal listened in tense expectancy as Leah ran to answer the summons.

"Is the king here?" came an anxious voice.

"It's Joab," David whispered, as he swiftly deposited Michal on her bed, and to meet the chief of his armies.

"I'm sorry, my lord, to disturb you, but the Philistines are coming. I fear we must march at once."

A cloud of irritation covered the king's face, but he answered calmly. "Of course, Joab; I'll be with you in a moment."

David went back to Michal, sat down beside her, and crushed her once in his arms. "I must go, my darling. It seemed to be the stoop of our lives. But never mind—husband, wives, children—nothing is important but that we are together again. No one has ever taken your place; no one ever shall. Wait on us. Pray for us. I'll be back."

And before Michal could utter a word or protect, her husband was gone again.

Chapter 44

The Philistines came and spread themselves in the valley of Rephaim. And David enquired of the Lord, saying, "Shall I go to the Philistines? Will you deliver them into my hand?"

And the Lord said, "Go up, for I will surely deliver the Philistines into your hand."

So David and his men went down under cover of darkness, and hid in the cave of Adullam. But Joab took thirty chiefs and deployed them and their men all around the valley; for it was the time of harvest, and David dared not risk destruction of the abundant crops in the fertile valley.

At the break of day, Joab's men attacked with a mighty shout from all around the valley.

The Philistines, startled from sleep, fled in disarray to the cave of Adullam. But David and his six hundred seasoned warriors stood back in the darkness of the cave and defended it. The Philistines made perfect targets against the morning light, so David slew his enemies, and the Lord wrought a great victory for Israel.

David followed the few stragglers who escaped to Baalperazim, where the reserve troops were camped, and smote them there. Where the last poacher was dead, the king gathered his men together to give thanks to God for their victory.

The fleeing Philistines left their pagan in the city, and David and his men gathered them and burned them.

But while the Israelites gave thanks to their God, the Philistines regrouped, called up more reserves from home, and spread themselves again in the valley of Rephaim. They were determined to gather the Israelites' abundant harvest for themselves.

When David enquired of the Lord again, he said, "You shall not go up, but surround them from behind, and come upon them over against the mulberry trees while they are resting. And let it be when you hear the sound of a rustling in the tops of the mulberry trees that you shall attack, for then shall the Lord go out before you to smile to smite the host of the Philistines."

And David did as the Lord commanded him, and he smote the Philistines from Geba even unto Gazer, for God gave them a great victory.

To show his gratitude to God, David called together his thirty thousand chosen warriors to go with him from Baale of Judah, to bring up to Jerusalem the ark of God, whose name is called by the name of the Lord of hosts that dwells between the cherubims.

And they set the ark of God upon a new cart, and brought it out of the house of Abinadab of Gibeah. Uzzah and Ahio, the sons of Abinadab, and accompanied the ark, and Ahio went before it.

And David and all the house of Israel played before the Lord on all manner of instruments made of firwood, and on harps, and psalteries, timbrels, cornets, and cymbals.

When they came to Nachon's threshing floor, Uzzah put his hand on the ark to steady it. The floor was rough, and the oxen shook the cart so much that Uzzah feared the ark would fall.

But the Lord was angry with Uzzah because all men were forbidden to touch the ark, so God smote him there for his error so that he died beside the ark.

David was frightened and angry because the Lord had punished Uzzah, so he stopped the procession, and he called the name of the place Perezuzzah in memory of his fallen friend.

And David asked, "How shall the ark of the Lord come to me?" But there was fear and resentment in his heart, so he got no answer from the Lord.

The king was afraid to move forward without God's direction, so he refused to continue on his journey to the city of David with the ark, but carried it aside into the house of Obededom the Gittite. And the ark remained there for three months, and the Lord blessed Obededom and all his household.

But David returned to Jerusalem in sorrow, his recent victories forgotten. He knew he had displeased the Lord or he would have received an answer to his prayer.

Since the day Samuel anointed him king of God's people, David had walked by faith. Unless God led the way, he refused to travel. So David went back to his city, and he mourned and fasted, and besought God that he would speak to his servant.

Abiathar the priest met David as he emerged from his prayer room at the close of the day. "Why is my lord sad? And why is his countenance cast down?"

"God is displeased with me, Abiathar; he turns a deaf ear to all my petitions."

"Did the king expect God to be pleased with him when he brought into his household the daughter of the bloody house of Saul?"

"Michal was not responsible for her father's sins; no one suffered more cruelly at Saul's hand than she did!"

"But my lord the king knows it is against God's law to return to his bosom a wife who has been wife to another man," countered Abiathar.

"I have been praying about that, too. I get no answer to any of my prayers, so I fear to move in any direction. But Michal is the love of my life; it does not seem fair that I should have to give her up. Neither of us ever wanted anyone to come between us. She loves me; I am all she has."

"I thought you said she had several children? Surely, my lord would not jeopardize his kingdom for one woman—when he has so many."

Chapter 45

Michal refused to allow the bliss and joy of her husband's visit to be dimmed by his by his sudden departure. He went because he had to—not because he wanted to go.

Every day Michal sent Leah out to learn the latest news from the army. The reports came in one day that the Philistines had been slaughtered and were in full retreat. The next day they were reported to be back in force.

A runner declared David had beaten the enemy completed, and burned their idol gods. Israel went wild with rejoicing; the people were certain the Philistines would never trouble their fertile valley of Rephaim.

With such conflicting reports, Michal knew David had more than he could handle in the field; he could not possibly get back to Jerusalem until the enemy was completely routed. Yet the waiting seemed longer and more unendurable than any she had ever experienced. Over and over consoled herself with the fact David loved her. As long as she was sure of his love she could endure any agony.

Michal really wanted to be friends with the other women in the compound. And if the children were not David's children, she would adore them. But her best efforts could not erase the resentment from her heart. She kept feeling they were intruders who had come into her home and cursed it.

The princess tried desperately to conceal her animosity, and only Abigail seemed to see through her courteous façade. She made every effort to welcome Michal to their midst, and make her comfortable, but she never intruded on her privacy. She did not ask curious questions, allude to the past, or inquire as to the first wife's expectations for the future.

In her usual gracious manner, Abigail informed Michal of the customs of the king's household. "The children are looking forward to their father's return," she remarked casually. "They know the first thing he will do when he returns to the city will be to come and bless his household."

Abigail never referred to David other than "the king" or "the children's father." And she never alluded to any personal relationship. Michal tried to follow the older woman's wise example, but David had been her whole life since childhood; she could discuss him with another wife.

What a miserable situation! Reluctant as she was to talk about family affairs with the servants, there was no one but Leah, and she had to talk to someone.

"Why does God approve such a sorry situation?" she asked, forgetting her handmaid had no husband at all.

"What makes you think God approves it?" Leah reasoned. "Did he not create only one women for one man?"

"That's what mother always said; why then does he allow it."

"Did you not allow your sons to do many things you did not approve?"

"But that was different," protested Michal, as she thought of the cruel way Merab's sons often teased little lame Mephibosheth. "I couldn't punish them all the time."

"And why not, my lady?"

"Because I loved them" And I wanted them to love me—and to be happy."

"Do you think God does not love his children, and want them to be happy—and to love him?"

"But disobeying God does not make his children happy. Mother frequently pointed out the trouble Father Abraham started when he took another wife. The children's children of those women still each other."

"Didn't your children's disobedience usually make them unhappy? Don't you remember the bumps and bruises they got when they climbed the forbidden mountain?" Sid always bringing suffering; God seldom needs to punish us more."

Michal regarded her handmaid thoughtfully. Leah had served her faithfully for many years, yet she hardly knew her as a person. She was still young and well favored; would she too like a husband and children?

"Breaking the commandments is not wrong because God forbids it," Leah continued. "God forbids us to/do the things that are wrong and will bring us suffering."

"Obviously, you know more about God's teachings than I do; Where did you learn?" asked Michal curiously.

"My father was a scribe, and he did not think it unseemly for a woman to read and write. He taught all his children to read the Scriptures."

"If your father was a scribe, why did you become a servant?"

"My father fell out of favor with king Saul—even as you did, my lady."

"But could a scribe not find others beside the king who would pay well for his work?"

My father was slain."

"Oh, Leah! I'm so sorry. And here you have served the wicked king's daughter faithfully these years."

"But you were not at fault, my lady. You have sheltered me and shown me every kindness. And your—the king's sins eventually caught up with him."

"No wonder God took the kingdom from Saul; his disobedience brought misery to so many in Israel."

"So you see, see, Saul's disobedience was wrong—not merely because he broke God's commandments you can break without hurting someone—yourself or others?"

Michal sat silent and thoughtful for a long while. "No, I can't. But I never thought about it before. You and I are suffering now because of the sins of Saul." Then she looked curiously at her maid, as if she were seeing her for the first time.

Leah's shoulder-length black hair was straight, but it was thick and glossy. Her black eyes mirrored the restraint of the well-trained servant, but her cheekbones gave her face pride and dignity. Any woman so well endowed must also have ambition.

"Leah, would you like to have a husband and children, and a home of your own?"

"Of course, my lady. But I have no father of brother to arrange a marriage for me, so I am grateful to have a place of service with you."

"Would you like me to arrange a marriage for you?"

Leah's eyes flamed with hope and happiness, but immediately the light was quenched, and the blank curtain of reserve came down. "You have no one else to serve you, my lady."

"Oh, forget about me. I can get a young girl or a poor widow."

Leah's eyes brightened again. "You are most kind, but I have served you so long—"

"Yes—too long. It's time you served yourself. I will speak to the king for you."

Chapter 46

The king's return, the city was not marked with the usual rejoicing. He had failed in his efforts to return the ark. The soldiers dispersed to their homes quickly. Soon the whole city knew David grieved for his friend who died in his service. And the thing pleased the people, as everything the king did pleased the people.

But as days passed, and David did not come to bless his household, uneasiness pervaded the compound. No one seemed to know why the king delayed. Michal met Leah at the door each time she returned from her errands. But there was no news. All she could learn was that the king spent all his time in the prayer room when he was not busy with affairs of state.

Ten days after his return, a messenger announced the king would dine with the royal family. But no personal word came for Michal. Abigail sent her handmaid to inform Michal the king requested her presence beside him at the head of the table, and she hoped nothing would prevent her attending.

Once more Michal's heart sang. God always seemed to remember her when she reached the depths of despair.

Arrayed in a scarlet gown trimmed in gold, and anointed with her sweetest perfume, Michal went to meet her husband. She watched from her window, and went to meet her husband. She watched from her window, and went out in time to meet him at the gate. His open admiration was balm to her soul. She saw love and longing in his eyes, and something else she could not fathom. Was it sadness? Regret? Guilt?

The children gathered around to kiss their father, and thoughts of Michal were obviously erased from David's mind. He was gracious and charming as usual, and the food was abundant and delicious, but in Michal's mouth it was like ashes.

There were so many things she had to discuss with her husband, but this was definitely not the time. The meal was almost finished, and nothing was said of a later meeting. In desperation, Michal whispered, "When will I see you again?"

His tone was his gracious, and his reasons ample, but the cornered look in his eyes frightened her, "King Hiram is coming to the palace tomorrow; the preparations must be made tonight. I don't know how long he will stay, or exactly the nature of his visit," David countered cautiously.

The king's answers were vague, yet he obviously did not plan to see Michal in the near future. The ache in her heart almost overwhelmed her, yet some things must be said. "I have been so troubled for the family in Mahaniam—for Ishbosheth's family," she added quickly.

David responded warmly. "Don't worry, my love. The house of Saul still occupies the palace in Mahaniam, and every provision has been made for their welfare."

"But—" Michal hesitated. The problem was much too complex to be discussed in such a public place. She simply must talk to David alone.

"Oh, I almost forgot," he said cheerfully, "your handmaid found such favor with Joab, he insists I ask if he might have her to wife."

"Does he already have a wife?" asked Michal quickly.

"No, Joab has been too busy fighting wars to think about women."

Michal bit her tongue to keep from saying wished David had kept as busy. "Then I will be happy for you to arrange the marriage," she said demurely. "Leah will make your nephew a good wife; I trust he will treat her well."

"I will see to it," the king promised.

David seemed so kindly disposed toward her and eager to please; why did he avoid her? Michal was increasingly puzzled, and her frustration and irritation intensified. The emptiness of her life simply must be filled. If only she had her nephews! They would at least keep her busy. What she really wanted, of course, was a son of her own.

David lingered and played with his children until their bedtime. Then when his seven wives turned seven pairs of anxious eyes upon him, he arose and fled back to his palace alone.

Chapter 47

Michal tried to drown her own disappointment in her joy for Leah. She was curious, however, as to how Joab recognized so quickly the qualities in her handmaid that escaped her observation for so long. Leah was available and undemanding as the air she breathed, and her mistress had taken her as much for granted. She knew she would miss her servant dreadfully, but she rejoiced in Leah's good fortune.

Joab had murdered her cousin Abner, but Michal could remember many times when she would have thoroughly enjoyed murdering him herself, so she could scarcely hold that against David's mighty man of war. Anyway, Leah would have a husband and children, and that was the important part.

Michal realized few women were fortunate enough to get to choose the men they married as she had. And in spite of war and persecution from the mad king, those first two years were heaven. The golden memories sustained her through ten years of loneliness. But now that her husband was within her grasp, and she still could not have him, it was almost more than she could bear.

For the first time, Michal began to realize how Phalti must have suffered. She could even understand his lack of appreciation for his good wife, Adah. The thought of having to endure the attentions of another man filled Michal with loathing. She wanted David or none. If he loved her as she loved him, how could he have taken other wives? She thought she had conquered the bitterness on that subject, but it welled up in her again until it almost choked her. Forcibly she put the thought from her, and concentrated so plans for Leah.

The eager bridegroom was at the compound gates before they opened the next morning. But Leah refused to leave until a suitable servant could be found for her mistress. Joab assured her he would find one if he had to go back to Bethlehem, and get a good, strong, country girl.

The veteran warrior could scarcely believe his good fortune, A charming bride, and no dowry to pay! There was no one to demand it; like Michal, Leah was all alone.

Michal managed to fill the next few weeks with plans for her handmaid. But as the days passed, and she saw David only when he came to the compound in the late afternoons to play with his children she made one decision; If her husband would not restore her to her rightful place as his wife, and permit her to bring her nephews to the palace, she would return to Mahanaim.

If the king would not give her permission to leave, she would run away. She could not go on day after day trusting, hoping, waiting. She had waited patiently for ten years without complain. But to know her beloved was within a stones throw of her—night and day—and never see him alone, or have an opportunity to even talk to him was unendurable.

Michal had to admit David treated her with utmost courtesy and deference. He showered her with jewels and fine raiment, and he frequently sent her sweet meats from the palace kitchen. Often as he played with his children in the garden, She caught him looking at her with his soul in his eyes as he looked the night he went out their bedchamber window, on the last night he was all her.

But if he loved her, why did he not invite her to the palace? Why did he avoid seeing her alone? He was her same loving David the night he came to her house. If only Joab had not interrupted their reunion! What happened since then to change her husband's plans for her?

Whatever it was, Michal had to know. She could not live in such torment. For days she thought: Today he will come. Today I will really see him—be in his arms again. Today he will love.

She had watched his children climb into her husband's lap, and enjoy his caresses the last time she could endure it. If she could not at least share his love, she could not bear to see it lavished on others. As far as Michal could observe, the other wives were faring no better than she was: and she had heard no complaints. But the other wives' relationship with David was their problem; at least they had children. If only she had his child!

As soon as Leah was married, Michal was determined to see David and find out exactly what his intentions were. Complete banishment would be preferable to the uncertainty under which she existed. She refused to think about the years Phalti lived under similar circumstances. But she never told Phalti she loved him or gave him any encouragement she ever would.

David had sword undying love for her; where was it? The pent-up love in her own heart must find release—or die.

Chapter 48

The day Joab took Leah to be his wife, Michal prepared for the visit to her husband she could no longer delay. She put on her royal robes, but added the veil she had not worn since her journey from Hebron. She was not sure what she would say to anyone who might question her mission, but the veil would enable her to see her questioner without being seen. Michal had not been outside the courtyard since her arrival in Jerusalem, and heart was filled with fear. But she must go; she could live no longer in suspense. At the gate, however, she refused to let her through!

"I'm sorry, my lady," he said courteously, "but no one is allowed to leave the royal compound without the king's permission."

"But my handmaid has come and gone through this gate freely since the day we came here," Michal protested.

"Yes, my lady, but Leah is a handmaid, and you are a wife."

"So the servants are free, but the wives are prisoners?"

The gatekeeper winced. "Suppose we say the wives are protected."

"I do not need protection; I need to see my husband."

"Then my lady should send a messenger with her request."

"Half blinded with rage, Michal turned away. She would not argue with a servant. How dared David subject her to such humiliation! And the knowledge that her shame would be the talk of the compound within the hour was unthinkable. A prisoner in her own home! The whole situation was unbearable, and to think she had waited ten years for this. Michal spent the rest of the day in angry indecision."

As soon as the eunuch opened the gate the next morning, Michal sent Bela, her new handmaid, to the palace. She carried a note to be delivered to the king. The note contained only four words: "I must see you."

"Remember, Bela." Michal cautioned, "give the message only into the king's hand regardless of how long you must wait."

As Michal watched her maid pass freely through the gate that was closed to her, she wished for the ten thousandth time she had been born a servant. The basest slave enjoyed more freedom than she had ever known, except for the first two years of her marriage. She was guarded as a child because she was the king's daughter. After she was taken from her husband, she was imprisoned lest she run away and join him. Now that she was back in his house, she was still a prisoner! The rebellious spirit within Saul's younger daughter was backed against the wall; enough was enough!

Michal paced her bedchamber like a caged tiger. She scorned the bed carved from ebony and ivory, and the rich tapestries that covered it. She stamped/ her feet on the thick Persian carpet, and tore the royal robe from her shoulders and threw it on the floor. She snatched up the box overflowing with rare jewels the king had so freely bestowed upon her, and flung it against the wall. How gladly she would exchange it all for a cave or a tent in the woods with the shepherd lad she married. Whatever made her think she wanted to marry a king!

The brothers and sister Michal aspired to impress were all dead. There was no one left to care whether she was princess of peasant.

In a matter of minutes, Bela was back—the note still in her hand. "I'm sorry, my lady, the king was not there. He has gone to the house of Obededom the Gittite to bring back the ark of God."

"But I thought he left the thing there because he was afraid to bring it here."

"The king was frightened because the Lord slew Uzzah. But everyone is talking about the way God has blessed Obededom's house since the ark has rested there, so the king has gone to try again to bring it here. He has already erected a tabernacle to receive it, and half the city went with him to bring it home."

"When will he be back?" Michal asked through clenched teeth.

"The palace guard expects them back before nightfall—if all goes well. They said the king took the Levites—thousands of them. This time the king is trying to move the ark according to God's law. He thinks he failed before because he did not follow God's instructions. It seems no one is ever permitted to touch the ark. Only the Levites are allowed to carry it, and they have to lift it with staves placed through the rings made to carry it by.

"All the people who did not go with the king are fasting and praying for his safe return." Bela said no more, but in her eyes was the unspoken question: Why did the king's first wife not know of such an important event?

Michal bit her lip. The king spent several hours in the compound only yesterday afternoon, but she had been too angry to trust herself out of her room. Abigail deliberately avoided all the family for weeks, and they respected her obvious desire for privacy.

Well, at least David planned to be back today. Surely could survive one more day. But try as she would to control her emotions, anger continued to boil her heart. Her husband had no time for a single word with her, but he could go traipsing off for a whole day to bring a silly little box to the city.

It was all right for a man to love his God, but didn't God command a husband to love his wife? All the messages David ever sent her were love notes to God—not to her. Perhaps her religion was on the outside, but at least she had room in her heart for her husband!

Michal was so filled with anger, the love she had cherished so many years seemed to shrivel and die. She would talk to the king if she had to do it before the whole world. Let him banish her; she hoped he would! She would go back to Mahanaim where she was loved and needed. She was sick of living like a bird in a cage—golden though it was. She had rather be a free peasant than a fettered princess. And free she was determined to be.

Chapter 49

Michal climbed to the upper chamber of her house, and looked out over the city. Sacrifices fires burned under family altars in every direction. A fire was burning under family altars in the royal compound. So much commotion over one little box!

No children played in the garden, and no smoke rose from the kitchen. Michal was so engrossed in getting a message to David, she failed to notice the servants brought no breakfast. So fasting and prayer was the order of the day? In spite of her emotional turmoil, she was immediately hungry, and she was certainly in no mood for prayer.

Michal recalled many times Samuel insisted Saul bring the ark of God from Kirjathjearim to Gibeah. But Saul reminded Samuel of the calamities that befell the Philistines while they kept the ark, and of the more than fifty thousand men smitten in Bethshemish while they are rested there. He wanted nothing to do with that little box.

Samuel's favorite argument in his efforts to persuade Saul to restore the ark to its rightful place in the tabernacle was quite a tale. He insisted it destroyed the Philistines idol God, Dagon, and so plagued the Philistines they sent it back to Israel without even being asked.

Saul always questioned that story, but Samuel vowed the ark came to Bethshemish all by itself. It had cursed the Philistines until they feared to go near it. So, according to Samuel, they laid it on a new cart, surrounded it with coffers of gold for a trespass offering, tied two milk cows to the cart, shut their calves up at home, and those cows were supposed to have carried the ark straight back to Israel—without stopping to crop a blade of grass or take a drink of water.

Michal agreed with—that was an unlikely story. But, apparently, David believed the box had magic powers. He was so upset when Uzzah dropped dead after touching the thing; why didn't he leave it alone? Why ask for more trouble by bringing it to Jerusalem?

But Michal didn't pretend to understand David's religious zeal. Religion was quite all right in its place, but there was no reason to be a fanatic about it. One could surely obey the laws of God without risking his life or making a fool of himself. She saw no reason to allow religion to interfere with one's happiness or welfare.

It was not quite midday when a commotion in the watchtower attracted Michal's attention. Immediately a messenger descended the tower, and ran toward the palace; he came directly from there to the royal compound. Soon the people began emerging from their homes, and surging toward the city gates. The garden below Michal's window came alive as the children swarmed out to play. The servants ran from the compound and joined the surging crowd.

"Bela," Michal called, "go out what the excitement is all about."

"Yes, my lady," said Bela eagerly, as she ran out the door.

But Michal hastened to the roof where she could see for herself. A huge procession was approaching the city gates from the northwest. There appeared to be thousands of marching men.

In a few minutes, Bela was back. "The king is returning with the ark. As soon as it is safely in the tabernacle, the king has a great feast prepared for all the people. Everyone is to get a loaf of bread, a big piece of meat, and a flagon of wine—the women as well as the men."

"Would you like to go the feast, Bela?"

"Oh yes, my lady, but I would not go and leave you all alone."

To be pitied by a servant! This was indeed the last straw. "But of course you must go, Bela; I wish it. And stay as long as you like."

"Thank you, my lady; you are most kind." Bela dashed out the door, and followed in the wake of the joyous crowd.

Michal wanted her maid to leave before she lost control of her anger, and conducted herself in a manner unbecoming royalty.

The lonely woman, who was neither maid nor wife nor widow, went back to her window, and watched in silent fury as the procession came into the city. The welcoming crowd moved back and formed a wall on either side of the cobblestoned streets. The sound of trumpets could be heard above the shouting throng.

Michal could see some silly fellow dancing his fool head off leading the parade. Behind him came four priests carrying a box on staves across their shoulders. She could see something gleaming in the sunlight in the center of the four men; that must be the great ark. Behind them marched thousands of men four abreast. But she saw nothing of the royal chariot.

Where was David?

Above the tumult of the shouting throng, Michal could hear trumpets, cornets, cymbals, psalteries, and harps. It looked as if everyone who has an instrument was playing it, and the rest of the people were singing and dancing. Never had she seen such wild rejoicing. Not even Israel's greatest victories in battle were greeted with such celebrating.

As the procession passed the palace and drew near the tabernacle, Michal could see that all the men marching sedately behind the ark were priests. The foolish fellow dancing in front of the ark also wore a linen ephod, but he lacked the other accoutrements of a priest.

But still no David.

With a loud clashing of the cymbals, the marching column stopped in front of the tabernacle. The dancing clown stood still and raised his arms in a gesture of silence. The four priests bearing the ark disappeared inside the tabernacle, and the next four stepped up to the light the fires under sacrifices already upon the altars. After the priests returned to their places, the jester with arms still upraised began to pronounce a blessing upon the crowd. Then Michal received the supreme shock of her shocking day; the giddy dancer was David himself!

Anger and shame struggled for mastery of the emotions of the proud daughter of Saul.

Chapter 50

Michal watched in silent fury as the king's servants dealt out bread, meat, and wine to the great multitude. The people did not partake of the feast in the streets, but each departed to his own house as he was served. When the crowd cleared away, Michal saw David, clad once again in his royal robes, flanked by his usual four mighty men, walking toward the court.

Trembling with rage, Michal descended the stairs. She met Bela coming into the house. The handmaid was carrying a loaf of bread, a flagon of wine, and a dish of meat.

"The servants have prepared a fatted calf, and the king is coming to dine with his family," said Bela. "It is all right if I go out to eat with the other handmaids?"

Michal nodded; she was too angry to speak.

"Thank you, my lady." Bela bowed and ran.

Michal walked firmly from the house, and out to the open gate; she was waiting when David arrived. She did not wait for his greeting. "How glorious was the king of Israel today," she said mockingly, "who uncovered himself before the eyes of the handmaids of his servants as one of the vain fellow shamelessly uncovers himself!"

David stood still; his face with shock, pain, and disbelief. When he spoke, the hurt in his voice slowly turned to anger. "It was before the Lord, who chose me before your father, and before all your father's house, to appoint me ruler over the people of the Lord, over Israel that I danced; therefore will I play before the Lord. And I will yet be more vile than this, and will even be base in my own sight. And the maidservants of which you spoke, of them shall I be had in honor."

Without another word, David wrapped his royal robes around him, and proceeded toward the porch where the banquet awaited him.

Shame and humiliation washed over Michal, taking away all her anger. She turned and ran back to the refuge of her house. She fell upon her bed and lay writhing in suffering to bitter for tears.

How well Michal knew the penalty for angering a king. Not until she experienced his wrath did it become real to her that her shepherd lad *was* the king. There was no question about it now; he would be forced to at least banish her. A less merciful king would have slain her on the spot because she had humiliated him in front of his men. No woman could expect to defy her husband with impunity—certainly not the king. How could she have forgotten her mother's warning about her sharp tongue?

The sounds of merriment coming from the garden failed to pierce Michal 'wall of misery. Her hunger, her impatience, her anger—all were forgotten. Her heart was too filled with shame to leave room for any other emotion. And there was no one to whom the suffering woman could turn.

After hours of silent agony, while her usually agile mind probed every avenue of deliverance, Michal arose from her bed, fell on her knees, lifted her face toward heaven, and cried out in desperation, "Oh, God—if there is a God—have mercy on me! I know my religion is all on the outside, but I don't know what to do about it. Please come into my heart; cleanse me; forgive me; and give me peace."

Michal bowed her head, sank down against her bed, and cried like a child. Eventually, slept.

When she waked, the sun was casting long shadows through her west windows. Sunlight glittered on the gold threads in the draperies around her bed. With wakefulness, memory returned, and Michal waited for the pain to descend once more upon battered heart. But the only emotion she felt was resignation, and a strange sort of peace. She knew what she must do.

Arising from her cramped position, Michal removed her royal robes and all her jewels. She donned again the simple raiment she wore to Hebron. She tried not to think of the high hopes that filled her heart when she last wore the garments. Could it have been only six months? It seemed like a lifetime. The ten years she waited in Gibeah and Mahanaim were nothing were nothing compared to the anxious months spent in her husband's house.

Perhaps she would never know why David sent for her only to keep her a glorified prisoner. Except for those few brief moments she spent in his arms, her life in his house had been torment.

Michal unpinned her long black hair, shook out the braids, and let if fall in a cloud of dark curls around her shoulder. She packed a few simple necessities and tied into a bundle, there sat down to await her fate. There came a faint knock at her door. She preferred to ignore it, but she was sure it was Bela, and she would be worried about her strange new mistress.

"Come in," said Michal calmly.

Like any well-trained servant, Bela ignored her mistress' tear-ravaged face and simple attire. "The hour grows late," said the maid timidly. "Would my lady like her supper?"

Michal smiled, a smile she feared expressed more heartbreak than her tears. "Yes, thank you, Bela. And you may bring it to me here."

Surprisingly, the food tasted good, and Michal felt better after eating. Suddenly she realized she had spent the day in fasting and prayer after all.

"You may go now, Bela. I'll need you again today," she added kindly.

"But," Bela hesitated, obviously reluctant to leave. "But—are you sure you are all—you don't need me?"

"Quite sure," said Michal with the best smile she could muster. "You may have the night off to do whatever pleases you."

"Thank you, my lady." But Bela withdrew with obvious reluctance.

The sun sank behind the mountain, and still no one came for the waiting women. As she wandered about the lavishly appointed house—it was never a home—that David built for her, she wondered who would occupy it after she was gone. Then her eyes lighted on the stone jar containing the psalms David sent her. Idly she took out the parchments, and listlessly scanned them. But one caught her attention. She went back to the first line and read it carefully all the way through;

> The Lord is my light and my salvation;
> > whom shall I fear? . . . .
> When my mother and my father forsake me,
> > then will the Lord take me up . . . .
> Wait on the Lord; be of good courage,
> > and he shall strengthen thine heart . . . .

Once more the forsaken women lifted her eyes toward heaven. "I'm waiting Lord," she said calmly; "I have no one else."

The darkness crept into the lonely house, but Michal refused to light a candle. The dark room matched her mood. She tucked the parchments into her bundle, carried it to the front door, and sat down to await the summons she knew would come. David would not rest until he carried out whatever decision he made concerning her.

The night was black outside her window when Michal saw two lighted torches approaching the gate to the court. After a brief delay, the torches passed through the gate and came straight to her door.

Chapter 51

Michal arose and flung open her door before her callers could knock. Silhouetted against the light stood a palace courier. Behind him, holding the torches were two huge, burly eunuchs.

"We have come for the daughter of Saul," said the courier, in a triumphant tone. "Summon her immediately."

Michal drew herself up to her full 5' 10", tossed back her black curls, lifted her chin to a proud angle, and said in ringing tones, "I am the king's wife."

"Dare you defy the king?" The courier strode forward arrogantly to push Michal aside. She quickly stepped out of his way.

One of the eunuchs moved in and held his torch so the light fell full in Michal's face. "She really is the king's wife," he said in shocked surprise.

"Are you sure?" asked the skeptical courier.

"Positive," said the big gatekeeper; "I talked with her only yesterday."

"You are to come with us," said the slightly wilted courier, "at once!"

Michal picked up her bundle, handed it to the gatekeeper, and with her head high and her shoulders squared, she walked out of the house before her callers.

The disconcerted courier dashed forward and took her arm roughly. Without missing a step, Michal disengaged his hand from her arm, and pushed it away. A bit uncertainly, he stepped in front of her and led the way out of the court.

Michal looked neither to the right or left, nor did she speak to her captors. She had no idea where they were taking her, but wherever it was, she did not plan to stay long.

They walked to the foot of the hill, and straight toward the palace gates. Something she thought was dead surged in Michal's heart. With David's forgiving spirit, was there hope for her yet? But the guards passed the palace without breaking stride, and continued on toward the gates of the city.

Was the king sending her back to Mahanaim? How she longed to see her nephews! And Phalti's kind and gentle face rose up before her. Why on earth had she not possessed the good sense to fall in love with him instead of David? She could not be his wife as long as David lived, but if merely having her near made him happy, she was ready to make him happy for the rest of her life.

Michal could see the torches burning at the city gates, but she saw no camels or other means of transportation. Surely, David did not expect her to walk to Mahanaim! Alone? In the dark of night?

Abruptly, the courier turned and began to climb the hill on the opposite side of the valley from which they came. At the top of the hill they stopped; they were at the gate of a large walled courtyard high above the city gates. The house inside the compound was a huge three-storied structure that appeared to be built on the city wall. One of the eunuchs unlocked the gate, took Michal's bundle from his companion, and motioned for her to pass through the gate. She followed her guide to the door.

Lights shown dimly from the two lower floors of the house, but the third floor was well lighted, and the sound of music, dancing, and feminine laughter wafted out the open windows. Michal waited silently beside her guide for a response to his knock.

A fat old woman opened the door. "Well, come in, dearie," she said, holding high the candle in her hand. "Why—they can't be Saul's daughter," she protested.

"They tell me she is," the eunuch shrugged.

"I am king David's wife," said Michal with royal dignity.

The old woman lifted her candle higher, and looked searchingly at Michal's face. Then she waddled around her, and observed her from all her sides as if she were a prize cow. "Then come along, dearie, come along; but you sure don't look like a princess to me. My name is Zervah," she added as sort of an afterthought.

Michal did not design to answer, but she followed her guide up the stairs. By the time they reached the third floor, the old woman was struggling and panting.

"These stairs get steeper every day; I do hope I don't have to climb them again today." She did not seem to expect a response, and Michal made none. Heaving and grunting, the old woman lifted an iron bar from its slots on either side of the door at the head of the stairs.

The door opened on a huge room filled with beautiful young women. A few were playing stringed instruments, others were singing and dancing, but a few lying listlessly on the beds on the beds that lined the walls.

Rich carpets were scattered over the marble floor, and marble pillars supported the high, beamed ceiling. Bright colored lanterns filled the room with the soft light. The women were dressed in rich garment—many typical of the heathen countries surrounding Israel.

"Come girls," coaxed Zervah, "greet Princess Michal, the daughter of king Saul."

A bold young Egyptian, who was dancing near the door, gyrated over and bowed before Michal. "Welcome Princess," she said mockingly, "to the end of the road."

Chapter 52

The young women gathered around Michal—not in any gesture of welcome, but in ill concealed curiosity. How different they were from the stately women in the king's court. They were all young and beautiful, but several were overweight, and a few were disgustingly fat.

Who were these women? Michal wondered. Why was she brought here? It was certainly not an inn. The old woman who escorted her up the stairs barred the door behind her when she left. All she said before leaving was, "Your bed is number 26."

Was the daughter of one king, and the wife of another expected to occupy a bed in the same room with all the vulgar females?

"The higher they are, the harder they fall," said the bold dancer as she gyrated around Michal.

"Oh, let her alone," said a sad-eyed beauty reclining on a bed. Languidly, she arose and came over and bowed to Michal. My name is Hadah," she said kindly. "May I show you to your bed."

"Please," said Michal gratefully. She followed Hadah, a young woman almost as tall and dark as herself, to a bed in the far corner of the room.

Hadah turned and held out her hands toward the bed in an expressive gesture.

Michal looked at the bed, and then her glance swept the crowded room. The women had returned to their pursuits, but they watched the newcomer with interest. "I am to sleep here with—with—?"

"I'm sorry, Princess, but I'm afraid you are. We've never had a wife here before; what did you do anyway?"

Michal's face flushed, but she ignored the question, and asked one of her own. "Who are these women? And what is this house?

"We are the king's concubines, and this is the second house of the women."

"These are? You are David's wives?"

188

"No, my lady—concubines. There is a world of difference."

"You mean—all these women—belong to the king?"

"That we do, Princess, body and soul, till death do us part. And there are several of us who would welcome even that kind of parting."

"Then why did you come here?"

Hadah laughed, but there was definitely no mirth in her laughter. "Our fathers brought us here and sold us like so many cattle—for money, favors, influence—whatever they happened from the king."

"Then why don't you leave?"

"Why don't we leave! Why don't you leave? Did you notice that big door was barred behind you? And did you happen to see those big brawny eunuchs who occupy the first floor? If you find a way out of this place, please let me know."

Michal was appalled. "Do you mean to tell me all these beautiful women are to remain prisoners here for the rest of your lives? To grow old and—all alone?"

"Oh, we are not alone—more's the pity. Rarely, when it rains all day, and we can't get out into the gardens, we almost go mad."

"You mean you have no privacy?"

Hadah motioned Michal to step aside. She walked around the bed drawing the sheer draperies until the bed was completely enclosed. Then holding back the curtain at the head of the bed, she motioned Michal inside. "You can see out from the inside, but you can't see in from the outside. It may not seem like much to you, but it is cherished privacy to us. There is an unwritten law here that you never pull back anyone's curtains but you own."

Michal felt the rage she thought was gone forever, flooding her soul. She sank down on the narrow bed and motioned Hadah to sit beside her. "How could anyone be so cruel as to subject another human being to such degradation?"

"Well—I'm sure it will come as a shock to you, but a few of these women actually like it here. Good food to eat, beautiful gardens, no work to do—even their children are cared for by others."

"These—? These girls have David's children?"

"Let's say they are supposed to—and a few of them actually do. There are seven children in the nursery on the second floor. But, as you know, the wives have houses where the king can visit, and where they can bring up their own children in privacy. We never see the king, after our initial visit to the palace, unless he calls for us by name. He has forgotten our names already—more than likely; how can he call for us?"

"He never comes here?"

"Yes. Occasionally. He comes to the nursery to see the children, and the mothers are allowed to be present. But he never comes up here."

"Do you have children?"

"No," said Hadah quickly, but she looked so embarrassed, Michal changed the subject.

"Do the girls ever try to escape?"

"Yes. But not often, and they always get caught."

"And then what happens?"

It all depends. If they simply run away and are brought back safely, they only get a flogging. If they are found with child—they are stoned."

To death?"

To death."

Michal shuddered. She could not believe such things happened in her native Israel. She knew there were such cruelties in the heathen countries of their neighbors—but Oh, God—not in the Promised Land! And that David, the Sweet Psalmist of Israel, could be responsible for such injustices was unthinkable.

Michal had planned to leave Jerusalem as quickly as she could find a way, but she changed her mind. She would not leave until this house was destroyed, or at least every woman in it was free to go or stay as she pleased.

Chapter 53

The sun rose bright and beautiful on Michal's first day in the second house of the women. But what a night! For the first time since her marriage, she had been told when to go to bed. Even without the turmoil in her heart, the hard, narrow bed in the crowded room was hardly conducive to sleep.

Silence reigned for a while in the hot, stuffy room after the lights were out. Eventually, Michal heard regular breathing, and a smothered sob here and there. She wondered in the evening. She wondered if the sobs came from the girls who danced so gaily earlier in the evening.

The fat Persian woman in the bed on her right began to snore. The Edomite on her left cursed softly under her breath. Michal thanked God that the lamps were out. If one had been available, she doubted if she could have restrained herself from hurling it against a wall, and burning this cubicle of human misery to the ground.

As the night wore on, Michal tried desperately to shut the noises in the room from her mind. She concentrated on the sighing of the wind through the tamarisk trees, and the lonely cry of the nightbird who sounded as forsaken as herself. She was relieved when the contented cooing of the pigeons, the mournful calls of the doves, and the raucous cries of the jays heralded the coming of the dawn.

Gradually the city below began to turn from ebony to purple. An occasional tree grew black against the reddening sky. The flowers and shrubs in the courtyard below separated into leaves that moved in the morning wind. The stars that had diamonded the sky through the dark hours faded as the inky blue was diluted with light.

Slowly the city began to take form below her. The buildings were a mass of masoned mountains, their roofs catching the light, their lower floors in a golden mist coaxed from the streets by the heat of the rising sun.

Moving into the dawn traffic were sleepy servant girls, hurrying shopkeepers, and reluctant donkeys laden with the days wares. It was if the dark blanket of the night had rolled back to welcome a new day. Even the squalid marketplace was painted in beautiful colors by the rosy dawn.

Jerusalem was built on terraced hills, tier upon tier. It was a city of marble, and yellow stone; of domes, porticoes, and spires; of narrow, cobbled streets; of olive, palm, fig, cypress, and tamarisk trees; of beautiful gardens and flowing fountains: and of noisy marketplaces and crowded tenements.

Surrounding the second house of the women was a courtyard enclosed by a high stone wall. In the center of the compound was sparkling fountain perpetually overflowing. Secluded benches were shaded by huge cypress trees, and hidden by grape arbors. Numerous tamarisk trees whispered softly in the morning breeze. So much ethereal beauty in the presence of such satanic baseness!

The concubines were herded down to a large dining room on the second floor for breakfast. Michal insisted she was not hungry, but the big eunuch who unlocked the door demanded she accompany them anyway. He also commanded her to change into the clothing that had been issued her.

After breakfast the women were escorted to the garden. The mothers took their children along.

Michal wandered through the garden as if admiring its beauty, but her eyes probed every corner for an avenue of escape. The house was not built on the city wall as she thought the previous night, but on the highest terrace next to the wall. The roof was high enough above the wall as she thought the window sills of the third floor were level with the top of the parapet. The Jebusites had used the building to house their elite guard, the men who directed Jebus' defense successfully for generations until David outwitted them.

After completing her tour of inspection, Michal searched for Hadah. She found her lying on a bench in a secluded grape arbor; she was weeping uncontrollably.

Not being addicted to tears herself, Michal was usually impatient with them, but the girl's grief seemed so genuine, and her sobs so despairing, it would have required a heart of stone to have rejected her.

Michal stood quietly for a moment. "Can I help?" she asked softly.

Hadah made a desperate effort to control her sobs. Finally, she said, "Not really. Nobody can help me; I am doomed. But thank you anyway."

"Have you tried God?"

"God!" Hadah exclaimed scornfully. "The king prates about God while he keeps us shut up here like so many animals. I don't want his God."

"God does not approve of everything his children do, any more than mothers approve of everything their children do," said Michal gently.

"Well—even if there is a merciful God, it's too late for him to help me."

"You could give him a chance; what do you have to lose?"

"Nothing! I've already lost everything."

"Not quite. You still have your life."

"Not for long—I won't."

"Would it make you feel better to tell me about it?

The girl shrugged hopelessly. "I was betrothed to a soldier. My brother brought him wounded from the battlefield to our home. We fell in love. But when he asked to marry me, my father said my beauty should not be wasted on a common soldier." Hadah began to sob again.

"Couldn't be wasted on a common soldier, but it can be thrown away on an empty garden," Michal sympathized. "You say there is no escape from this place, but what's to keep you from propping a bench up against the wall, and climbing over?"

"If you stay here long enough, you'll find out. You are not the first one to think of that."

Suddenly there was an anguished cry from across the garden. Michal peered through the arbor in the direction of the sound. One of the concubines was cowering against the wall. Her arms were suspended above her head; her wrists were bound with a rope tied to a spike on top of the will. A big eunuch was lashing the girl's bare back with a whip. Each time the whip descended, the flesh erupted in ribbons of blood, and the helpless woman screamed in agony.

Michal whirled and started out of the arbor. Hadah grasped the hem of her garment.

"Don't go out there; you'll get some of the same."

"We can't let him beat her to death."

"We can't stop his beating her, but he won't kill her."

And even as Hadah spoke, the cries ceased. Michal looked back through the arbor. The eunuch was dragging the battered girl toward the house. "What will become of her now?"

"There is a room reserved for the sick; she will stay there until her back heals."

"David does not know about this sort of thing; he would never tolerate it."

Hadah laughed her mirthless laugh. "He keeps us here in a living death, which is far worse. I'd rather be beaten to death today—here and now—than to grow old and die here."

"Ah, but as long as there is life there is hope. Don't give up so easily. You, like almost everyone, are anxious to change your circumstances, but unwilling to change yourself. Don't lie and cry—something!"

"I have done something," Hadah shrugged; "that's why I have no hope."

"What have you done?"

Hadah sighed. "I don't suppose it can make things any worse if I tell you. I decided I could bear this living death if I could have a child—Judah's child; he is still my betrothed. But that was before I learned how the system works here. That fat vulture you saw last night keeps a strict account of each concubine's visit to the palace. Any baby that arrives here had better correspond to its mother's visit with the king. I'll not be able to conceal the fact much longer that I am with child, and I've not seen the king since I came here."

"Then you have committed adultery?

"With the king—yes! With—no!" Hadah cried. "Before God, Judah is my husband; I wanted his child. I didn't know I would get us both killed."

"There are no scars on your back; how did you avoid the flogging when you ran away?"

"I didn't leave; Judah came here."

"Here? How?"

"He climbed over the wall in the darkness and hid in the shrubbery until I came to the garden the next day. He has been here several times. His visits are all that have made my life bearable."

"Then you must get out of here and go to your Judah; he can't leave you here to die!"

"But how? wailed Hadah."

"I don't know. But we'll find a way."

"There's no use in your getting killed too."

Michal shrugged. "Some people face life as if it were a storm; they find a safe place to sit down and wait for it to end. I can't do that. I must leave this world a little better place for my having lived in it. I cannot go until I do."

"But what good would it do you or the world to get me out of here?"

Michal smiled, but it was a smile so sad brought back tears to Hadah's eyes. "I'm reconciled to the fact I'll never be able to do much, and I have no children to accomplish for me. But all God requires is that we do our best and trust him with the result. After all, it was Pharoah's daughter who brought up Moses, and your little Judah might be another Moses."

"What do your think you can do shut away in this prison?

Michal arched her heavy black brows. "God does not expect me to change the whole world, but he does expect me to change my little corner of it. And I'm going to change it if it's the last thing I do. Now let's start with you. Can you get a message to your Judah?"

"He'll be here tomorrow."

"Good! Tell him to get two camels, and be waiting by the city wall beneath our windows tomorrow night."

"It's no use; we'd be caught within hours."

"You would not be missed until morning; you could be far away by then. Flee to Philistia if you must. The king would not provoke another war to reclaim you."

"But we are checked every night. We never know when, but Zadoc, that big brute who was beating Bithia, checks on us. He peeps behind every curtain; he would be on our trail immediately."

"He didn't check us last night."

Hadah looked puzzled, then understanding lighted her eyes. "He knew you would be awake. New girls seldom sleep well at first. After a while, sleep is the only happiness we know. We can at least dream of the time when we were free."

"How could Zadoc trail you? Many roads leave Jerusalem; how would he know which one you took?"

"He knows every girl will try to get back to her city; where else could she get help?"

"And what is your city?"

"I am from Hebron, and my Judah lives there also."

A sly look came into Michal's eyes. "Then let's send Zadoc toward Mahanaim."

Chapter 54

The concubines returned to their beds for naps in the afternoon. Hadah whispered to Michal as they climbed the stairs. "It's no use; Judah and I would get caught, and you might be punished for helping us."

"You have to try," Michal whispered back. "You can't stay here and without a struggle. God does not require us to succeed in life, but he does command us to try."

"But I have tried, and everything I've tried has failed.

"You'll never win a race, you know, unless you run. And you'll never know how fast you can run unless you try."

"I'm sorry, but I can't do it."

Michal shook her head sadly, and went on to her bed. She had not slept at all the previous night, and very little the night before. From sheer exhaustion she fell asleep.

The princess was awakened by a commotion in the room. The concubines were dashing by about in a wild disorder. Many were crowding around the windows facing the street. A few were face down on their beds with their pillows over their heads. Wild shouts and shrill laughter wafted up from the street below.

Hadah moved back up from a window, came over to Michal's bed, and whispered, "I'll try! I'll try!" She motioned Michal toward the window.

Michal hesitated, but curiosity conquered her dignity. She went to the window and peered out over the heads of the concubines, who were all much shorter than herself. She saw a mob streaming out of the city gates, and converging on a spot where a heavy stake was driven into the ground.

On the far side of the stake, which was some six cubits high, stood a priest, flanked on each side by a tabernacle guard. Four soldiers marched up, dragging a barefooted woman clothed in flowing white garments. The guards stepped forward, stripped the woman of her outer garments, and covered her with a scarlet robe.

One of the soldiers drove several nails into the stake, while another bound the woman's hands. Then they lashed the prisoner's hands to the nails. Their work finished, the soldiers moved back behind the priest, and stood at attention.

The priest stopped forward and shouted, "This woman is an adulteress! She was taken in the very act. She has played the harlot in Jerusalem! She is an insult to all men revere God and his laws. We submit her to the judgment of the men of Jerusalem."

The priest turned and walked solemnly away. The guard followed.

Immediately an Edomite in the forefront of the mob picked up a stone and hurled it at the helpless woman. Then many men in the crowd began stooping to find stones, and soon all seemed to be armed and throwing.

If the victim made any outcry it could not be heard above the shouts of the rabble. But a huge, jagged stone caught her in the breast. Blood spurted through the torn red robe, and she screamed in agony.

"Oh, God, please," Michal moaned; make somebody do something."

Several of the concubines glanced at her uncomprehendingly. A few with sympathy; but no one said a word.

"The soldiers," cried Michal, why don't they help her?"

But the men in uniform watched objectively while the mob on all sides scurried about gathering more ammunition. The hapless woman's body sagged as she pelted with missile after missile. By then she appeared to be mercifully unconscious. The big Edomite who had cast the first stone, rushed up and motioned for the others to stand back. He took careful aim, whirled his arm, and launched his rock. It struck the victim full in the face.

The blow tore the prisoner's hands loose from the nails, and she collapsed in a shapeless blob of bloody rubble at the feet of the stake. As she fell, the mob rushed upon the fallen body, smashing it with stones too heavy to throw. They continued to drop huge rocks on the crumpled body until it was complexly covered.

Slowly the mob began to drift away. Silent the concubines withdrew from the windows, but Michal continued to stare at the mound of stones, her eyes blazing with anger.

"Where is the man?" she demanded of no one in particular. "Did that woman commit adultery all by herself?"

No one answered.

"Where is the man?" she screamed at the heedless mob.

"He was probably the one who cast the first stone," muttered the Persian.

A few stragglers behind the retreating mob looked toward the window, but it was obvious Michal's meaning had not prevailed above the noise in the street.

"That was horrible!" Michal protested, turning back toward the young women in the room. "Why is it permitted? Why doesn't the king stop it?"

"If anyone tried to stop it," said the Edomite, 'the men you watched today—would storm Jerusalem, and kill the heathen."

Michal was suddenly assaulted by the terrifying thought that this was the fate of the lovely Hadah. Her eyes quickly sought the unhappy girl. She was lying prone on her bed, apparently oblivious to her surroundings.

Many of the women were white with fear; several appeared to be in a state of shock. A few wept openly; others stifled sobs in their pillows. The fat Persian lay supine on her bed gazing at the ceiling.

"If no one else will do anything, I will," Michal said angrily. Wait and see if I don't

Chapter 55

After the evening, the women were permitted to return to the garden until dusk. Michal and Hadah found a secluded bench, and completed their plans for the following night.

"Whatever happens, I want you to know I'm grateful for your help," Hadah assured Michal.

"If you get away safely, give God the glory; we'll succeed only with his guidance and protection."

"What if Judah will not agree to our plans?"

"Tell him, said Michal grimly, "to go look at the pile of stones outside the city gates."

Hadah shuddered.

Michal slept fitfully that night. It was several hours after she went to bed that she be heard the door open softly. She could hear stealthy footsteps padding around the room. She felt rather than saw someone pull back the curtains around her bed. After a brief hesitation, the silent figure padded on.

The following morning, Michal wandered back and forth in the garden between Hadah's trysting place and the other women in the vicinity. Once she stooped and picked up a large smooth stone. She brushed the dirt from it and held it concealed in her sleeve.

Michal watched and listened, but she could detect no movement behind the dense cypress trees that hid the wall and the area where Hadah's beloved was supposed to wait. No sound emerged except the rustling of the leaves on the trees.

When the gong sounded, and the women began moving back toward the house, Hadah came out of the cypress grove and joined Michal.

"He didn't come?" whispered Michal.

"He came," Hadah said softly. "And he will be back tonight with the camels. He sent you his humblest gratitude.

The remainder of the day dragged slowly by. Hadah was so agitated, Michal went over and sat beside her as she lay shaking on her bed. "Be careful," she whispered to the frightened girl. "If you don't calm down, someone may get suspicious. You have trusted me; you can surely trust God more."

Hadah heaved an exhausted sigh. "Thank you. And if I do get away, I'll ask your God to deliver you too."

"Now that's the spirit. You rest while you have a chance; it will be a long night, and you can't sleep too well on a camel." Michal hesitated a moment. "And thank you for your prayer," she whispered softly. "If God wants to deliver me, I'm sure he will—in his own good time. But right now I think he needs me here."

After a few whispered instructions from Michal, Hadah rose from her bed, and went out to the center of the room where several of the women were idly strumming on the stringed instruments. "The daughter of Saul is sad tonight," she said. "Why don't you play something lively? Perhaps it will cheer her up."

Apparently delighted to have an assignment to direct their aimless ways, the women immediately launched into the army's marching tune. The ones who were not playing, clapped their hands in time with the music.

Michal hastily stripped the sheets from Hadah's bed. She folded one in half and tried to tear it in two pieces; the stout linen would not tear. Then she set her teeth in the edge and pulled with all her strength; the material would not give. She looked around in desperation. The brass bedposts were pointed on top. Perhaps? She laid the middle of the sheet over the metal point, and jerked hard; the brass pierced the linen a mere inch.

Quickly, Michal hooked her forefingers in the hole and pulled; the sheet began to rip. When the hole was big enough to admit both her hands, she tore the sheet apart. When she had repeated the process with the other sheet, she tied the four pieces together. Then she slipped them around the bedpost, and pulled with all her weight against each knot; they all held.

Michal folded the torn sheets as flat as she could, concealed them in the folds of her dress, and returned to her own bed. After she pulled her curtains, she took the stone she found in the garden and tied it in end of her "rope." Then she lay down on her bed and waited impatiently for the lights to go out.

When the lights were finally out, Michal listened in the thick darkness for the sobs to give way to the snores. She pulled back her curtains and watched the stars. There would be a moon later, but now only millions of stars lighted the clear black sky.

The night was perfect for her plan—she hoped.

Chapter 56

As soon as Michal decided the concubines were all asleep, she crept from her bed. Cautiously, she picked up her pillow and the wooden bench beside her bed and carried them to the open window. Placing her pillow on the window sill, she turned the bench upside down, and pushed it slowly across it rested on top the city wall. Folding the torn sheets into a tight bundle, she pitched them to the top of the parapet.

Carefully, Michal stepped out on the bench, and crept across the chasm. Safely on the wall, she unfolded the sheets and let the weighted and down until she felt it touch the ground. Then she slipped the other end through the aperture in the end of the bench, and tied it securely.

Her work finished, Michal lay flat on the wall and peered at the ground. The camels were there!

As quickly as possible, Michal recrossed the bench, crept over to Hadah's bed, and gently touched her shoulder. The girl was shaking, whether from eagerness or fear, Michal could only guess. Without a word passing between them, Hadah followed her guide to the open window. Michal crept across the bench; Hadah followed.

When they were both safely across the chasm, Michal lifted the bench, turned it right side up, and eased it down across the top of the wall.

"Now, get a good grip on the sheet with both hands, and walk down the wall. I'll sit on the other end of the bench so it can't tip up. Don't be frightened; just hold on to the sheet, and let yourself down hand over hand. Be careful—and may God go with you."

"And may your God grant you the desires of your heart," whispered Hadah fervently.

Michal sat down on the opposite end of the bench; Hadah clutched the sheet, climbed over the edge of the wall, and slowly disappeared from sight.

After what seemed an eternity, Michal felt the tension go out of the bench. She waited and listened until she heard the soft plop of the camel's feet. Hastily she retrieved the dangling sheets, put the bench back across the chasm, climbed back through the window, replaced the placed the bench and pillow, and crept into Hadah's bed. She whispered a prayer for the fleeing couple's safety, pulled the coverlet over her head, and fell asleep.

Michal was awakened in the middle of the night by a commotion in the room. A lamp was burning, and the concubines by a chattering in a hubbub of excitement. She peered out through the curtains. Zadoc was questioning the women on either side of Michal's empty bed.

"I don't know a thing," said the Persian; "I go to bed to sleep."

"I know nothing," shrugged the Edomite. "She was in bed when the lights went out."

Zadoc turned to face the room. "Any of you? Did you hear or see anything of the daughter of Saul?"

His questions met with a stony silence.

"She could not have gone out a window without some help or leaving some evidence behind. Now somebody must know something."

"She was very sad last night," said a timid little Benjamite, still huddled in her bed. "Perhaps she jumped out the window."

Zadoc uttered an exclamation of disgust, and bolted from the room, barring the door behind him. Michal could hear the stomping down the stairs. She turned over and went back to sleep.

When the chattering of the birds waked Michal the next morning, she arose and crept silently back to her own bed. The torn stomping, she tucked beneath her mattress. She dressed within her curtained bed at rising time, and waited until the concubines were being herded down to breakfast by the fat old women, who was complaining at every breath as she counted the women passing down the stairs, Michal followed close behind the last one.

No one noticed her until they were seated. The women sitting beside her looked as if she had seen a ghost, but she said nothing. Soon the concubines were all nudging one another, and whispering, but no one commented aloud. Michal kept her head down and ate her breakfast.

Zadoc was nowhere to be seen, but the other eunuchs were all there. When the women went out to the garden, Michal kept her head down, and stuck close to the fat Persian.

"So he caught you," the woman whispered.

Michal gave her a black stare.

"Didn't he whip you?"

"What do you mean?"

"I mean—well, where were you last night?"

"In Bed. Where else if there to go?"

The woman's eyes narrowed. "Look, Princess, I don't know what you are up to, but I do know you were not in your bed when Zadoc checked us last night."

Michal smiled. "What you don't know can't get into trouble, can it? But I assure you I did not run away."

A slow smile replaced the suspicion on the women's face. "You are right; forget I asked. My name is Vesta. I only hope you don't get into trouble when Zadoc gets back."

"So do I," Michal shuddered, but she knew she had another friend.

As soon as they reached the privacy of the garden, the other women crowded around. "How did you get out?" asked several at once.

"Where did he catch you?"

"Did he whip you?"

"Wait a minute!" Vesta held up her hands for silence. "The princess is here, and she did not run away. Now scatter before we all get into trouble.

Chapter 57

Michal escaped detection again at noon. But when the women laid down for their naps, Zervah lumbered from bed to bed checking them. She pulled back the curtains on Hadah's bed, and turned toward the room with a puzzled look. All the girls were in their beds.

"Where is Hadah?" she asked the woman in the next bed.

Michal watched closely as can as the pretty concubine shrugged her shoulders and shook her head.

"I know she was at dinner. I counted twenty-four of you. Bithia is still in the sick room; Michal has fled, so that leaves twenty-four. You were all there; I counted twice."

Michal pushed back the curtains from her bed. "Did someone call me? She called innocently.

Zervah grasped her fat, heaving bosom, and almost collapsed. "The—the daughter of Saul! Where did you come from?"

"I've been here all the time."

"Where were you last night?"

"In bed asleep; why do you ask?"

Here? In this room?"

Here. In this room."

"And you didn't know Zadoc was on his way even now to Mahanaim to find you?"

"Zadoc seldom informs me of his movements."

The concubines tittered.

"There is something strange going on here," Zervah opined. "And when Zadoc gets back, someone will likely get a taste of his whip." She lumbered to each of the other beds. Stared at every occupant with fishy eyes, and went out muttering.

When the women heard the bar on the door slam into place, the rolled out of their beds and surrounded Michal. "Come On! Tell us! How did you do it?" they pleaded on every side.

"Will you get me out?" begged the timid little Benjamite.

"And me? And me?" they chorused.

"Please—girls! Be quiet! You'll get us all into trouble," Michal cautioned.

"But you got Hadah out," persisted the Benjamite. "I know she would never have tried it alone; she was too scared."

"Shhh," pleaded Michal. "I'll talk to you this afternoon in the garden." She drew the curtains around her bed and lay down.

The concubines drifted back to their beds. But they were still talking and laughing. For the first time, Michal detected a note of hope in their voices. She closed her eyes, and lifted her heart toward heaven. "Oh, Lord, deliver us all from this prison."

It was dusk on the third day when Zadoc rode dispiritedly up to the courtyard gate. He talked briefly with Ramah, the gatekeeper, and fell off his camel for the group surrounding Michal, coiling his whip expectantly.

"Uh oh! Here it comes," hissed Vesta.

"Let's all jump him," suggested Rachel, the timid little Benjamite. "He can't whip us all."

"No! No! Girls—please? Let me handle it; you might get hurt," pleaded Michal.

Zadoc strode up to the women with all the righteous indignation of an avenging angel. "So—the daughter of Saul defied her father, and get with it, defied her father and got by with it, so now she thinks she can defy Zadoc!" The big eunuch flicked his leather whip with his right hand, and drew it though his left hand caressingly as he spoke.

The concubines shrank back in terror. Michal rose to her full height, lifted her chin, and asked calmly, "Wherein have I defied Zadoc?"

"You know perfectly well how you defied me; you helped Hadah escape!"

"Have you any evidence to present to the king that I helped Hadah escape?"

Zadoc hesitated a moment. "I collected ample evidence that you defied your father."

"I had a choice," said Michal in ringing tones of pious devotion, "of defying king Saul or defying the Lord God of Israel. Which would Zadoc have had me make?"

You defied king David, the savior of Israel," he blustered.

"Did I not come here in humble obedience to the king's command?"

Zadoc was discomfited in the manner men usually are when defeated by a woman. "Tell me what you know about Hadah, and I'll let you off this time," he countered.

"What could I possibly know about Hadah? I never saw the girl until I entered this—this place last week."

Zadoc's temper began rising again. He snapped his whip viciously. "You tell me where Hadah went—or you are going to regret it!"

"How can I tell you where Hadah went, when I don't know any more of her whereabouts than you do?" asked Michal, without flinching.

Accustomed to cringing fear and instant obedience from the women he is so despised, Zadoc looked at a loss to know how to handle the situation. "You send me on another wild-goose chase like that, and you will taste Zadoc's wrath." He turned on his heal and strode away.

The concubines began to titter.

"Shhh! Girls—please!" Michal whispered.

There was an abrupt silence.

Michal knew she had won the first round.

Chapter 58

David stood disconsolately by the east window of his palace, and looked across the hills toward the second house of the women. Abiathar the priest regarded him with disapproval.

"How long will the king of Israel mourn for the daughter of the bloody house of Saul?"

"How many times do I have to remind you," David retorted, "that Michal was not responsible for her father's evil deeds? She was a victim of his madness as well as the rest of us."

"Perhaps," said Abiathar placatingly. "But she is responsible for her own deeds. If you had permitted her to defy you and go unpunished, all your wives have defied you. Can you imagine what it would be like to have seven wives and twenty-five concubines rebelling against you?"

David shuddered.

"And if the king's wives could defy him, all the wives in Israel would start defying their husbands. Surely, my lord, you can see that you did only what you had to do. You should have put her to death as your counselors advised. The king's tender heart does him disservice."

"Michal was not really; she was angry. And she had every right to be angry. I neglected her—yea even ignored her for months. I should have told her why I could not make her my queen. Because I didn't have the courage to deal honestly with her, I avoided her; she resented it. Bereft of father, mother, brothers, and sister, she had only her children; and I took her from them. How can I punish her when she has been more righteous than I?"

"How can you do otherwise?" Abiathar pleaded. "Hasn't God blessed you in every way since you banished that woman? Has he not given you victory over all your enemies? Daily, Joab reports more victories. Ammon is destroyed, and Rabbah cannot withstand the siege much longer. Surely you would not risk the wrath of God on Israel for a woman!"

"But if she cannot assume her rightful place as my queen, then she should be allowed to return to her children. Everyone has to have someone to love or life is not worth living."

"If the daughter of Saul is half the woman my lord says she is, she will do well wherever she goes."

"To be honest, Abiathar, I need Michal as she needs me—perhaps more."

"But if six wives and twenty-five concubines are not enough to keep my lord happy, Israel is full of beautiful young women who would be honored to comfort the great king who had delivered Israel so gloriously."

"But I don't want a strange young woman; I want the wife of my youth, who never brought ought but joy to my heart."

"You know God's answer to that, my lord. You cannot take back a wife who has lain in the bosom of another man."

David sighed in utter dejection, and retired to his bedchamber. He tossed and turned on his gold and silver bed, but could find no relief in blessed sleep. The thought of Michal bearing children for another man always filled him with murderous rage. How could she! She promised to wait for him, however long it took.

David would never have looked at another woman if Michal had remained faithful. If only he could quit loving her! How could she still be so young and beautiful after bearing six children? She was even lovelier than he remembered her. Her beauty had matured and blossomed beyond his fondest dreams. But he must forget her. He must! He must!

A lopsided moon burst into the starlit sky; it cast warm rays across the king's bed. Unable to endure his loneliness and misery any longer, David arose form his bed and climbed the stairs to the palace roof, where he could walk in the moonlight unobserved.

The moon would be full in another day or two. The palace garden was lighted almost as bright as day, but the king could not thrill to its beauty as he usually did. He wondered if Michal enjoyed the lovely garden at the second house of the women. Why should everything remind him of his first love? He simply had to forget her.

Momentarily, David wondered if Michal ever thought of him. Then his face burned. She probably thought of him constantly. And what she must be thinking!

David turned his back on the serenity of the garden and walked swiftly to the back of the building. The parapet protected him from the sight of anyone below, but he had an excellent view of all the houses across the narrow street behind the palace.

A man and woman sat peacefully on the grass in the first yard; several children romped and played beside them. If only God had allowed him to live out his days in Bethlehem, with Michal as his only wife and the mother of his children.

The king sighed and walked on. In the next yard two young lovers, locked in each other's arms, were gazing at the rapidly rising moon. Less than a half mile away his Michal was probably watching the same golden moon. But there was no magic in watching the moon all alone. Quickly, David moved on.

In the next yard directly behind the palace, secure within her courtyard walls, a woman was bathing herself. From that distance she could have been his Michal. She was tall, slender, dark, and very beautiful. When she finished her bath, the woman wrapped herself in a shimmering white garment, lay supine on the grass, put her hands behind her head, and gazed at the moon.

For a long time, David watched the reclining woman. Apparently, she was all alone, and she appeared as lonely as himself. Abruptly, the king whirled and returned to the bedchamber. But he did not go back to bed. He paced the floor for a few minutes, then he put on his royal robes, and summoned a servant.

"Who lives in the house within the courtyard directly behind the palace?" the king asked when the servant arrived.

"I have no idea, my lord," said the servant in an obvious attempt to conceal his curiosity.

"Then find someone who does, and send him here immediately."

"Yes, my lord." The servant bowed courteously and departed.

David paced the floor impatiently until the servant returned; he was accompanied by a chambermaid.

"Do you know who lives in the house in the courtyard behind the palace?" the king asked eagerly.

"Yes, my lord. It is the home of Uriah the Hittite. But he is not at home; he is a captain in the king's army with Joab."

"And the woman I saw there?"

"I'm sure it was Uriah's wife, Bathsheba, the daughter of Eliam."

The king was silent.

"Is that all, my lord?"

"That will be all; you may go," said David absently.

As the servants left the room, the king called after them. "Joel."

The manservant returned.

"Joel?"

"Yes, my lord."

"Is it true that women in the kingdom are anxious to be of service to the king?"

"Quite true, my lord."

"Then you take Hosea with you, and go and ask the wife of Uriah if she would like to come and talk with the king."

"Tonight, my lord."

"Tonight—now!"

"Yes, my lord." Joel bowed hastily and turned to go, but not before David noted the disapproving look in his.

"If she chooses to come, bring her to the palace waiting room."

Joel hesitated. "Yes, my lord," he said stiffly.

Chapter 59

David was still pacing the floor impatiently when the woman was ushered into the palace waiting room. The king had to admit she was as beautiful as his Michal.

"Thank you for coming," said David graciously. "I understand you are the wife of Uriah the Hittite, a brave captain in the army of Israel.?"

"Yes," the woman answered in a low musical voice.

"You know, of course, that you did not have to come here just because the king sent for you?"

"Yes," she said in the same sweet tone.

"How long have you been married?"

"Five years."

"What is your name?"

"Bathsheba."

"Do you have children, Bathsheba?"

"No."

"You are an Israelite are you not?"

"Yes."

"From what tribe do you come?"

"Benjamin."

"Why did you marry a Hittite?"

"He asked me."

David was about to exhaust his resources in an effort to make conversation with the woman. "Do Hittites place the same value on children that Israelites do?"

"No."

"You are very beautiful."

Apparently, Bathsheba did not feel that statement needed comment; she said nothing, but smiled in agreement.

"It will be sad if you have no children to perpetuate your beauty.

The woman wrinkled her brow in an apparent attempt at thought, but said nothing.

"Do you live all by yourself while your husband is away?"

She appeared relieved by a question she could answer. "Yes," she said eagerly.

"Does he come home often?"

"No."

"What do you hear from Uriah?"

"Nothing."

"Do you get lonesome?"

"Yes." A slow seductive smile lighted Bathsheba's face, and enhanced her dark beauty.

An hour or so later, David sent the woman home. "She may have Michal's beauty, he mused to himself, but she is a long way from having her brains." He looked thoughtful for a moment, then said slowly: "I don't believe I have a single concubine who does not have more personality. No wonder her husband seldom comes home. That woman would bore a man to death. Oh, well," he yawned, "She is beautiful."

And with Bathsheba's dark beauty before his mind's eye instead of the disturbing image of Michal, he turned over and went to sleep.

Chapter 60

One by one, the concubines who had no children besought Michal to help them escape the harem.

"But where would you go?" she asked. "If your fathers sold you here to begin with, would they not be honor bound to return you if you went home?"

Rachel sought Michal out in the garden. "I don't have to go home; I have a cousin who wanted to marry me. I could go to him."

"Why didn't you marry him to begin with?"

"He had no dowry."

"How long have you been the king's concubine?"

"Almost a year."

"How do you know your cousin still wants you? He may have found another wife by now," Michal added hastily.

"Our grandmother had moved here to Jerusalem. She came to see me less than a month ago; she said my cousin still pines."

"Would your grandmother be willing to hide you until your cousin could take you away?"

"Oh, yes. She grieves that I am here."

"Where does your cousin live?"

"In Carmel"

"And where do your parents live?"

"In Gibeah,"

"Good! That will send Zadoc in the opposite direction."

"Then you will help me?"

"Can you find your way to your grandmother's house after dark?"

"Oh yes!" Rachel beamed with joy. "She lives on the street behind the marketplace; she showed me the house from the window of the visitor's room on the second floor."

"We are allowed to have visitors are we?"

"With Zervah's permission."

"Then she knows your grandmother lives here; that would be the first place Zadoc would look."

Little Rachel's face fell, and big tears welled up in her eyes.

"Do visitors have to tell Zervah where they live?"

"Yes." Then a ray of hope lighted Rachel's face. "But my grandmother told Zervah she lived in Hebron. You see, her home really is in Hebron; she came here to live with my uncle because she is too old to live alone."

"Then it might work. Zadoc is still out looking for Hadah. Let's get you out tonight before he comes back."

Rachel said nothing.

"That is—if you are sure you want to go."

"Oh yes!" cried Rachel. "I'd rather die than stay here, but it just sounds too good to be true."

"Is being the king's concubine that bad?" Michal asked curiously.

Rachel's face turned a dull red. "You are a wife; you don't understand."

"Try me."

"Well—I've never seen the king but once. He was very kind and gentle. But I don't want to be any man's plaything—even the king. I want a husband and children all my own."

"Of course you do, because that's the way God intended people should live. Did he not make only one woman for the one man? Any other arrangement results in misery for everyone concerned."

"Well—the king is supposed to be a man of God, so why does he have so many women?"

"I wish I know," said Michal grimly. "I wish I knew."

Before Michal and Rachel left the garden, they carried one of the benches to the cypress grove in the corner of the compound. Propped at an angle against the wall, it gave easy access to the top of the parapet.

Timid little Rachel, who usually huddled on her bed and cried in the evenings, surprised everyone that night; she sang louder and danced faster than the bold Egyptian.

"My, my! Aren't you the gay one this evening! Has the king sent for you?"

Rachel stopped abruptly and stared at Dinah. "Would that be an occasion for rejoicing?"

"I would rejoice over anything that got me out of this place," said Dinah frankly. And you must admit a night in the palace is fun."

Rachel stared at Dinah in amazement.

"Well," Dinah shrugged, "A man is a man, and the king is the only man available to us."

Rachel silent shook her head.

Michal bit her tongue to keep silent.

As soon as Michal was satisfied the concubines were all asleep that night, she turned back her bedding, retrieved the sheet rope she used to liberate Hadah, picked up her pillow, and crept over to Rachel's bed. The shivering girl was sitting up in her bed waiting for her.

Michal bound one end of the sheet securely to the bedpost beside the open window, and dropped the other to the ground. The full moon lighted the garden like day, but Rachel's bed was against the north wall; she could stay in the dark shadows of the house and trees until she was safely outside the courtyard. From there to her grandmother's house she would risk being seen. But the hour was late; few people would be in the streets.

"Take it slow and easy," Michal cautioned. "And whatever you do when you reach the street—don't run. Remember now, wrap your cloak around you; go slow, and walk bent and stooped like an old woman."

"I won't forget," Rachel assured her deliverer. "And I'll never forget you. Whether it is a boy or girl, my firstborn shall be called Michal."

"Thank you, Rachel; I'd like that. Now go, and may God go with you and keep you safe."

Rachel crept out the window and slipped slow hand over hand to the ground. She waved to Michal, and disappeared among the trees.

Michal swiftly hauled in the sheets, and rolled them into a loose bundle. She placed the sheets and her pillow in Rachel's bed, and drew the coverlet over them. She unfastened one of the curtains from the rod, tucked it under the cover, and spread out the dark fringe on the pillow. Swiftly, she plumped the pillow, folded one end under the other and partially covered it with the coverlet. She spread the dark fringe over the exposed portion of the pillow, gave it a final pat, and went back to her own bed.

Michal listened intently that night until she stealthy footsteps make the round of the beds. When she heard the door close, and the bar drop, she went to sleep.

At the first sound of the harbingers of the day, Michal slipped over to Rachel's bed, replaced the curtain, retrieved the torn sheets and her pillow, and went back to bed. She was sound asleep when Zervah called them to breakfast.

Michal dressed as quickly as possible. She was already seated at the table when she heard Zervah bellowing from the top of the stairs. The last concubine came down with Zervah pushing and panting behind her.

"Sit down—all of you!" the old woman screamed.

The young women hastily found their seats. Zervah lumbered slowly by, counting each one carefully.

"All right! Who's missing this time?" she yelled.

The concubines looked searchingly at each other. Michal observed their expressions. Surprise, curiosity, envy, hope, fear, exhilaration—the whole gamut of human emotions was registered on their faces. Suddenly, she noticed Zervah was reading them as clearly as she was. Quickly, Michal endeavored to replace her expression of satisfaction with one of curiosity. She was, however, either too late or too obvious.

Zervah waddled over and towered above her threateningly "All right, tricky daughter of Saul, who have you sneaked out this time?"

Michal's brown eyes widened with surprise. "What do you mean?" she asked in shocked indignation.

The concubines tittered.

Zervah's fat red face grew redder. "You know perfectly well what I mean. No one ever escaped from this place until you came here. Run away? Yes. Escape? No! Now if you want to know what's good for you, you will tell me where she is."

Michal rose from her chair, drew herself up to her full height, and looked coldly down into the angry face of her accuser. "Don't you think you should at least tell me who it is you want me to find before I start looking for?"

The big woman shrank under Michal's haughty stare. She turned and waddled from the room.

The concubines began to giggle. Michal silenced them with an upraised hand.

Zervah reappeared with a parchment scroll. "You will answer when I call your name!" she bawled.

"Number one—Hazel."

"Here."

"Number two—Naomi."

"Here."

"Number three—Vesta."

"Here."

"Number four . . . .

"Number seventeen—Rachel. Rachel!"

Several exclamations of surprise broke from the concubines.

"So!" Zervah waddled back to Michal, who was calmly eating her breakfast. "The timid, whining, little Benjamite managed to escape herself?"

Michal shrugged. "Don't ask me; I barely knew the girl."

Zervah advanced threateningly toward Michal as a big eunuch entered the room.

"You sent for me, Madam?" he asked.

"I did. You checked the beds last night like I told you?"

"In the middle of the night as you instructed."

"And the concubines were all there?"

"Twenty-four, Madam; I'll swear to it."

"Well—only twenty-three came out of there this morning. Rachel is gone. I'd suggest you find her before Zadoc gets back. Come," she beckoned the eunuch from the room. "We'll check on Rachel's family. She can't have been gone long; she should not be hard to find."

Chapter 61

After three weeks of relentless searching failed to reveal any trace of the fugitives, Zadoc felt compelled to report the missing concubines to the king.

"Why would my concubines want to run away? Are they mistreated?"

"Oh—never, my lord, never! They have the best of everything, and live a life of ease."

"Good. That's the way I want it. Now. What makes you think the Princess Michal is responsible for the runaways?"

"Who understands women, my lord? Not I! But I do know no one ever managed to escape me until she came. And I'm sure she occupied Hadah's bed to send me toward the north, while Hadah fled south."

David stroked his beard. "That sounds like Michal, all right. But you know princess has several—has a family in Mahanaim; why would she help strangers escape while she remained behind?"

"I don't know. But I do know something strange is going on, and I'm sure she is behind it."

"You could be right. If anyone could get out of there, the princess could. The fact she is still there simply means she did not choose to leave. But why? Why does she not want to return to her family? That's strange, not like Michal at all."

"I have never understood women, my lord, but I do know we must get them back, or at least find out how they got out, or others will be gone."

"Very well, Zadoc; as soon as Joab returns from Rabbah, I'll send him over to help you. In the meantime, double the guard.'

"Is that all, my lord?"

"No. You make sure the Princess Michal is treated with every courtesy."

"Oh yes, my lord, of course. All the concubines are treated with every courtesy."

"The princess is not a concubine; be sure you remember that."

"Yes, my lord. She is every inch a princess. I saw it right away."

As soon as Zadoc left, a messenger asked to see the king. When the man was admitted, he bowed low before the throne, and handed David a small parchment scroll. The king untied the scroll and read the message: "I am with child." No signature.

"Who sent this message?" David asked.

"Bathsheba, my lord; the wife of Uriah the Hittite."

David closed his eyes and tried to pray. No prayer would come.

"Is that all, my lord?" asked the messenger.

"That is all; you may go."

"Yes, my lord." The messenger bowed and turned to leave.

"Wait—tell your mistress I received the message."

"Yes, my lord."

David turned to his servant. "Bring me pen and parchment, and prepare to run to Rabbah with a message for Joab."

"Yes, my lord."

David wrote one line on the parchment: "Send me Uriah the Hittite." He folded the message and sealed it with the king's seal. "Make all haste," he commanded the servant, "and give it to no one but Joab."

And Joab sent Uriah to the king. And when Uriah arrived at the palace, David demanded of him how Joab did, and how the people fared, and how the war prospered. After the captain gave a full report from the battlefield, David said, "Go home now; enjoy a good bath and some well deserved rest. My servants have prepared a feast for you and your family, and have taken to your house. Go now and rest as long as you like before you return to the battle."

"Thank you, my lord," said Uriah. "The king is most kind. It is an honor."

The following morning, the king's servants reported Uriah was ungrateful for all the king's kindness. He did not even go to his house to enjoy the feast prepared for him. He spent the entire night in the servants' quarters, without even seeing his wife.

David sent for the captain immediately. "What's this I hear that you slept on the floor in the servants quarters last night?" Were you not tired from your long journey and all those weeks in battle?"

"Of course, my lord."

"Then why didn't you go home?"

"But, my lord," Uriah protested, "The ark, and the men of Israel and of Judah abide in tents; and my lord Joab, and the servants of my lord are encamped in open fields. Shall I then go into my house to eat and to drink, and to sleep with my wife? As surely as you live, I will do no such things."

"Well, that's all right, Uriah. Those are noble sentiments. You rest up today, get a good night's sleep, and I'll let you go back to the battlefront tomorrow."

That night David insisted Uriah dine with him. The king served his strongest wine and persuaded Uriah to drink hearty. The moment the captain's glass was empty, David refilled it himself; he would not take no for an answer until the captain was almost too drunk to walk. But again Uriah slept among the king's servants at the palace.

The following morning, David wrote a letter to Joab, and sent it by the hand of Uriah. In the letter he wrote: "Set Uriah in the forefront of the hottest battle, and retire from him that he may die."

In obedience to his king's command, Joab selected the most dangerous place near the city's gates. He knew the bravest men had been assigned to defend them. And the men came out and fought with Joab's forces. Several Israelites were killed, and Uriah the Hittite died also.

Then Joab sent a report to David concerning the war. And he told the messenger if the king became angry and should ask, "Why did you approach so near the gates? Did you not know they would shoot from the wall?" Then you say, "Your servant Uriah the Hittite is dead also."

But David did not rebuke the messenger. Rather, he consoled him. "You tell Joab not to be discouraged, because the sword devours one as well as another. Tell him to fight a little harder and overthrow the city. I know he is doing his best, and that he will eventually prevail."

When Bathsheba heard her husband was dead, she put on widow's garments and mourned for him. The king sent messengers to convey his official condolences.

Chapter 62

The atmosphere grew more tense each day in the second house of the women. Bithia returned from the sickroom. Her back was covered with angry red scars. She was still forced to sleep on her stomach. Several of the concubines were more insistent than ever that Michal help them escape. But a few asked her to count them out; they prefer to stay.

The bold Dinah approached Michal in a secluded corner of the garden. She bowed to the princess, and spoke without her usual mocking tone. "If my lady can forgive my past impudence, I would like to ask you to get me out of this prison. I've decided you have more than grit and backbone; you also have brains."

"Thank you, Dinah; what do you want me to do?"

"I don't know, because I don't know what you did for Hadah and Rachel. But I agree with Zadoc; you got them. Will you get me out too?"

"If you go home, your father will be honor-bound to bring you back—"

"I won't go home," said Dinah defiantly.

"Where will you go?"

Dinah shrugged. "There is always room for one more in woman's oldest profession."

Michal shook her head firmly. "No, Dinah! I will on help you become a harlot."

"What's the difference in being the king's harlot, and choosing my own partners?"

Michal shrugged. "You do have a point. But there are a few differences, and they are most important. In the first place, concubinage is legal. So—you have respectability, and that is important."

"To whom?"

"To you. It is important to your family and your friends, and for the welfare of Israel's God."

222

"If I was important to my family, would they have sold me here? And how many of my friends have been to see me? Would you really like to know?"

Michal said nothing.

"Well, I'll tell you anyway. Not one—that's how many. A lot of family and friends care about me. And as for the welfare of Israel and Israel's God—to perdition with them both. I'm an Egyptian. I want no part of Israel or her God."

"But," said Michal gently, "Israel's God is your God too. We worship the Creator of the Creator of the universe. He is your Creator as well as mine, so he is also your God. And he loves Egypt as surely as he loves Israel. He would lead and bless Egypt if Egypt would only follow him."

Dinah's big black eyes almost popped out of her head. "Why, Princess Michal! I never heard of such a thing."

Michal sighed. "No, probably not; because Israelites have not told you. God called Abraham and his seed to give the message of God's love to all men. I'm Israel has forgotten her commission. And if my people do not remember that they are a channel of God's love instead of a receptacle, I fear we will be destroyed, and God will give his message to a people who will give it to the world."

"Where did you get all that? I'm sorry, Princess; I don't mean to be impudent. But what you say is so amazing! And as you probably know, Egyptians are a bit skeptical of everyone except Egyptians, and we trust mighty few of them."

Michal smiled. "It's all right, Dinah; I'm glad to explain, David told me."

"Ha!" Dinah sneered derisively. "So our kind and loving jailer is showing us the love of God! How much has he shown you?"

Michal could not conceal her embarrassment, but she recovered quickly. "I know how it must look to you, Dinah; and I'll admit there are many things I don't understand. But I do know David. I know loves God, and I'm sure he loves me. He could have had me killed for humiliating him in front of his men. My—king Saul would have killed me for far less."

"So you still believe the king wants to do what's right?"

"I do. Take you, for instance; your father actually sold you to the highest bidder. If the king had not bought you, some other man would have. You are protected and cared for here. And I'm sure David does not know Zadoc abuses his concubines. He would never tolerate such conduct from anyone. He has killed in defense of his God and his country, but I have never know of his torturing anyone."

"After all that man has done to you! And you can still defend him?"

"David was a kind and tender lover, and a wonderful husband until he was forced to flee for his life and leave me behind. I don't know what happened during the ten years we separated. I know there's a misunderstanding somewhere, but I can't clear it up because I don't know what it is."

"Well why don't you ask him?"

Michal's eyes glistened, but no tears fell. "You have no idea how hard I've tried. I never had one single chance to talk to him alone."

"With all the wives and children the king has acquired, I can believe that."

"I came here prepared to accept David's wives and children. I realized even God could not erase them. But I did expect to be restored to my rightful place as his first wife, and be made the queen of Israel."

"And instead, you end up on the trash heap."

"I didn't say that."

"You didn't have to. And while I'm eating crow I may as well have a second helping. You are every inch a princess, and a tall one at that—no matter where you are."

"Thank you, Dinah." Two dimples softened Michal's cheeks momentarily. "Your kind words are balm to my spirit; I'll try to live up to them."

"Then help me get out of here."

"I'll gladly help you, Dinah, if you have somewhere to go. But I will not help you enter a life of shame, where your lovely young body will be ravaged by disease, and your children grow up on the street without a father. Here you are at least protected, and your children will have respectability."

"What children?"

"You are right again," Michal conceded. "But no children are better than miserable, neglected ones. Children have rights and feelings too, you know."

"If I could write," said Dinah thoughtfully, "I'd have a place to go. The guard who brought me here asked to marry me, but he could offer only a small dowry, so my father refused."

"But a member of the king's guard could not get by with stealing one of his concubines; you'd both be killed."

"Not if we went back to Egypt. And that's what we both want."

"I can write," said Michal calmly. "Who is this guard? And how do we reach him?"

"You are indeed a princess!" Dinah's bold dark face took on a soft/glow Michal had never seen before. "If believing in your God makes people like you, tell me more."

Chapter 63

When the concubines arose from their afternoon naps, Zadoc announced the Princess had a visitor in the waiting room. Michal calmly followed Zadoc down the stairs, but she was as excited as a child. Who could it be?

The waiting room was lavishly furnished, and it opened to the south on a vine-covered balcony. The visitor, a thick-set, richly dressed woman, was standing on the balcony overlooking the garden. As Michal entered the room, the woman turned, ran toward the princess, and fell on her knees at her feet.

"Oh, my lady! My lady! It is really you! Thank God you are still alive."

Michal did not recognize the face or the figure, but the voice she would know anywhere; Leah, her beloved handmaid! Her face appeared to be bloated, and she was obviously with child. Michal lifted the kneeling woman and embraced her warmly. "Leah! How good to see you! I'm so glad you've come. Here—sit down."

"Oh, my lady! I'd have been here long ago, but I didn't know where you were. I didn't even know you were alive. I went to see you as soon as Joab went off to war. No one knew you were."

"Did you ask the gatekeeper?"

"Bela asked him the first thing when she found you gone. He vowed he knew nothing except the king had sent for you. Even Abigail said she didn't know a thing. But all the servants were certain you had been put to death. They said—" Leah hesitated.

It's all right, Leah, what did the servants say?"

"They said you defied the king, but I'm sure my lady would never do such a thing."

Michal's dimples played briefly in her cheeks. "I'm sorry to disappoint you, but I suppose I did defy the king. And if he were not more merciful than kings usually are, I probably would be dead."

Leah looked thoughtfully at the princess. "My lady has changed."

"Oh?" Michal smiled. "That's interesting. In what way?"

"I don't know. I've been trying to decide what is different about you. You are even more even more beautiful, but that's not what I mean. There is a gentleness—perhaps it's patience—that I never saw in my lady's face before."

Michal laughed. It was a merry sound that had been missing from her laughter for many years.

Leah's face reddened. "I'm sorry, my lady; I didn't mean—"

"Never mind, Leah; you're right. I never was very long on patience—or gentleness either. My mother warned me my sharp tongue would dig my grave—and it almost did. Because the king has a forgiving spirit, I'm still alive, but I have been banished here to the second house of the women."

"I know. Locked up with the king's concubines. I couldn't believe it." Tears welled up in Leah's eyes.

"Never mind, Leah. And don't you cry. I've discovered something here: Prison is a matter of the heart and mind—not of locks and bars. Many of the women are suffering such cruel imprisonment they must be freed or die. Others are quite content; they would not leave if the doors were unlocked."

"And to which group does the lady belong?"

Michal laughed again. "Let's say I'm where I want to be at the moment. But I don't want to talk about me; I want to hear about you. Are you happy with Joab?"

Leah's puffy face glowed. "Oh, my lady! I can never thank you enough for arranging my marriage. And as you can see—"

"I'm so happy for you both. And Joab?"

"You'd think he was the first man ever to become a father."

"That's wonderful! But you never did tell me how you learned where I was."

"Quite by accident, really. I was afraid to go ask the king. I planned to get Joab to ask him as soon as he came home. But this morning my neighbor, and old lady who wanders in her mind, told me her grandson's wife was with child. She said the child would be called Michal with delight.

"Rachel!" cried Michal with delight.

Leah looked puzzled. "No. The old lady said her granddaughter's name was Hadah."

"Hadah! What else did she tell you?"

"That Hadah is certain you are an angel sent from God."

"She didn't say where Hadah knew me?"

"At Hebron, she said. But she also said you were one of the king's concubines. I knew saw no one at Hebron that I did not see also, and I never heard of Hadah. So I suspected she might have met you.

"Yes, Hadah was here. But she ran away.

And the king didn't catch her?"

"The king would never miss her. But that big brute who brought me here is determined to find her, so please forget what you heard. Whatever you do—don't mention her to Joab."

"I've already forgotten her name."

"Good. Keep it that way. Now, tell me; do you know a guard at the palace named Farah?"

"I know none of the guards by name."

"He's an Egyptian."

"Oh, yes! I know which one he is. Joab questioned him loyalty; he wanted to send him back to Egypt. But the king insisted the Promised Land is for all men who worship Jehovah."

"An Egyptian worships our God?"

"He says he does."

"Would you be willing to take a message to that Egyptian for me?"

Leah hesitated.

"Don't do it if you had rather not; I don't want to get you in trouble with the king too."

"It's not that, my lady. The king has all the troubles of his own handle right now anyway. But that big ugly eunuch who brought me in, warned me not to try to help you get out."

Michal laughed. "Poor Zadoc! Perhaps I *have* been giving him a bad time. But what kind of trouble does David have?"

Again Leah hesitated. "I hate to tell you, but if you don't already know, you are probably the only one in Jerusalem who doesn't—perhaps in the all Israel by now."

"What do you mean? I've heard nothing."

"Well—it's a long and ugly story.

"Tell me! Michal insisted. Perhaps I can help."

"You my lady? You are still willing to help him after all he has done to you?"

"If I can."

"Will you please tell me why?"

"For several reasons. In the first place, he is a human being, made in the likeness and image of God. Then, he is my husband and my king."

Leah sniffed with disdain. "I thought the word husband meant to 'take care of.' Would you say the king is taking care of you?"

Michal sighed. "There are many things I don't understand, but I'm sure David is doing the best he can do for me. I have talked much with the Lord about it; I believe God has forbidden David to make me his queen because I am of the house of Saul. I remember Samuel said Saul and his house would be destroyed. Except for Merab's five sons, Rizpah's two, and Jonathan's little lame Mephibosheth, I am the only one left. And it is only by the king's mercy that I am alive. Life is sweet, Leah, and David a son."

"He doesn't seem to be very particular about the other women who bear his sons."

"I know." Michal's eyes glistened with unshed tears. "But they are not of the house of Saul. I shall always be loyal to David as my king. And even if I can't be his wife, I can still love him."

"My lady—you have changed!"

"Thank you, Leah; I hope so. I hope so. I needed changing. Now, what's David's problem?"

"With seven wives and twenty-five concubines, you may find this hard to believe."

"Another wife?"

"No—another *man's* wife."

"Another man's wife?" Michal stared at her visitor in unbelief."

"See what I mean? You can't believe it. Several weeks ago, the king sent for Bathsheba, the wife of Uriah the Hittite; he was a courageous captain in the king's army."

"Was?"

"Yes. He's dead now. The king had him killed."

"Leah! Are you trying to tell me that David had a good man killed so he could get his wife?"

"No, my lady, but that's the way it looks. And that's what almost everybody else believes."

"Why?"

"Well—well, let me start at the beginning. The king sent for Bathsheba. She knew she didn't have to go to him. She was a married woman, and even a king can't legally take a woman from her husband. The messengers said the king told them to tell her to come only if she wanted to. They told her; she came."

"But why? What did she have to gain?"

"You would have to meet her to understand. She has that rare classic beauty that all Hebrew women want, but she is just as stupid as she is beautiful. Stayed at the palace about two hours. I'm sure the king couldn't stand her any longer; she can't even carry on a conversation. But they probably weren't talking anyway."

"Oh?"

"About three weeks after Bathsheba's visit—mind you, he never sent for her—she sent him a message that she was with child."

"Oh—no!"

"Oh yes. She was married to Uriah for five years, and no children, but spent less than two hours with the king, and she's having a baby."

"And then David had her husband killed? That was foolish. Why didn't he just send her to her husband?"

Leah smiled admiringly. "Probably because he didn't have you there to advise him. He tried the other way—to get Uriah to go home. I got the whole story from a chambermaid at the palace."

"So David didn't want her or he would not have sent for Uriah," Michal said defensively.

"Of course he didn't. But try to convince anybody in Jerusalem. They say it serves him right to get stuck with that dumb woman. Why she can scarcely say more than 'yes' or 'no' unless some man puts words in her mouth. If a man isn't satisfied merely to look at her—and sleep with—she would probably bore him to death. And let me assure you, my lady, she is no more beautiful than you are."

"Thank you, Leah. But I've not felt very attractive lately; even a flower wilts when there is none to admire it."

"Oh, my lady! All who know you admire you. You have been blessed with great treasures. You have the beauty of an angel, the intellect of a scribe, the grace and wisdom of priest and prophet, and the common sense of a shepherd. How rare indeed to find such gifts of grace and talent combined in one person—and a woman at that."

Michal's eyes opened wide in amazement. And for once she was speechless.

"And may I add, you are clever as a fox. Now it appears you have acquired a little of the greatest grace of all: humility. But then you never seemed to know you were a great woman; you were always too busy being one."

The tears Michal had not shed in sorrow poured forth in joy. "Leah, how sweet you are! It's pretty obvious I could not be all those things or I would not be here, but your encouragement could not have come at a better time. I've been feeling rather unnecessary of late. And I can't tell you how much I miss you. You were such a blessing to me, and I took you for granted like the air I breathed. Now I'm so glad you're getting the happiness you so richly deserve. My God bless you always for the years of devoted service you gave me."

"Thank you, my lady; he is blessing me. And I'll be glad to deliver any message for you if I can."

"Oh, I almost forgot; I was thinking of David. So no one really knows if he had Uriah slain?'

"They know it—even if they can't prove it yet. Given time, the truth usually comes out."

"But even if he did have him killed, it was not to get his wife; it was to save the king of Israel from disgrace—to prevent a scandal"

"Perhaps. But it's a little late for that. Servants always know everything that goes on in the households where they work. And most of them talk too much. The king may think he averted a scandal, but the whole story is all over the country by now."

"O my poor David!"

Leah regarded Michal skeptically. "That may be you sentiment, my lady; but most people are saying 'poor Uriah.'"

"I know. And I'm sorry about the captain. But he is, we trust, safe in heaven with God. If a Hittite fought with Israel's army, I'm sure worshipped Israel's God. But poor David; how God will punish him! Pray for him, Leah. That's all we can do. Let's ask God to spare his life and forgive his sin."

"Even God does not forgive us until we repent. And the king shows no evidence of repentance. You may forgive his without his repenting for the way he has treated you—but God won't."

"Then let's pray God will bring him to repentance—and not crush him to death in the process."

Leah smiled and shook her head. "If *you* can pray for him, I'm sure God will hear and answer your prayers."

God always answers prayer. Because he does not grant our every request as soon as we make it, we are prone to think he is ignoring us. Never! God is wiser than we are. He is often forced to say "no" to our requests for our own good. Faith means that we believe God will do what he says he will do—keep his promises. How can we claim the promises of God if we do not know what he has promised? That was one of the reasons I was so determined to learn to read; I wanted to see for myself what God has to say to his people instead of depending on the priests."

Leah smiled again. "Has my lady finally managed to get her religion on the inside? It does not seem to be a burden any more."

Michal was shocked! But her religion really was no longer a burden. Instead of being an unknown power she feared and resented, God was her friend and comforter. When did such a radical change take place? When? When?

Late that night, when all others were asleep, Michal found the answer. Of course! That last night, alone in her house in the royal compound, when she reached the very depths of despair! God came in and soothed her aching heart. She must read again that psalm David sent. What was it he said? "When my mother and my father forsake me, then will the Lord take me up. David was right! God was there when all others had forsaken her. God was indeed loving and merciful.

"PLEASE, God," she whispered into the thick darkness of the crowded room, "have mercy on my David."

Chapter 64

When Zadoc discovered Dinah was gone, he literally went berserk. He herded the concubines back to their quarters without allowing them to eat breakfast. Then he stormed up and down the room breathing out threatenings and slaughter. Drawing his whip expectantly through his left hand, he raged, "I know Dinah did not get out of this room without help! Now whoever helped her escape can step forward and tell me all about it, or I'm going to lash every one of you within an inch of your lives."

No one moved.

"All right! Who wants to be first?" Zadoc viciously cracked his whip.

Bithia ran forward and fell on her knees at the angry eunuch's feet. "Please don't whip me. I have no idea how Dinah escaped or I'd tell you. All I know is that she seemed especially happy last night. She danced faster and sang louder than ever before," the cringing girl sobbed.

"All right, Bithia; I'll leave you till the last. Suppose we begin with the daughter of Saul." He walked menacingly toward Michal.

The princess stood tall and straight, and said with biting scorn, "Hold—Zadoc. You have beaten these defenseless girls, and gotten by with it. You dare lay one hand on me, and I'll see that the king takes off your head."

Zadoc reconciled as if Michal had struck him. For a moment he stood as if he were stunned. Suddenly, he whirled and left the room.

When the bar slammed in place behind the departing eunuch, the women gathered around Michal. Bithia fell at the princess' fact and began to kiss them." She was crying hysterically.

"That was telling him," said Vesta. "How I wish you had come here sooner. No offense, my lady," she said respectfully; but several of us would have prettier backs if you had.

Michal lifted Bithia up and held the sobbing girl in her arms. "There, there, the big bully is gone; you are all right now. Come and lie down."

233

Gently, she led the sobbing girl to her bed. After she tucked her in, Michal turned to the others. "I want you girls to promise me something.

"Anything, Princess," they chorused.

"The next one of you who is called—who gets to see the king, tell him how Zadoc abuses you."

"And what if he whips us too?" asked Bithia.

"Why do you think he would whip you?"

"For the same reason Zadoc did—for running away," said Vesta.

"David would never do that," Michal declared emphatically. "He is kind and gentle. I'm certain he does not know how you are being treated here."

The concubines looked skeptical as they muttered among themselves."

"Show the king your backs—you'll see. If he doubts you, tell him to ask me."

After a half-hearted search for Dinah, Zadoc reported to the king. "If my lord will not permit me to put bars on the windows, then I must have enough guards to keep one in the room with the women at all times," the eunuch insisted.

David thought for a long while. "No, Zadoc; we cannot do either. You tell the women that anyone who is not happy to be the king's concubine, is free to go. They are not to take my children, of course; but those who have no children may go, and if any mother wants to go without wants to go without her child, I won't stop her."

Zadoc appeared stunned. "But, my lord! It—it—isn't done. You can't free your concubines—just like that!"

"Who says I can't? As long as I am the king of all Israel, I can surely do what I please in my own house!"

"Yes, my lord. Of course. Whatever you say, my lord."

Zadoc was more surly than ever with the women, but a bit subdued. They surmised he was sleeping in the daytime; he frequented their room at all hours of the night.

Seven of the women had children; two others were with child. And fat Vesta frankly admitted she preferred to stay. The other twelve were earnestly seeking contacts on the outside, which might enable the to escape. When they asked Michal if she wanted to leave, she merely smiled and kept her own counsel.

Leah was Michal's only visitor but she came regularly until her baby was born. She kept the princess informed on affairs at the palace, and brought her all the news she could get from Mahaniam. It was from Leah that Michal learned David had brought Mephibosheth, Jonathan's lame son, to the palace to live as his own son. Michal longed to see the boy, and her heart ached to see Merab's sons, who were more her own than her sister's. She chafed under the many restraints, yet she could not leave until the others were also free to go.

Regretfully, Leah brought Michal the news that David married Bathsheba. He even placed her in Michal's house. Resentment raged in the city, but nowhere was it higher than in the king's own household. The other wives resented the eighth wife occupying the first house—even if they were identical. They seethed to have so little time for the ones he already had.

But who dared rebuke the king?

Chapter 65

When Bathsheba bore David a son, all the courtiers came and exclaimed over the new baby. No one seemed to notice anything strange about the marriage or the baby's early arrival.

But the thing David had done displeased the Lord. So God sent Nathan the prophet to see the king. Nathan did not mention the newest prince. Apparently, he came to complain about some misconduct of one of the king's subjects.

"There were two men in one city," said Nathan; the one was rich and the other poor. The rich man had vast flocks and herds. But the poor man had nothing except one little ewe lamb. The lamb was an orphan, which the poor man had brought up in his own house with his children. The lamb ate with the family, slept on the man's bed, and was like a daughter to him.

"The rich man had company. He would not take a lamp from his own vast herds but took the poor man's lamb and dressed it for his guest."

"David was furious. He said to Nathan, "As God is my witness, the man who did this thing shall die. But first he shall restore the lamb fourfold because he did this cruel thing, and because he had no compassion on his neighbor."

Then Nathan said to David, "You are the man. The Lord God of Israel says to you, 'I anointed you king over Israel, and I delivered you out of the hand of Saul. I gave you your master's house, and I gave you the house of Israel and Judah. If that had not been enough, I would have given you whatever else your heard desired.

"Why have you despised the commandment of the Lord, to do this evil in his sight? You killed Uriah the Hittite with the sword of the children of Ammon, and have taken his wife to be you wife.

"So the Lord says, 'The sword shall never depart from your house because you have despised the commandments of the Lord, and have taken Uriah's wife to be your wife.'

"Furthermore, the Lord says, 'I will raise up evil against you out of your own house, and I will take your wives before your very eyes, and give them to your neighbor, and he shall lie with them under the sun for all to see. You did this evil secretly, but I will punish you before all Israel, for everyone to see.'"

And David cried out to Nathan, "I know I've sinned against the Lord, and I'm sorry. I did wrong; then I tried to hide it by a greater wrong. Oh my God forgive me; I can never forgive myself!"

"God has heard your prayer and granted your petition; you shall not die."

"Would God have me put away this woman?"

"No. Two wrongs do not make one right. After slaying her husband, putting her away would be worse than the other evil you did her. But because God's mercy endures forever, and as an assurance of his forgiveness, God will give you of this weak and foolish woman a son whose wisdom shall exceed that of any man who has gone before him. And through this wise son of yours shall all nations of the earth be blessed."

"God's mercy is greater than I dared to ask."

"However, because your evil deed has given great occasion to the enemies of the Lord to blaspheme, this child that Bathsheba has borne you shall surely die."

So Nathan the prophet returned to his own house. And the Lord struck the child that the wife of Uriah bore unto David, and it was very sick.

David believed the prophet, yet he besought God earnestly for his son. He fasted and prayed the rest of the day. And when night came, he went out and lay all night upon the earth.

The wise men of his household tried to raise the king up from the earth, and to persuade him to eat or drink.

For seven days the king fasted and prayed, and on the seventh day the child died, according to the word of the Lord.

The servants feared to tell the king his son was dead. They said, "While the child was still alive, we tried to reason with him, and he would not listen. What will he do when we tell him his son is dead?"

But when David observed his servants fearfully whispering, he asked, "Is the child dead?"

"He is dead, "the servants answered.

Then David arose from the earth, and washed and anointed himself. He changed his clothes, and went into the house of the Lord, and worshipped. Afterward he went to his own house and asked his servants to prepare food for him. Even as he ate, his servants could not contain their curiosity.

"We don't understand," said their spokesman; "you fasted and wept for the child while he was alive, but after he died your calmly arose and asked for food."

"While the child was yet alive," said David sadly, "I fasted and wept, for I said, who can tell whether God will be gracious to me that the child may live? But now he is dead, why should I fast? Can I bring him back again? I shall go to him, but he shall not return to me.

"God is merciful, but he cannot let sin go unpunished. I fear what the future holds for your king, but my prayer is that he will spare the kingdom."

Chapter 66

David was so preoccupied with the birth and death of his son, he had no time for his wives or his children, certainly not for his concubines. Joab took a brief leave from the battlefront to come home and offer his condolences to the king.

Leah was careful to say nothing to her husband about the king's problems or Joab's part in the sorry drama. But his guilty conscience needed no accuser; Joab attempted to defend the king's conduct anyway.

"David would never have married all those women, and brought all this trouble on himself and his kingdom if the daughter of Saul had remained faithful."

"What do you mean? asked Leah.

"I mean that David would never have looked at another woman if his wife had not gone to be the wife of another man," Joab insisted.

"You know the princess could not avoid going with Phaltiel. King Saul would have killed them both if they had refused. But she was never his wife. The captain succored and protected the princess, but never did he lie with her."

"Then pray and tell me where she got all those children. Does she not have six sons?"

Leah looked shocked, then she laughed. "Oh—that! Yes-she does. Five of them are Merab's sons that the princess brought up for Adriel the Meholathite, after her sister died. The sixth one is Mephibosheth, Jonathan's little lame son the princess took to the live with her after his father and mother were slain."

"Are you trying to tell me Michal has no children of her own?"

"The princess has never borne a child."

"But she was Phaltiel's wife."

"No! No! She was never his wife!"

"How do you know?" persisted Joab stubbornly.

"Did I not sleep every night at the princess' feet? And many times have I heard Phaltiel plead them with her to become his wife. Always she gave him the same answer: Never as long as David lived would she be wife to another man."

Joab gave a long whistle. "If only David had known that."

"Why didn't he know it? The princess promised to wait for him, didn't she?"

"But everyone said—"

"I don't care what 'everyone said.' The king should have believed the princess. Why didn't he ask her?"

"But he was so sure."

"So he was sincere—but he was sincerely wrong. The king condemned his own wife without a hearing; he would not treat the humblest beggar in the kingdom so unjustly. And God only knows what the poor princess had suffered. Do you know where she is right now?"

"She is not at her house in the king's court?"

"No! That—Bathsheba is living there. The princess is in the second house of the women with the concubines."

"Oh, no!"

"Oh, yes. Now what do you think of your good king David?"

"But he didn't know. David, too, has grieved and suffered; I must tell him at once."

"While you're at it, would you also tell him how that brute, Zadoc, beats the concubines? If the king is such a man of God, he will surely show mercy to the helpless women."

Joab's right hand dropped to the hilt of the sword at his side. "I'm sure he will," he said grimly. "I'll be back shortly."

"Joab, wait; it's too late to talk to the king tonight. Anyway, you should wait until the period of mourning is over."

"I can't wait. I must go back to the battlefront tomorrow. And this news will do David more good than any medicine. It will take his mind off his grief. The daughter of Saul was the love of his life. I can think of nothing that would rejoice his heart more than to have her returned to his bosom."

"It may be too late."

"What do you mean?"

"The last time I visited the princess—three days ago—I took her several things I'm sure she wanted to help her escape. I begged her to let me help her; she refused. She was so afraid the king might vent his wrath on me."

"What did you take her?"

"One of your old—it was in the rags, an old turban, a pair of sturdy sandals, a piece of cheese cloth, a goatskin bag, and a waterbag containing a small measure of fine flour."

"That doesn't sound dangerous. How could she escape with that?"

"I don't know. And she refused to tell me. But it is certain she would have no use for any of that where she is."

"You are probably right. And it is best we not tell David you took the princess anything. You never know what may incur the wrath of a king. It is late; perhaps I had better wait till morning. How I wish you had told me all this sooner."

"But I didn't know the king had heard such a monstrous lie about the princess—nor does she."

Chapter 67

Joab saw nothing sinister in the harmless items his wife had taken to the princess. But even the wily Joab knew he was no match for the ingenious daughter of Saul.

Michal observed that Zadoc relaxed his vigilance over the concubines in the waning hours of the morning. But he watched them so closely she forced to make her preparations within the limited privacy of her curtained bed. She was convinced it was no longer possible to help the women from inside the harem, so she would try from the outside.

It was easy to secrets enough bread, cheese, and parched corn to fill the goatskin bag Leah brought her. She cut the cheesecloth into a mask for the mask for the lower part of her face, leaving long strings at the top and bottom. In her drinking cup she mixed a small amount of flour with water to make a thin paste. Then she unbraided her long thick curls and cut off about a finger's length. Carefully, she pasted the hair to the mask, and laid it under her bed to dry.

Michal went to bed early that night. She slept soundly until the late-rising moon began to shine in her face. Immediately she was wide awake. Cautiously she peered between the curtains into the moonlit room. The chair beside the door where Zadoc maintained his nightly vigil was empty.

The princess lay back on her pillow and listened intently. Nothing but the usual night sounds met her ears. Quietly slipped from her bed and tiptoed around the room. When she was satisfied every woman was asleep, she hastily removed her night clothes, and put on the plain dress she had worn from Mahanaim, still in her bare feet, Michal silently pulled two bundles from beneath her bed, and stacked them on the broad window ledge. Placing her pillow across the window sill, she packed it down firmly on both sides. Next she pulled the mattress from her bed and placed it beneath the window. The sheets that lowered three of the concubines to freedom would serve again. When one end of the sheet had been securely bound to the bedpost, she dropped the rest into a loose pile on top the other bundle.

Finally, Michal picked up the bench at the foot of her bed, turned it upside down, and pushed it across the window sill. When the other end of the bench was firmly planted on the city wall, she took the two bundles and crept across the bench to the top of the wall. Laying her bundles down on the parapet, she stepped off the bench, raised it up, and pushed it back until it dropped soundlessly from the window to the mattress below.

Michal unrolled the sheets and swiftly lowered the end with the rock to the ground outside the city wall. Then she dropped the other bundle to the ground beside the sheet. Without a moment's hesitations, she breathed a silent prayer, firmly grasped the sheet, and lowered herself over the wall.

The rough stones were cold and bruising to Michal's bare feet; but clinging to the sturdy shed, she made her way steadily down the wall—hand over hand. The journey was perilous, nerve-wracking, and slow. While she comforted herself with the thought that the sheets had held for three others before her, she recalled that none of the concubines was as heavy as herself.

When her feet safely touched the ground, Michal uttered a fervent prayer of thanksgiving. Then in the faint moonlight, she hurriedly untied the bundle, took out the sandals and strapped them on her bruised and bleeding feet. Grasping the rock in end of the sheet, she walked long the city wall until she passed the northeast corner of the house she had so recently vacated. She drew back her arm, and with a quick thrust threw the rock over the wall. She heard a faint thud as the rock-bound sheets fell back beneath the window between the house and the wall.

Michal hurried back to her bundle. She extracted the piece of cheesecloth to which she had pasted her shorn looks. After liberally dusting the hair with flour, she tied the mask over her face. Hastily she donned a tattered robe, and wound an old turbine around her head. She tucked her bag of food and the empty flour bag in her pocket, and started walking south along the wall toward the city gates. When she came to the well outside the city gates, Michal rinsed the remaining flour from the waterbag and filled it with fresh water. After sprinkling her clothing with water, she rolled in the sand until color and pattern disappeared beneath the dirt and grime.

Daybreaks found a dirty, tattered, gray-bearded beggar huddled down beside the city gates, waiting for the day's traffic to begin.

Chapter 68

The same daybreak found Joab pacing the floor of the ball of justice awaiting an audience with the king. The palace guard assured the captain the king would be conducting no affairs of state until the morrow. Being captain of the army gained Joab entrance to the court, but even he must await his king's pleasure.

The sun was climbing the sky when a servant brought word to the nervous captain that the king would have him join him for breakfast. With difficulty Joab restrained his urgency and forced himself to eat a little food to keep David company. As soon as they finished, Joab poured out his story.

The king sat with bowed head as if turned to stone. He made no response.

Joab squirmed uneasily in the silence.

"Would you like to talk with my wife—hear the details from her?"

"No," David said thoughtfully. "Your story clears up many things. How could I ever have doubted Michal! I was amazed that she kept her youth and beauty after bearing six children. I expected her to go back to them—or have them brought here; she did neither.

"When I asked Mephibosheth where Michal's song were, he said they were with Adriel in Mehola. I wondered why they were not with Phalti." Again David bowed his head and was silent.

When the raised his head again, his eyes were filled with anguish such as Joab had seen before. "Oh, Joab! What have I done to my beloved?"

"Michal loves you," said Joab soothingly. "She will understand when you tell her you didn't know."

"But I promised never to lose faith in her; I'm sure it never occurred to her that I did. Oh tangled lives! The wasted years! Quick, Joab! Bring my love to me at once."

"Yes, my lord!" said Joab with a broad grin, as he sprang to obey his king's command.

Before the door closed behind the captain, however, David called after him, "Wait—I'll go with you."

By the time David and Joab reached the courtyard gate of the second house of the women, they heard agonized screams coming from the third floor. The eunuch who admitted them appeared almost paralyzed with fright. David did not wait for explanations; he ran up the winding flagstone path to the door.

Zervah unlocked the door to the king's imperious summons. Her florid face turned ashen when she saw her callers. Brushing past the sputtering woman, David dashed up the stairs to at a time, with Joab at his heels.

When the two men burst through the doorway at the top the stairs, Zadoc was cursing the women, and lashing them with his whip at random. They were screaming and running in wild confusion in a vain effort to avoid the cruel lash.

"Hold," cried David.

At the sound of his master's voice, Zadoc's whip halted in midair, and he crumpled in greater/fear than the frightened women.

"What is the meaning of this?" David demanded.

Uh—uh—uh—" Zadoc stuttered, obviously too frightened to speak. The whip dropped from his nerveless fingers.

"How dare you lay a hand on these women! You were placed here to protect them—not punish them."

"Vesta, the fat Persian, approached the king and bowed before him. "If my lord please, Zadoc was trying to force us to tell him how the daughter of Saul escaped. We cannot tell him because we do not know."

"Michal is gone! When? Where?" Then turning to the cowering eunuch, David asked in angry tones tinged with curiosity, "What do mean—escaped? Did I not command you to tell you to tell my concubines they were all free to leave the harem if they pleased?"

Zadoc was visibly shaking. He opened his mouth but no words came.

Sobbing and trembling, Bithia crept up to the king, fell on her face at his feet, and without her head, asked: "Did my lord say we were free to leave here?"

The king reached down and tenderly lifted up the trembling girl. Holding her gently against his bosom, he replied: "Yes, Bithia. I want you to be happy. If you are not happy here, you are free to return to your family anytime they will come for you. You cannot, of course, go out unprotected."

Struggling to control her sobs, Bithia began fervently kissing the king's hand. "Oh, thank you, my lord; the blessings of our God be upon you."

Other concubines began pressing in upon the king. "Are we really free to go?" they chorused in joyous unbelief.

As David looked around at the excited women, he saw the skulking eunuch slicking toward the door. Quickly he released Bithia, and pushed his way through the bevy of beautiful women crowded so beseechingly around him. "Hold, Zadoc! Tell me! Why did you not tell my concubines they were free to go as I instructed you?"

Too frightened to think up a plausible lie, Zadoc blurted out the truth. "But—but—I—if they left, where would I go? What would I do?"

"You miserable, sniveling coward! Your own mouth has testified against you." Turning to Joab, David commanded: "Get him out of here and take off his head. No! Wait! Do it here; these women should enjoy it."

After David convinced his concubines they were indeed free to go if they chose, and ten of them assured him they preferred to stay, he began to question them about Michal.

"All we know for sure," said Vesta, is that she was here last night and she was gone this morning. Zadoc said she was still here when rose."

"The moon rose late," said David thoughtfully, "so must still be in the city. Do you knot how she got out of here?"

"Come," said Vesta. She led the to the window from which the sheets still dangled. The mattress, bench, and pillow, however, had been removed.

As David gazed at the dangling sheet, his mind fled back through the years to the night Michal risked her life to provide the same kind of escape for him. And he lifted up his voice and wept.

Their own troubles forgotten, the concubine tried to comfort their weeping monarch.

"She can't have gone far," said Joab. "I doubt if she has left the city. We'll find her if we have to comb every inch of Jerusalem. I have already sent a guard to the gates to see that she does not get away."

"But the king said we were all free to go," said Bithia apprehensively. "Why must you search for her?"

"Will the princess be punished?" asked Vesta cautiously.

"The princess," promised David solemnly, "will be made the queen of all Israel—as she should have been long ago."

"I'm glad," said Vesta generously. "The princess loves you. She also loves your God, and she loves Israel—it that—I think."

"Only God and Israel have ever been dearer to me," said David. "Michal was the first woman in my life, and the most enchanting one I have ever known. God grant I may be able to recompense her for all the sufferings she has endured.

"Come, Joab; let's find my love."

Chapter 69

As soon as the city gates were opened, the traffic began to move. Merchants and sellers of all kinds of ware waited without the gates to enter the city. The shepherds brought fat lambs from the flocks, and the tillers of the soil brought of the fruit of the ground to sell in the marketplace.

The merchants waiting without the gates stood aside to permit the traffic within the city to pass out. The first one to emerge was a Jebusite beggar. When he saw a beggar already sitting in his favorite spot, he began to rail on him. He cursed him by his gods, and threatened dire bodily harm if the usurper did not leave at once.

"Jewish dogs has taken away our city; must you also take away our living?" he screamed angrily."

The gray-bearded beggar arose quickly for one so old and infirm. Humbly he made signs he could neither hear nor speak. Then he limped over to a less prominent place beside the city wall, and sank down in a heap upon the ground.

Somewhat mollified, the Jebusite took his accustomed place, but he continued to mutter under his breath. The only distinguishable/ words were, "Jewish dog."

The displaced beggar sat patiently against the wall, as the broiling sun climbed higher in the heavens. He made no effort to solicit alms, but bowed gratefully to the generous merchants who cast a few coins in the dust at his feet.

About the third hour, a soldier approached the gatekeeper. "Has a woman passed through the gates this morning?" he asked.

The gatekeeper shrugged. "Several merchant caravans left the city; it's possible a woman could have been among them, but I don't recall seeing one. Who are you looking for?"

"The daughter of Saul! She fled the harem; the king is searching the city for her."

"And when he finds her?"

"She'll be put to the sword—I suppose, as she should have been long ago. Nothing but evil ever came from the bloody house of Saul. However, Joab said the king freed all his concubine this morning, so there's no telling what he may do."

For one who could neither hear not speak, the gray bearded beggar took avid interest in the conversation.

At midday, the Jebusite beggar arose to return to the city. He shook his fist at the gray bearded Jew, and uttered dire threats should he or anyone else attempt to usurp his place while he was gone. The Jew ignored him. The other beggars drifted back into the city as midday slowed traffic to a trickle.

Safely hidden behind her disguise, Michal pondered her next move. If the concubine were free, there was no need to linger in Jerusalem. And if the soldier was right about her being put to the sword, she had no time to lose in fleeing the city.

Rising dejectedly, the dirty beggar limped down to the city well. After drinking deeply of the clear cool water, Michal sat down under the palm trees. From inside her dirty robe she drew the goatskin bag suspended from a leather thong around her neck. Taking out bread, cheese, and parched corn, she ate with relish.

When she finished eating, Michal cleared the rocks from the sand beside her, pushed up a small mound of sand for a pillow, and lay down for a nap. The city was sleeping; she might as well sleep with it until it bestirred itself again.

A few travelers came and went from the well. They paid scant attention to the dirty beggar sleeping on the sand.

When the city began to stir again, Michal was waiting beside the road that led to Jericho. Surely some kind merchant would allow a poor beggar to join his caravan for the trek across the desert.

While she waited, the royal chariot, pulled by two white horses, burst from the city gates. It was followed by four soldiers on horseback. A cloud of dust boiled from beneath the chariot wheels and almost obscured the passengers, but they looked like David and Joab. Perhaps the king was escorting his captain back to the battlefront.

If, however, David was on his way to Mahaniam to look for her, at that rate he would be back before she reached Gibeah. Michal watched the chariot until it disappeared from her sight. Would God the lover of her youth might disappear from her heart as easily.

Michal had crossed the desert many times, but never on foot. Before her spread the boulders shimmering and baking beneath the burning sun. The realm of drifting sands was not visible from the city; it was farther out, but the region where the vegetation began to dwindle stretched before her. The surface was strewn with granite boulders and rocks of every hue from gray to black. Interspersed among the stones were languishing acacias and wilted tufts of camel grass. Behind them grew the oak bramble and trailing arbutus almost to a line. It looked as if they had peered over into the rock-strewn waste and cowered in fear.

After being imprisoned in the second house of the women, however, for so many months, Michal felt even walking across the burning desert would be a welcome change.

How good to breathe free air again, to be alone, and to think her own thoughts. But one thought kept hammering its way into her consciousness. Over and over she seemed to hear the same refrain: "Till death do us part."

Taking a long look at the peaceful desert with its promise of freedom and adventure, Michal peeled the gray beard off her face, dropped the grimy, tattered robe from her shoulders, and unwound the turban to let her long black curls fall around her face.

Turning back toward the gates of Jerusalem, she breathed a prayer toward heaven: "And if I perish, I perish."

THE END